MEET
THE
PARENTS

BOOKS BY EMILY SHINER

The Wife in the Photo

The Hotel

DETECTIVE FREYA SINCLAIR SERIES

Three Drowned Girls

One Liar Left

EMILY SHINER

MEET
THE
PARENTS

bookouture

Published by Bookouture in 2024

An imprint of Storyfire Ltd.
Carmelite House
50 Victoria Embankment
London EC4Y 0DZ

www.bookouture.com

ISBN: 978-1-83525-585-8
eBook ISBN: 978-1-83525-584-1

For my Dad.
You're a great Doc in more ways than one.

PROLOGUE

Flames lick the sky.

They crackle, shooting up into the air, lighting up the night, casting an eerie orange glow around the house. Fingers of them twist when the wind blows. Heat from the fire burns my face, the dancing light causing the rise and fall of shadows on the lawn.

Wood splinters. Blackened pieces of the house's framework appear like broken teeth. The entire structure groans as the roof caves in, sending more flames shooting into the sky. A cascade of embers sprays, winking out before hitting the ground.

I did this.

By the time a neighbor calls about the fire, the house will be too far gone. If anyone were left alive inside, they would be dead from the fire or from smoke inhalation. Firefighters could make it in. But they wouldn't make it back out.

There will be no rescue mission.

A thick layer of ash covers the car in the driveway. Ours is out of the way, parked on the road, waiting for me. If any ashes land on it, they'll blow off as we leave.

A large ember flies from the house, floating like a falling

star, landing on the ground. With a sigh, I shift my weight and grind my toe into it to put it out.

It's time to go.

I reach into my pocket and finger the car keys. My passenger is strapped in, waiting on me.

Turning, I run down the driveway, exchanging the heat from the inferno with a cool breeze blowing directly in my face. When I reach the car, I pause and look back.

How much longer do I have until a neighbor notices what's going on? How long until this place is crawling with firefighters, with EMTs, with any first responder on duty?

I need enough time to get down the road. Put some distance not only between us and the house but also between us and what happened here.

After that? I don't care what happens here, but I have an idea.

They'll run their hoses, lay them like thick snakes on the ground. Smoke will get in their lungs, and they'll cough, rub their eyes. They'll stand around, hard hats on, squinting against the heat and light, aiming for containment.

And, when it's burned out, when they've sprayed it down, fully saturated whatever's left, when the fire marshal comes and tells them they can enter *as long as they're careful—watch your step right there*, they'll go in.

They'll look for bones.

See who didn't make it out.

ONE

GINA

Stress eats away at me. I'm not paying attention to the road in front of us, so I don't see the pavement change to gravel. I feel it though, my teeth clattering together as Owen's brand-new Lexus drops down off the smoothly paved road onto the small rocks.

"Whoa," Owen says, reaching out to squeeze my hand. "Sorry, I didn't think to mention the gravel. It's pretty rough going from here on out, but the good news is that we're almost there."

"Great." I smile as I speak, hoping to take the edge off how I feel. "I was wondering how much longer we had to go. It's been just woods for miles. So we have to be close." I squeeze Owen's hand back. We've only been together seven weeks. It's a whirlwind love story for the books, but although I fell head over heels for Owen, being this close to actually meeting his parents makes me feel... well, ill.

"We are. Right... now." He taps the brake and lets go of my

hand to turn the wheel. "You can't see it through the trees, but it's here, I promise. The driveway is just insane."

"Noted," I say, but I'm not really paying attention. I'm leaning forward again, doing my best to see out the windshield. So far, all I can see are thick trees. Briars. Gnarled rhododendron.

Then, right as we go round a curve in the driveway, the trees open up. There's a clearing, not totally unexpected, sure, but much bigger than I anticipated it would be. I inhale sharply and frown, looking up, up, up.

At a house.

Not a cabin.

Hell, maybe not even a *house*. Is the correct word a mansion? Or is this a little on the small side? What's the slightly smaller sibling of a McMansion? A MiniMansion?

That's what it is. A MiniMansion. Two stories, both of them fully lit up; even the front porch lights are on so I can see the huge wrap-around porch, the rocking chairs lined up like sentries, the hanging ferns that still somehow look healthy, like it's the middle of summer and not pushing November.

"Here we go." Owen taps the brakes and stops us next to a...

I turn my head to look. Brand-new Range Rover. With a vanity plate. *MARTA#1*. Of course.

"Wow, this is not a cabin," I say, keeping silent about my internal debate regarding what kind of mansion the place really is. "You really downplayed it, Owen."

He shrugs. I feel more than see the motion since it's dark in the car, and I'm still staring at the house. An American flag juts out from the eaves, but there's no wind so it hangs still and silent. Off to one side of the porch is a dog house that—get this— is a replica of the house itself.

"You didn't tell me your parents have a dog." That feels like a normal thing to say. It hides how completely overwhelmed I am; how much this place feels like a joke to me. I'm fully expecting an aging celebrity with a microphone to jump out from behind one of the thick porch columns so everyone can laugh at me.

Brad Pitt? No, he's too classy.

Owen Wilson? No, too busy surfing.

It'll come to me.

"Well, they did. Pickles. But he died last summer, and Mom said she just isn't ready to open her heart to a new animal. He was her shadow. Absolutely followed her everywhere. Honestly, I don't think Dad liked him that much, and the feeling was probably mutual, but Mom adored him, and Pickles was obsessed with her."

"I get it." I'm grabbing for anything to say that might make this feel more normal. "I had a dog growing up. My therapist said having one would probably be good for me. Help me heal from the trauma."

Now he turns to me, his bulk shifting in his seat, and he lightly cups my cheek. I lean into his touch.

"You're so strong, Gina. Trust me. I know you can handle anything."

"Even meeting your parents?" My words are dry, and he laughs.

"Even that. They've been looking forward to meeting you for months now."

I pause, surprised. "But we've only been dating a few weeks."

He opens his mouth to respond, but before he can, there's a knock on my window and I jump, a small scream on my lips. Owen just breaks into a smile, whatever he was going to say forgotten.

"Speak of the devil!" His hand drops from my cheek and he turns, getting out of the car faster than I really think is necessary.

I watch him throw himself into his mother's embrace.

"Mom! Dad!" Excitement pours from him, and I take a deep breath. Steel myself.

I wanted this. Even when Owen waffled about taking this trip, I pushed hard to make it happen. There's no backing out now, not when I've come this far. Gotten this close to getting what I want.

When I get out of the car, I have to walk around the hood to where Owen is currently in the middle of a parent Oreo. He extricates himself and pulls me forward, his hand closing around my wrist as he does. "This is Gina. Gina, these are my parents."

"Grant," his dad says, thrusting his hand in my direction. I grab it, surprised as my hand seems to disappear inside his paw. He pumps my arm up and down a few times. "It's nice to meet you," he says to me. Then, to nobody in particular: "She has a firm handshake. That's good. No dead fish here."

"Thank you?" I mean to sound confident, but it comes out as a question. While I'm busy kicking myself for that, his mom steps forward. Her handshake is light, flighty. It matches her appearance. Owen and Grant are huge men, the kind that would easily be tapped to play a game of pickup football, but Marta is shorter than I am. She's thin, the type of thin that women get when they have more self-control than desire, when they can force themselves to look at dessert, imagine what it tastes like, then willingly throw it in the trash.

I am not one of those women.

"I'm Marta," she says. Her hand flutters against mine, and I have to fight to wipe away the feeling when we let go. *Dead fish. Now I get it.* "Owen has told us so much about you, and we're elated he was able to come visit for a few days. You must feel so lucky that he brought you with him."

"I'm really excited to be here," I tell her. "And your house, wow. Owen downplayed it a little bit. In fact, I think the exact words he used were 'a little cabin in the woods.'" I make air quotes around the words.

Owen throws me a wink, then turns to talk to his dad.

Her face goes tight for a second before it relaxes. "Owen always downplays things so he doesn't make people uncomfortable, especially if they grew up in a different socioeconomic class. There isn't anyone quite like Owen in the entire world. He's always been so special, and we've always been close. I'm sure he's told you that."

"How close the two of you were?" I nod. "Of cou—"

"How close we *are*. Boys and their mothers have a special kind of relationship, Jenna."

"It's Gina."

"Of course it is."

My mouth drops open as my mind races for a response. Before I can come up with anything, she loops her arm through Owen's and tugs him away from his dad and towards the house.

"I'm sure you two are starving."

At first, I don't realize she's talking to Owen, not me. But he's turned to his dad, so I answer.

"Actually, we're not that hungry." I feel her stiffen next to me, but she's still walking, so I hurry to keep up. The huge wooden steps up to the porch groan a little under our weight. "I'm so sorry—is that a problem? We got hungry an hour ago and stopped for Subway."

She pauses and pulls her hand free from his arm, then turns on me. "You ate already?" There's ice in her voice. Her eyes narrow and her mouth tightens. "But it's tradition. When Owen comes home, I make a big meal. I've been cooking all afternoon for my son. I always do this. Every time he visits."

Next to her, guilt flashes across Owen's face. It's there and gone in a moment, carefully hidden behind the Very Serious Surgeon face I see him wear at work. "I'm sorry, Mom. We were both really hungry, and I couldn't wait any longer." He turns her by the shoulders, pulling her into a hug before throwing me a wink.

She murmurs something into his shoulder that's probably meant just for him, but I still hear every word.

"This is how we always do it, Owen. Why would you let her change that?"

Her. Derision drips from the word, and I can't help but frown. No, I didn't expect her to rush to me with open arms, but I certainly didn't think she'd be so obvious about the fact she doesn't like me.

But maybe this is exactly what I should have planned for. Honestly, knowing what I do about her, how evil she is, maybe this shouldn't have been a surprise. From my research, I hoped Marta would be quiet. Mousy. A pushover.

But from what I've just seen, getting revenge might be a lot harder than I thought.

TWO

MARTA

I know Grant and I came up with this plan together, but actually having Gina in our house is different than just talking about it. It's worse. When the plan was ephemeral—just something we were talking about—I could stomach the idea of her here. But now she's in my house, and I feel like I'm trapped in a nightmare.

I hate the way she looked at Owen during dinner, like he was a prize that she'd won; like just because he brought her here, she'd be able to stay in his life forever. She can hope for that all she wants, but I won't let it happen. Gina thinks she's got it made, but I'm not letting her walk out of here.

Pain shoots through my hands, momentarily drawing my mind away from Gina. I'm too young to have arthritis, but nobody bothered to inform my knuckles. They're swollen and achy, and I bite down on my lower lip as I massage a CBD salve into them. If I hadn't spent all day in the kitchen making dinner for Owen, then they wouldn't hurt like this, but...

No, I'm not going to ruminate on that. Owen's a big boy now, and if he wants to stop at Subway on his way to come see me, then he can do that. I'm not going to guilt-trip him about it.

I'll just heat everything up tomorrow and serve leftovers for dinner. Grant won't love that, but Grant can get over himself. He wasn't the one standing at the stove all day.

He never has been, and at this rate, he never will be. Men never change, do they?

"What did you think of Gina?" I ask. I wrinkle my nose a little bit when I say her name. I don't like her. Doesn't every mother find the woman her son falls for lacking in some way? I can't help myself. It's just the way it is. Mothers are wired like this. Our brains don't have the right synapses.

That's what I tell myself anyway. The truth is I wouldn't ever like Gina. Not knowing what I do about her, about her past.

Not when she might know the truth of what happened. That fear—that she might be aware of what happened when she was younger; that she might know why her life fell apart—gives me chills. It doesn't matter what she knows; it's the threat that she might know something.

I'll do anything to get rid of her.

That thought is all-consuming, and it's only when Grant speaks that I snap back to reality.

"Gina's what I expected." Grant has his back to me. He's sitting on the edge of the bed, hinged forward at the hips to stretch and release some pressure in his spine before lying down. A groan escapes him. When I flip back the covers and climb in, he turns and does the same, repeating what he said a moment ago. "She's fine."

I hear the words he doesn't say, but only because I've heard them so many times in the past that they're ingrained in me.

She's fine really means *she's quite pretty*.

Gina is Owen's type, but she's also Grant's. Like father, like son.

I can use that. Get rid of her. And get rid of Grant.

Have Owen all to myself.

I shift position, the thought exciting, a new plan taking root. It's one thing to know what happens when your husband is away and surrounded by women, and to turn your head, look the other way, ignore the behavior. I did that for years. Years! And look where it got me: Gina here and me having to deal with her. But now it could happen under my roof, and I won't be the dutiful wife sitting at home waiting on my husband.

I can be the one pulling the strings. I dig the fingernails of my right hand into the back of my left. If Grant notices the movement or my sharp intake of breath as I try to calm down, he doesn't respond.

He's quiet. Thinking. Lost in his own head. Thinking of Gina—I know he is.

So am I, but what he's thinking is different than what I am.

We're both keeping our voices down so they don't hear us, although I don't believe it's really necessary. Our bedroom is on one side of the house; theirs is on the other.

"He seems to really like her," I say, pushing that out of my mind. "She's the first woman he's ever brought home anyway. So I feel like that must count for something."

Never mind the fact that we've been pushing him to bring her home since they first met.

"Do you hear wedding bells?" Grant asks, then speaks again before I can respond. "Alexa, turn out the lights."

There's a soft ding in response, and the room goes dark.

I don't answer him. Not because I don't hear wedding bells. I heard them from the moment Owen told me he'd moved her into his apartment. But I don't *want* to hear wedding bells.

Not with her. Not when I know who she really is.

Not with... anyone, if I'm honest with myself. As soon as Owen marries someone, I lose him for good. I won't let that happen.

"I do," I say, needing to keep talking. Needing to plant the seed. "She's the prettiest girl I've ever seen him with. And so young."

Grant doesn't respond.

"What is she, probably about twenty-eight? In the prime of her life. And Owen's forty-one this year. She likes older men."

Now he chuckles. "And Owen obviously likes them younger, Marta. What of it?"

"Just that she's got a lovely smile. Those full lips. And did you see the leggings she had on?" I prop myself up on my elbow and turn to face Grant. It's too dark to make out the expression on his face. "They were painted on. Nothing left to the imagination."

"Shameful." Grant sounds tired, and I know it's time to pull back. No reason to show too much of my hand.

"What's the plan for tomorrow?" I ask him. He always falls asleep faster than I do, so if I want to talk to him, I need to do it now. That's men for you. They do whatever they want during the day and then pass out at night, a clear conscience, unhampered by any concerns from the day.

But me? I'll stay awake for a long time. As still as possible, of course, so I don't accidentally shift around too much and wake him up.

"I figure we'd let the two of them take the lead on that." Grant's voice is already fading. "Owen might want to take Gina out hiking—might want to show her the river through the woods. As long as the weather's good, that is. There's supposed to be rain tonight, so the trails might be slick, but they'll be fine. He'll take care of her."

The idea of my son taking care of Gina makes me grimace.

"And you? If they go out exploring, what do you think you'll get into?" I reach out and touch his side, making him jerk a little.

"Oh, me. Reading probably. And I went to town this week

and picked up that new band saw, so I'd like to see that in action."

Right. I forgot Grant's new woodworking hobby. *I made the money, Marta, and I can spend it however I want.* "What are you going to make?"

No response.

"Grant." I lightly poke him again. Not too hard, not hard enough that it'll actually wake him up if he's asleep, but just enough to pull him back from the edge of slumber if he hasn't tipped over it. "What do you think you'll make? Remember I told you I want a new bookcase?"

No response.

Huffing, I roll over, pulling the blankets with me. Let him freeze a little tonight. All my life I've done everything I can to make Grant's life as easy as possible, so for him to be cold for one night won't kill him. But even when I close my eyes, I can't seem to turn off my brain.

All I can think about is Gina. And Owen. And Gina and Owen together.

Not necessarily what they're doing right now, although that thought does keep trying to creep in. I hate it, hate imagining what they might be doing while under my roof, but that's not my worry right now. What I'm worried about goes far deeper than the possibility of an accidental pregnancy.

We know how to take care of those. A little money, a small vacation for Gina, and all would be well again. Grant always wondered why I never got pregnant again after getting pregnant with Owen was so easy.

But after I found out about him and the other women, I couldn't allow myself to have more kids. I already had Owen; he was my focus, and I didn't need another baby to distract me from taking care of him. The plan has been for him to take me away from all of this.

If Gina were to get knocked up, I'd be more than happy to foot the bill.

But it's not going to get to that point with her. Not if the plan works.

What worries me is more than a positive pregnancy test, a trip to the doctor, a payment made in cash. It's the fact that my son, so innocent and trusting, fell for Gina.

I know I'd made it very clear—he doesn't need a woman.

Especially not Gina.

He doesn't need anyone else but me.

THREE

GINA

I don't have much time.

As soon as Owen's breathing evens out, I lift the covers back, swing my legs over the side of the mattress, and slip from bed.

He doesn't move. I'm aware of how I'm breathing: trying to hold my breath and only let it out in little puffs. Fear tickles the back of my neck, and the house settles, the sound making my stomach flip.

Nobody's coming. Old houses settle, even ones that look like they belong on the front of a magazine. Just because the house is groaning doesn't mean anyone else is on the move.

Just me.

I pull a tiny flashlight from my pocket and turn it on, shielding the beam with my hand so the sudden light doesn't wake Owen up. He groans and rolls over.

I freeze.

Count to ten.

Only when I'm sure he's still asleep do I move.

I walk around the bottom of the bed, carefully stepping over the clothes we scattered on the floor in our hurry to fall into bed together. At the door I pause, angling the flashlight out into the hall. There's a bathroom directly attached to our bedroom, so I don't have a good excuse of having to pee if I run into Marta or Grant.

But what are the chances either of them will be up? If anything, I can tell them I have trouble sleeping in new places, that the sounds of the house kept me up, that I needed a midnight snack.

Carefully, so I don't accidentally trip on one of the wide rugs lining the hall, I make my way to the stairs. Grant and Marta's bedroom is directly in front of me, and I pause. What I wouldn't give to go in there.

I'd love to stand over Marta. Stare down at her. The mental image of her waking, fear in her eyes, the knowledge that I know what happened filling her up, makes my hands shake. I take a deep breath and rest my hand against the wall for balance.

As wonderful as that sounds, I need to stay focused. Owen would love for this to be a relaxing family trip where the four of us sit around and sing "Kumbaya," but I have other plans.

For both of his parents.

And that's why I'm here.

My steps are light as I hurry down the stairs. Now that I'm off the second floor, I stop covering half of the flashlight and let the beam dance around the room in front of me. Honestly, I could probably get away with turning on the lights down here, but I'd rather not.

When you're digging up dirt on someone, the last thing you want to do is draw attention to your actions. And keeping it dark in here will allow me to see if there are any little red lights from security cameras. They're tricky to see in the light but should be bright in the dark.

Owen was so excited to sit and talk to his parents that he didn't give me a tour of the house, so I explore now, moving as quietly as possible through the library, the living room, and the dining room. At each bookshelf I pause and investigate the books. I pick up knick-knacks and look at them, but there's nothing that seems incriminating. Nothing I wouldn't expect to find here. After leaving those rooms, I poke my head into the kitchen, but what are the chances anything damning is hidden in there?

No, what I'm looking for isn't going to be left out for company to stumble onto. It'll be hidden, tucked away. *Private.*

Turning from the kitchen, I walk away from the front of the house and cut around the living room to the left. There's a bathroom here, a huge one with a garden tub, but I continue past it to the one door at the end of the hall.

If I'm right, and I think I am, it's Grant's office. Before we left his apartment, Owen was more than happy to tell me all about the house he grew up in, and there's nothing else this could be.

And I have to get in there.

"Please be unlocked," I whisper to myself as I reach out and take the knob. Exhaling slowly, I turn it to the right, then to the left.

Nothing. It's locked tight.

"Come on," I mutter, giving it a jiggle and trying again to no avail.

Anger flares in me. I told him. I told Wade I might run into this problem, and he'd pooh-poohed it. He'd said that we'd done our research, that there wasn't any way we could be wrong, that I should listen to him because we're family, but I wanted to see for myself. Even with all the proof he had, all the information he had tying it all together, ensuring he couldn't be wrong, I didn't want to act rashly.

I wanted verification. After meeting Owen and accidentally falling in love with him, I still wanted revenge—of course I did. But I had to make sure we were right.

Without thinking, I smack my open palm into the door. The

sound is loud, and I jump back, my heart hammering in my throat.

There's an answering bang from directly above me.

I freeze, then look up, like I'm going to be able to see through the ceiling into the room above me. We tried to get blueprints of the house and failed, but after hearing Owen talk about the house ad nauseum, I know what's overhead.

Grant and Marta's bedroom.

"Crap," I mutter, turning and hurrying back down the hall. "Crap, crap, crap." My voice is a whisper. I'm still trying to be as quiet as possible, but when I turn from the hall into the library, my foot catches on the edge of a rug.

All of the other rugs in the house have perfectly flat edges, but this one is curled up just a little, just enough to catch my toe. I go sprawling, hitting the hardwood floor first with my knees, then my hands.

My flashlight flies free from my grip. I watch in horror as it bounces away, then rolls under a sofa.

The sound of my heart hammering in my ears makes it hard for me to hear anything else. I take a deep breath, then another, filling up my lungs and holding it before slowly exhaling.

Nothing. There's nothing. Whatever I heard—or *imagined* I heard—it's gone. Maybe it was the house settling. Or perhaps someone rolled over; knocked their phone to the floor. Or they had to pee. Pipes can rattle and bang, can't they?

Whatever it was, I need to move. No way can I stay here on the floor. My palms hurt, and I grunt as I reach under the sofa for the flashlight. The beam is a little dimmer than it was before I dropped it, and I whack it against my thigh.

It doesn't help, but I don't care. All I want now is to go to bed before someone knows I'm up and snooping.

As quickly and quietly as possible, I hurry across the room to the stairs. At the bottom I pause, glancing up.

The stairway is inky black. It's silent upstairs. I jiggle the flashlight at my side, deciding whether or not I want to see if anything waits for me at the top. The light dances around me, and I take a deep breath, forcing myself to shine it up the dark stairs.

For a moment, I hold out hope there won't be anything there.

Then the light hits a shape at the top.

Marta.

FOUR

MARTA

Gina hurries up the stairs and brushes past me, but I don't move.

If I do, I'll shove her down the stairs—I know I will. Bump her with my hip, stick my foot out and trip her... whatever it would take, I'd love nothing more than to see her fall.

But if I do that, I won't be able to use her later. As much as I hate to admit it, I need her.

For now.

She turns into Owen's bedroom, her flashlight bobbing around as she does, but I still don't move. The house creaks and settles around me, but I stand still. My muscles are tight, and my breath comes in little gasps.

What was it I'd heard that got me out of bed in the first place? Something, some... noise. A disturbance. Maybe just the knowledge that she was in the house with us, and she doesn't belong here.

Minutes pass before I take a deep, shuddering breath and walk back to our bedroom. My steps are silent as I walk down the wide hall. Unlike Gina, I know exactly where you can and can't step without making any noise.

When I slip back under the covers next to Grant, he doesn't move. I shift closer to him, seeking his body heat, then I turn on my back and stare up at the dark ceiling.

We don't have any lights in the bedroom. No clocks to upset our circadian rhythm, no glowing blue dots telling us things are charging. It's the only way to get optimal sleep, and optimal sleep is the only way for me to handle what's going to come next.

My body feels tight, like I'm ready to run a race, and I force myself to close my eyes. I slow my breathing, but I don't relax. All I can picture is Gina next to Owen, her eyes open as she stares at the ceiling.

What was she doing poking around?

I heave a sigh and slip back out of bed, grabbing my phone as I do and turning on the flashlight. True to form, Grant doesn't move, not even when I slide my feet into my slippers. The floor was colder than I expected when I was out of bed earlier.

In the hall, I pause and turn to Owen's room. Gina's awake in there—I can almost guarantee it. Rage sweeps over me, and I force myself to turn away and hurry down the stairs. Putting a floor between us sounds like a good idea right now.

I haven't gotten this close to getting what I want by being rash, and I'm not going to start now.

At the bottom of the stairs, I pause, then slowly turn and look through the room, using the light on my phone as a guide. What in the world was she doing down here? Knowing Gina, she had to be looking for something. I doubt she would be wandering around for no reason.

A chill races up my spine, and I slowly walk through the room, shining the light around me as I go. Yes, I could turn on the overhead light, but the last thing I want is to draw Grant or Owen's attention to the fact that I'm down here and not in bed where I should be.

I walk through the living room, dining room, and library. In the hall, I pause, then walk towards Grant's office. Without slowing down, I reach out and grab the knob on his door and twist it hard.

But it doesn't open.

Of course.

"What were you looking for, Gina?" I whisper to myself as I walk back down the hall to the kitchen. Everything is in place here. I never go to bed with dishes on the counter or in the sink. There are few things more overwhelming than getting up in the morning and having to clean up the kitchen before I can start cooking breakfast.

Nothing's out of place. The floral towel I used to dry dishes after dinner hangs on the oven door. There are flowers on the counter, but they don't look touched.

My eyes fall on the door across the room.

Gina wouldn't care about messing up my flowers or my towel. If she came downstairs for a reason, then there's no way she would waste her time with something like that, even if she knew how much it would drive me nuts to have things moved or touched.

I cross the kitchen as quickly as possible, my steps long, my eyes still locked on the door. When I reach out for the knob, my hand trembles, but I push away any worries and grip it.

I yank it hard to the left. Then to the right. It doesn't give. The door doesn't swing open, and I exhale hard, turning to lean against it for support.

Whatever Gina was hoping to find down here, she didn't.

Whatever dirt she thinks she has, she doesn't.

My mind and heart race as I hurry back up the stairs and to my bedroom. A quick pause in the doorway lets me turn off my flashlight, then I kick off my slippers and slide into bed. Even as I try to still my body, my mind races.

Grant turns towards me and throws his arm over my stomach. He presses his face into my neck. "Everything okay?"

I freeze. It isn't so bad that Grant knows I was up and about, but I'm tired, and tired people make mistakes. The last thing I want is to accidentally slip up about my plan.

Not our plan. *My* plan.

"Do you think she knows?" I decide to answer his question with a question. When he doesn't immediately respond, I continue. "Gina. Do you think she knows what we've done?"

Grant exhales hard and rolls away from me onto his back. I reach down and lace our fingers together. I'm diverging from our original plan, but I still want his assurance that things are going to be okay.

"No," he finally says. He exhales the word into the silence of our room. I'm about to reply, but he continues before I can. "Even if she does, we're going to take care of it. Of her."

Our mantra runs through my mind. It's what the two of us have said to each other over and over while we worked through what to do, how to fix this.

"No loose ends," I whisper.

FIVE

GINA

Saturday

I'm still alive.

That's my first thought when I wake up. The words dance through my head, making my stomach turn. I reach over to the side, looking for Owen but only smacking the empty mattress where he should be. A groan escapes my lips. Light filters in through the soft white sheer curtains in the windows, but the entire house sounds still. If I didn't know he'd been in bed with me last night and that his parents went to bed when we did, I'd wonder if I were the only person in the house.

Sure sounds like I'm the only one here anyway.

Exhaustion hits me, and I close my eyes, taking a deep breath as I think about what happened last night.

Snooping downstairs. The frustration at finding Grant's office locked. Hitting the door, then falling as I made a run for the stairs.

But worst of all: Marta at the top of the staircase. She hadn't said a word to me as I ascended. Instead, she stood perfectly still, her arms crossed, her eyes locked on me. I'd had to sidestep her to get around her, and even then, she hadn't made a sound.

For a moment, I had a terrible mental image of her arm flying out, hitting me in the chest, knocking me back down the stairs. I'd pinwheel my arms, try to grab on to something—anything—then crash into the floor. My neck would snap. My eyes would glaze over. She'd watch it all happen, not moving. Not helping.

And Owen would never know what really happened to me. She could tell him whatever she wanted—that I tripped, that I must have been lost, that I was sleepwalking.

Her eyes followed me down the hall where I closed and locked the bedroom door. Climbed into bed. Pressed myself hard into Owen's side.

I can't stay in bed any longer. I need him.

I sit up and tug the curtains to the side and am greeted with trees. Driving here last night, I knew we were deep in the woods, but I hadn't realized how secluded we really are. There's nothing outside, just a deep forest, browns and shadowed greens, the colors dark, the sunlight barely able to fight its way through the canopy.

Even when I go up on my tiptoes to try to see over the trees, there's nothing breaking up the monotony. No roof, no chimney, no sign of any civilization beyond the window I'm staring through.

I force myself to get dressed. After brushing my teeth and pulling my hair into a ponytail, I tug on my favorite NY Giants hoodie and wander out of the room to find Owen. The smell of fresh coffee greets me when I'm halfway down the stairs and I pick up the pace, hurrying through the library and dining room, and into the kitchen.

"Good morning," I say, fully expecting Owen to be right there, for him to sweep me into his arms and give me a morning kiss, but the kitchen is mostly empty.

Except for Marta.

Crap.

She sits at the kitchen counter, her back to me, bent over something. I'm not entirely sure how to play this, given she caught me sneaking around the house last night, but I'm going to start by being as friendly as possible. I'm still here for a purpose, and playing dumb might be the only way to get what I want.

"Hi, Marta," I say, walking around the island.

She slowly turns to look at me, pushing her reading glasses up on her nose as she does. "Oh, Gina. You're actually awake this time. I thought for sure you must be sleepwalking again, although I'm confident Owen would have told me if you were afflicted with such a malady."

I force a smile. "I wasn't sleepwalking, Marta. I was looking for something."

"What were you looking for?"

I pause. "My ChapStick. It must have fallen out of my pocket yesterday."

She doesn't smile. "So you took a flashlight and nosed around downstairs while everyone else was asleep? I can't say that sounds very unfeigned of you." Her responses are rapid-fire. I wonder how long she's been up thinking about this conversation.

"What can I say? I needed ChapStick and didn't want to wake Owen." She doesn't respond, so I continue. "Anyway, that coffee smells amazing. Just what I need to wake up." I don't want to turn my back on her, but I do so I can walk over to the coffeepot.

"Because you were snooping around all night."

My hand is right above a coffee mug, but I pause. "I wasn't snooping, I was—you know what? It doesn't matter. I just hope I didn't wake you." I close my eyes for a moment and take a deep breath. *Where is Owen when I need him?*

"Actually, I was awake. I don't sleep well with strange people in the house." There's ice in her voice. "Is there something you want?"

"Just coffee. Mind if I grab a cup?" I'm already flipping over one of the mugs by the coffeepot, but it still feels polite to ask.

"We have instant. That seems more your speed."

I frown. "No, this is great. Thanks. I'm going to finish it, if that's okay."

She sighs. "If you must. The guys already took some with them on their trip. Don't bother starting a new pot; you have to get the proportions of water to grounds perfect, and I don't trust you to do it."

I ignore the jab. "Where did they go?"

I fill my mug to the brim and replace the pot, then turn and lean against the counter while watching her. Before she responds, I take a sip of the coffee. It's... wow. Insanely good. Much better than the no-name stuff I grew up drinking, and better than the Folgers I could afford before meeting Owen. Even he doesn't have coffee like this, and he likes the best of the best.

"Just for a walk around the erf." She glances up at me, then her face brightens. "Oneiric! That's it."

"I'm sorry?" I step closer to her, then see what she was bent over as I walked in. "Oh, a crossword? You're a fan?"

"Of course. It's the best way to keep your brain sharp." Her pen flies across the paper, and I frown, trying to figure out what it is about her doing a crossword that doesn't feel quite right.

Then it hits me. She's using a pen, not a pencil. There's no soft scraping sound of lead on paper, just a smooth glide as she writes in the letters. And... I look closer, checking for any letters she's written and then scratched out. Yep, no mistakes. What kind of a monster completes a crossword with a pen and doesn't make any mistakes? And then uses the words from the crossword in everyday life?

"Do you do the crossword?" She's talking to me but doesn't look up from the paper in front of her. Her hand flies across the screen as she fills in the little boxes.

"I don't," I say, "but I do the Wordle. That's more my speed actually. Owen and I compete every morning to see who gets it in fewest tries. It's about fifty-fifty who wins." I shrug. Take a sip.

No response.

"Sooo, what's the plan for the day?" I know Owen has every right to disappear with his dad for as long as he wants while we're here, but I can't help but wish I'd at least had a heads-up. Growing up, I always had this dream that my future mother-in-law and I would get along perfectly.

Not that I ever imagined Marta would be my mother-in-law. Honestly, that was never the plan when I met Owen. Meet Owen, have him fall in love with me. Meet his parents. Deal with them.

That was my plan from day one. But I didn't take into account how quickly I could fall for him. Meeting him was on purpose. Falling this hard? That was an accident. I've had to adapt.

"Oh, I don't know." The exhalation that leaves her lips tells me just how annoyed she is at having to look up from her cross-word. She puts her pen down and pushes the paper away from her. "It's the first time Owen has brought anyone home with him, so we're not really used to having to share him. Normally, it's just whatever the three of us want to do." A pause. "On a normal visit, I'd be out there walking around with them, but *someone* was obligated to stay home in case you yenned for anything when you woke up."

Obligated. Yenned. Most people don't talk like Marta, do they? I'm feeling a little stupid talking with her.

No, not talking. *Conversing* with her. Take that, Marta—I can use big words too.

"Well, I appreciate you being willing to wait around for me." I throw her a winning smile, the one I always use with patients' families when they look lost and in need of extra care. "I was so excited to get to come here with Owen, to get to know you and his dad. He goes on and on about how much he loves the two of you, you know."

"He's a good son." Now that the conversation has veered away from being about me and is firmly in Marta's interests, she fixes her blue eyes on me. "Always has been. Willing to do whatever Grant and I ask of him. There aren't many children nowadays who are willing to listen to their parents like he is. And we've been so close since he was little. I'm sure you know about that."

"He's told me Grant traveled all the time for work and it was just the two of you. It must be hard to see him grow up and find someone else he wants to spend his time with."

Marta purses her lips. "Sons always need their mothers, Gina, and woe to the woman who tries to come between them."

That... wasn't really an answer, but I move on, unsure if she'll answer my questions when she obviously doesn't like me. "Did you ever travel with Grant?"

Her eyes flick to mine and she holds my gaze for a moment before responding. "Once or twice when Owen was older and out of the house, but it wasn't really my thing."

"You didn't like being holed up in a hotel room while Grant knocked out business?"

Her lips tighten. "I didn't like interacting with the locals as much as he did. Although there was once or twice I got... personal with people on the trip."

My heart hammers. *I knew it.* Marta acts so innocent. I think back to the nights my dad would come home smelling like another woman and my stomach twists. Before I can say anything else, she continues.

"But that's in the past. When Owen was younger, I never

would have left him. He needed me. We've always done every-thing possible to make Owen's life run smoothly and to take care of him. I highly doubt he'll ever forget that."

"From what I've heard, it's a two-way street." I take a sip of coffee. "Owen's told me before how Grant encouraged him to work at Mercy Mission. He's made it pretty clear to me that without your support, he wouldn't be there, not when there were so many other places he could have gone. And then I never would have met him. So I guess I should thank you for that."

"Grant really wanted him to get a job there," Marta confirms, but she's speaking slower now, as if carefully choosing her words.

"Why is that?" My mouth waters for another sip of coffee, but I don't dare move to lift my mug. It feels like Marta's about to tell me something important. The air in here has changed; there's electricity crackling between the two of us. I don't know what it is. All I know is that I really want to hear from her why Grant pushed Owen to work at that one hospital.

I just want to hear the truth.

Marta frowns at me. She gives her head a little shake, then plasters a smile on her face.

It's almost a mirror image of mine.

"Is that really something you need to be vexing yourself with? As his mother, I'm privy to everything Owen thinks is important. But you're just the girlfriend."

Just the girlfriend? I frown, but before I can respond, she continues.

"You know how it is between sons and their fathers," she tells me. "Grant just wants the best for Owen, as I'm sure your parents want for you. Mercy Mission is—"

"It's good," I say at the same time she says, "—exactly where he needed to be."

I add, "But honestly? For cardiac care? There are better hospitals." I take a sip and stare at her over the edge of the mug.

This has bothered me from day one of meeting Owen. The man could easily be top in the country, if not the world. And I'm not just saying that because of that thing he can do with his tongue. He's that good. Owen doesn't know this, but I saw the letter on his desk inviting him to come work at Sacred Grove Hospital.

Sacred. Grove. Hospital. The best in the country for cardiac care. Owen could have gone there right after residency, but instead he ended up at Mercy Mission.

He hasn't mentioned the letter, and it's been a month.

"Mercy Mission is precisely where Owen needed to be at this point in his life." Marta gives a little sniff and nods at me. "I think you'll do well to remember that."

She pushes back from the counter, grabs her coffee mug, and walks to the sink to rinse it out. "Owen has always had the two of us looking out for his best interests. I know you think you're important, and you think you know what he needs, but trust me. You don't. Not like I do."

All I can do is sit and stare at her as I try to work through what she said as well as any implications.

Grant and Marta pulled the strings to get him employed at Mercy Mission, but I'd been doing my research well before Owen walked through that front door. His parents getting him a job at the hospital where I worked made it that much easier for me to run into him.

Kismet, some might say. But I don't believe in fate, or luck, or karma.

She wouldn't admit it, but I believe they put him there for a reason: to meet me.

SIX

GINA

Marta's onto me. She knows I was snooping last night. I just have to hope she doesn't figure out why.

There's an icy chill in the house while we wait for Owen and Grant to come back home. I could text him and let him know I'm up and that I miss him, but it can wait. Marta could be dangerous, but that's what I'm trying to figure out. Even if she is, I don't think I'm in danger right now. Not in the daylight. Not when Owen could return home at any moment.

Besides, there's one thing I read that I have to keep reminding myself of: anytime there's a disagreement between a girlfriend and the boyfriend's mom, the girlfriend needs to remember she won. She's the one he takes home at night; she's the one he falls into bed with. She's the one he tells all of his dreams and fears to, not his mother.

So while Marta might have been more than a little bit of a bitch to me in the kitchen, I'm going to let it roll off my back. Not because I want to, but because of the plan. I'm the one her son chose to spend time with. He has to spend time with her because she's his mother.

But in the end, I'm going to win.

Which is why I'm currently curled up in a massive armchair by the roaring fire, a smutty romance novel I found tucked on a shelf between classics like *Old Yeller* and *Pride and Prejudice* in my hand. I'm not currently reading it because while heaving bosoms and ripped gentlemen are a fun thing to read about, I can't tear my eyes away from this room.

Because it's insane. Over-the-top. Decked out to the nines.

It's what I think an eighteenth-century hunting lodge would look like, mounted deer heads included. There are three leather armchairs up close to the fireplace and a pair of sofas turned to face each other directly behind where I'm sitting. Behind that is the pool table, then the bar.

But it's the stuff on the walls that has me agog. Deer heads, with antlers so big they look fake. Old guns hung up like artwork. Paintings of bird dogs out in the bush and a gold-leaf embellished turtle shell. Yeah, that's right. A huge snapping turtle shell that someone brushed gold leaf on.

I'm definitely going to have to ask Owen about that one. Was it an arts and crafts project when he was a little kid? Was it an inside joke? Or is it something his parents take seriously? Now that I've seen how intense his mom is with crossword puzzles, nothing would surprise me.

Just as I'm ready to continue reading about Amelia and her illicit affair with Marcus, the king's best friend, I hear the front door open and then slam shut. A burst of cool air shoots down the hall, wrapping around me. Shivering, I stand, put the book in my seat, and go find Owen.

He's right there by the front door, his cheeks bright pink, his eyes sparkling. For a moment I pause, surprised at just how happy he looks after walking around outside in the freezing air, but then he turns to me and his face lights up even more. Grant's next to him, unwinding a scarf from around his neck, but I ignore him and race to Owen.

"Good morning!" I say, jumping up and wrapping my legs

around his waist. He laughs, grabbing me so I won't fall. "Ooh, you're cold. I think there's still some coffee left if you want. Or I can make another pot."

"More coffee sounds great. And breakfast, if you don't mind." Owen kisses me, his hands spread on my back. "I told Dad last week about that herby frittata you make, if you think you can whip it up for brunch."

"I had Marta pick up the ingredients for you," Grant offers. "Owen's been going on and on about what a good cook you are, and now I can't wait to try it."

I grin at him as Owen puts me down. "He bragged on my cooking? No, he didn't." *Of course he did.* I've been studying Julia Child, Gordon Ramsay, Pierre Gagnaire. For Owen, I had to become the perfect woman. It was all part of the plan. It's meant long hours in the gym, longer hours in the kitchen learning how to cook and bake. I spent hundreds of dollars at the salon to prepare for the first time I spoke to him, giving my credit card a run for its money, and look: it all worked out.

Owen laughs, and I whack him in the arm. "Okay, if that's what y'all want, that's what y'all will get. Brunch sounds perfect."

"I can't wait." Grant smiles at me. "Owen, why don't you get her all set up in the kitchen? I'm going to change my wet socks, then find your mother and tell her that you and I survived a chilly morning outside."

Grant leaves us, his voice trailing off as he walks down the hall.

"I'm starving," Owen tells me, pulling me by the hand towards the kitchen. "But how did you sleep? Did you have a chance to talk to Mom this morning?"

"Slept great," I say. "And yeah, I saw your mom for a bit while I had some coffee. She was obliterating a crossword, so I didn't want to interrupt her."

There. That's a nice way to tell Owen that I saw his mom

but we didn't really chat because she's a bitch. The last thing I want is to make him feel bad about leaving me here with her, or for him to pick up on the fact that she doesn't like me. You don't need to be able to read minds to know the truth: no woman Owen brought home would be good enough for Marta.

"She's convinced they're going to keep her young." Owen's voice is soft. Conspiratorial.

"Well, she tore through it this morning."

We reach the kitchen as I'm about to say something else, but my words fail me. The smoke from the fire in the reading room must have been so strong that I couldn't smell what Marta had in the oven, but now she turns to us, gently knocking the oven door closed with her hip as a delicious smell wafts over me.

She's holding a frittata in her hands, her bright-red oven gloves carefully cupping the red pie plate like it's made of gold.

"Owen! You're back! I made brunch, so this is perfect timing." She grins at him, then carries the dish to the table, carefully depositing it on a trivet. "Nothing fancy, of course, but I figured you'd be famished after your stroll."

"Is that a frittata?" Owen asks. He's let go of my hand and walks over to the table to look.

I follow, unable to help myself.

"A frittata?" She laughs, reaching out and touching his arm. "Goodness, no, how pedestrian. This is a quiche, darling. Have you not had one recently?"

In addition to the quiche, there's a huge fruit salad on the table. Croissants. Three different types of jelly. Orange juice—"Freshly squeezed, of course," I hear her say—and a bottle of champagne on ice for mimosas. And everything has little hand-written labels in front of it.

When did she put all this out?

"This is too much," I say, interrupting whatever else she was saying. "Amazing spread, Marta, but you didn't have to go to this much trouble."

"No trouble at all," she says, but she's not looking at me. "I'd spend all day in the kitchen cooking if that's what Owen wanted. I'm sure you'll understand one day if you ever have children."

I've had a long line of therapists since I was a little girl. Some of them weren't nearly as great as others. They only wanted to get close to me to hear as many terrible details about what happened when I was little as they possibly could.

My mom usually rooted those out pretty quickly. It was clear when a therapist wanted a salacious story and when they wanted to help me.

But the good therapists I had, the ones who cared about me and not about what my story could do for them? Some of them really helped me. I draw on my time with them now, carefully taking deep breaths through my nose, holding the air, then exhaling it.

It's that or I lunge at her and throttle her.

Marta looks thrilled with herself. She doesn't glance at me but is staring at Owen like she won the lottery.

Another breath.

"I wanted Gina to make her frittata for us," Owen says slowly as he reaches back for my hand. "That's why Dad gave you a shopping list. So you'd have everything she needed."

"Well, I wanted to cook for you." Marta frowns. Glances at me, then flicks her eyes away again. "Why aren't you happy? You love quiche. And you love my cooking." She looks back at me. "Owen, every time you come home, you tell me how good my cooking is. That it's better than anyone else's, even Gina's, I'm assuming. So why would I make you eat her food while you're here when I know how much you love mine?"

"Mom. Please don't do this." He squeezes my hand, blood rushing into his cheeks. I return the pressure. "Gina is an amazing cook." Her face tightens, and he continues. "There's no comparison between the two of you—I love both of your cooking. This is lovely, but next time, ask. I want you to get to know Gina and how amazing she is, not steamroll her with what you think I want."

She huffs. "I don't see why I have to ask permission to cook something in my own house. But fine, if Gina wants to cook, she can cook." Her hands are behind her back now, and she unties her apron, then rips it off over her head before wadding it into a ball and throwing it on the counter. "I'll get your father for brunch. At least he appreciates the hard work I put into meals."

I wait until she's stomped out of the kitchen to turn to Owen. "Hey," I say, grabbing his other hand as well. "Thank you. I don't want to be the reason you don't get along with your parents. This trip—"

"Is important because I wanted them to get to know you." He kisses me, then lets go of my hands. I step to the side as he pulls out my chair, then settle into it. "My mom is controlling. Don't let her get to you, okay? I'm on your side here."

"I love you," I say, but I don't really pay attention when he says it back because I'm too busy thinking.

He said his mom is the controlling one, but Owen told me his dad is the one who pushed for him to leave the hospital he was at and work at Mercy Mission. Usually in a couple like this, one is the puppet and one pulls the strings.

But who is who?

SEVEN

MARTA

Owen keeps choosing her over me.

My hand tightens on the knife I'm washing. Grant keeps my knives sharp, the edges so keen it's like I work in a fancy restaurant, and as a result, I barely feel it slice into my skin.

Red blooms across my palm.

"Shit!" I drop the knife with a clatter. Leaning forward, I turn off the water and grab the fluffy white towel from the dish drainer, quickly wrapping it around my left hand.

"What happened?" It's Grant. Always Grant, even though I want Owen to check on me right now. He takes me by the shoulders and turns me to him, carefully cradling my hand in his.

A shiver races up my spine at his touch. "I slipped washing the knife," I say, gesturing behind him to the sink. "I'm fine. It was really sharp, that's all."

"I'll get Owen."

Grant lets go of my hand, but I reach out with my good one and grab him by the arm to stop him.

"He's a cardiologist, Grant. Not a general surgeon."

"He could still stitch you up."

"With what? A sewing needle? Did you see him bring a full med kit with him?" I shouldn't snap at him, not when he thinks we're in this together, but I can't help myself. "Just let me handle it, Grant. I always do."

He blinks at me. "What the hell is that supposed to mean?"

My hand throbs. The towel is slowly turning red. Instead of running to the bathroom to look for a bandage, I force myself to swallow hard and answer him.

"I'm sorry," I lie. "I'm just... stressed. This, with Gina? It's stressful." My voice is quiet, but I take a step closer to him to ensure nobody will overhear me. "I had no idea—"

"You knew what we agreed to do. To handle this." He eyeballs me. When he reaches out and cups my cheek, I have to fight to keep from pulling back.

Yes. I do know what I agreed to do, and if Grant pushes me to go over the plan again, I'll happily do it. But there's one thing he doesn't know, and that's that plans change. This plan? The one I came up with and he put into motion to clean up what happened before? It's changed.

It's time for my plan now.

"You're right," I say, resting my hand on his chest. The throbbing in my cut hand is enough to make tears spring to my eyes, but I don't want to let on how badly it hurts. "You're always right, Grant. It's just that we've been planning this for so long, and now it's finally here..."

"Don't get cold feet." His voice is a warning. In an instant, his eyes are darker, his mouth set in a line.

I shake my head. "I won't."

"Good girl. I love you, Marta." He kisses me, then grabs my hurt hand. "Are you sure you don't want help with this?"

"I have it under control. Don't worry about me."

Another kiss, then he's off, probably headed to his office.

What he needs an office for now that he's retired, I don't know, but I'm not going to push him on it. From what I've seen over the years, it's best for him to think he's in control and getting what he wants.

Like this trip. Grant thinks we're in this together.

But I'm the one who's going to come out on top.

EIGHT

GINA

Then

It's raining outside, huge fat drops that splash on the car and race down the windows. I have my hands spread wide, pressed against the glass, and I peer outside.

We're almost to my Aunt Bethany's house.

There are few things in this world I love more than when my dad takes time off work to take my mom on a date night. They keep telling me that when I'm older they'll leave me at the house by myself, but I'm not looking forward to that. Most kids probably would. They'd love the opportunity to dip into the ice cream without someone knowing, to stay up late watching TV, to steal a little money from the stash in their mother's bottom dresser drawer.

But not me. Not that I don't want to do all of those things, but I'd rather spend the evening with Aunt Bethany.

She's younger than my mom, the *oops* sister that wasn't ever supposed to happen. I love her red hair, the way she snorts when she laughs, and how she lets my cousin, Wade, and me run the house when I come spend the night with her.

Wade never comes to our house, not because Aunt Bethany doesn't trust my parents, but because she doesn't have anywhere to go. No boyfriend, no money for date night. Wade was an *oops* baby too, something I've heard my parents whisper about when they've had too much to drink or they think I'm not paying attention.

Well, it's mostly my dad whispering about it. He likes to remind my mom how he saved her by scooping her out of the gutter. Nobody's ever done that for Aunt Bethany, but I don't care. I love her worn-out sofa, the way it never matters if I put my shoes on it. I love eating microwaved meals for dinner because that's something I'm never allowed to have at home. And I love the way all of her clothes are so soft because they're old, so when she hugs me, it feels like I'm being wrapped in a cloud.

Aunt Bethany doesn't have any sharp corners. It's nice.

"Okay, we're here." Dad announces with a sigh, and Mom turns around, reaching back for me. The new bracelet Dad gave her for their anniversary sparkles in the light despite how dim and gloomy it is outside.

Real diamonds do that, honey. They look pretty, no matter what. Be like that.

"You have a good time with Bethany and Wade, okay?" Mom purses her lips at me. Her makeup is perfect. This evening I sat on her bed and watched her put it on, but I wasn't allowed to make a sound in case she messed up. "Be good, Gina. Show Wade what someone a little more grown-up is like."

I fight to roll my eyes. Wade is just as grown-up as I am, especially because he's two years older than I am. I know how much he helps out around the house so his mom doesn't have to do all the work and cleaning on her own. If that's not grown-up, then I don't know what is.

Dad pulls to a stop, and I grab my backpack, unbuckle, and

throw the door open in one fluid motion. Before he can tell me goodbye, I wave, then hop out of the car, running to the porch.

This is where I belong. Right here. With Aunt Bethany.

She's standing on the porch, a faded old blue apron wrapped around her waist, and I feel a jolt of excitement. An apron means more than just a microwaved meal. It means fresh cookies or brownies to go with it.

"Aunt Bethany!" I crow her name, and she throws her head back, laughing. When I slam into her legs, she braces herself, then pulls me closer, dipping her head down to kiss me on the forehead.

"Sweet Gina," she tells me. "Do you have any idea how long I've been waiting for you to come see me again? It's been too long!"

"It's been two weeks," I correct, then slip my arm around her waist and turn to wave goodbye to my parents. Dad flicks his lights at me, making the falling rain sparkle, then slowly backs down the driveway. I turn back to my aunt. "Two weeks! That's not so long. Dad doesn't always get time off that easily, so I'm happy about it."

"Me too, Gina." Her words are quick, falling on me like the rain. My parents speak slowly, always carefully choosing their words, like they're afraid they're going to use them up. Aunt Bethany isn't like that. I never feel like I'm taking up too much of her time or that her words will run out when I'm with her.

"So, what's first? Dinner? Or cards?" I look past her at the house. The front door is open, but the screen door is closed to keep out mosquitos. It hangs crooked on its hinges, but I don't care. It wouldn't matter to me if the entire house leaned a little to the side.

"Cards first," she announces, turning and opening the screen door with a flourish. "Wade is getting everything set up, but then he's going to go to a friend's house."

There's a moment of sadness that washes over me as I walk past her. "He doesn't want to stay here with the two of us?"

"That's not it."

She shuts both doors. I watch as she throws the deadbolt. It makes a thick sound as it slides into place. We have an alarm system, something three men in suits came out to the house to install a few years ago. I know Mom hates that Bethany doesn't have one, but it's not like she can afford it. That's what Mom says anyway. When I asked her one time why she and Dad don't just buy an alarm for Aunt Bethany, she told me to hush.

It's the same thing she did when I found the papers on her counter from the credit card company. She'd gotten red in the face and told me to stop snooping.

How can anyone owe another person that much money?

And if they owe that much money, how did Dad buy Mom a new bracelet?

I can't make it make sense. Mom always swipes her credit card at the fancy stores in town. Acts like it's no big deal. Like it's free money.

"Well, if he's not staying while I'm here, then it feels like he doesn't want to." I drop my backpack to the floor with a thud and cross my arms to prove my point.

"Oh, kiddo. Wade got invited to a sleepover tonight, but he's headed over late so he could see you! You don't really think he would give up a chance to hang out with his favorite cousin, do you?"

"I'm his only cousin," I grumble, but I can feel a smile tugging at the corners of my mouth as I follow her into the kitchen. Rows of cookies cool on the counter, the chocolate chips in them still melted and glossy. I move quickly and grab one, stuffing it into my mouth before she has a chance to react.

Wade sees me though. He always does.

"Gina!" He's sitting at the table shuffling the cards for the three of us to play poker. Mom would die if she knew I was playing a betting game, but Aunt Bethany said that since we only play for pennies, it doesn't count. I've gotten pretty good and have a Ziploc bag of pennies in my backpack to show for it.

"Hey, Wade," I say around the cookie in my mouth. He hops up and hugs me, then grabs us each another cookie. "I heard you're going to a sleepover tonight. What gives?"

He pulls a face as we sit back down. Aunt Bethany's digging in the freezer for something for us to eat. Probably microwave pizza. Or lasagna, if it was on sale. She got me this kid's meal last time that had lasagna, green beans, and garlic bread. It was amazing.

"It's Jeremy from school," he tells me, his wrist a blur as he flicks cards across the table. "He's nice, but needy. But he doesn't really have any friends, so I told him I'd be his friend."

"You're a good guy," I tell him, grabbing my cards and peeking at them. Not bad.

"So good I'm going to kick your butt."

"Language." Aunt Bethany mashes some buttons on the microwave and it starts to whirr. "Now, Gina, why don't you grab your pennies and I'll take you two to the cleaners?"

I turn and grin at her. There's dim light coming in from the window behind her, giving her something of a halo. It's so cheesy, like something I would have read in a book as a little kid, but at the same time, it makes sense. Aunt Bethany is the best.

I love my parents and I know they care for me, but they'll never understand what it feels like to come here. I don't care that the food is all microwaved or that the cookies were baked out of that plastic tube you can buy in the refrigerated section of the grocery store.

This is my safe place. Nothing bad can happen here.

NINE

GINA

The wide wood planks under my feet don't creak or moan as I walk slowly down the hall. Marta's in the bathroom, wrapping up a cut on her hand, Owen's helping her, and Grant... well, Grant wandered off to his office. I gave it long enough for him to get settled in before following him. After poking around and trying to get into that room last night while everyone was sleeping, I figured he must keep his office key on him at all times, so the only chance I have to see in there is when he's inside.

Nothing in the house was out of place last night. That tells me I have to get behind a locked door.

Right outside Grant's office I pause, then take another step forward, craning my neck to look around the doorframe. If he's facing me, I'll make up some lie about wanting to know more about the history of the house, but I get lucky.

His desk faces the large windows on the other side of the room, and I watch as he leans back in his leather chair, his hands behind his head, and lets out a sigh. It's the sigh of a contented man, one who hasn't ever run into a single roadblock in his entire life. In that way, he and his son are the same.

My fingers tighten on the doorframe as I watch him, but it

isn't long before my gaze wanders around the rest of his office. Bookcases loaded to the point of groaning line one wall. There's a low table on the other wall with a globe as well as some papers spread out on the surface. I lean forward, afraid to actually enter the office but determined to see what's on those papers.

A list? Maybe. I take a deep breath and lean a bit farther into his office. I squint, trying to make out the handwriting. You know what it looks like? A grocery list, which is the least exciting thing I could imagine finding in here.

I shake my head. *Idiot.*

What was I really thinking? That he would have a list incriminating him just sitting around? I shake my head. Nerves of being in this house are getting to me. Wade told me I didn't need a list, that we were right, but I'd still like to—

"Gina? What are you doing?"

Owen's voice behind me causes me to whip round, my heart kicking into high gear. I let go of the doorframe and run a hand through my hair, forcing myself to smile.

"Just taking myself on a house tour," I tell him. "After the bathrooms looked like something out of the Taj Mahal, I got a little curious about what the rest of the house looked like."

"Oh." He frowns, glancing past me into the office. Even though I didn't hear the squeak of Grant turning around in his chair, I have no doubt he's no longer looking out the window. "All you had to do was ask. You should have known I'd be more than happy to take you around. Give you the tour."

"Oh, but you were helping your mom." I go up on my tiptoes and give him a kiss. "I didn't want to interrupt." Grant hasn't said a thing, but I swear I can feel his gaze boring into my back. Goosebumps break out on my arms.

"You're fine. I got her all wrapped up." He pauses, thinking, then gives a little nod, like whatever idea he just had was perfect. "Why don't we walk around the property? I'd love for you to see the place—really get to know it. There's a stream out back where I used to fish as a kid, and I can show you my old treehouse."

Right now, this happy, he looks less like the formidable Dr. Whitlock and more like the happy little kid I know he was. He grins at me, then runs a hand through his hair while he waits for my response.

"You know what? That sounds great. Let me run upstairs and get my shoes." I point down at my socked feet to prove my point, then hurry away before he can change his mind and question me about what I was really doing spying on his dad. Behind me, I hear one of them speaking, but I can't tell if it was Grant or Owen.

I pause, listening, but they're too quiet.

Shivering, I race up the stairs to the bedroom. For a moment, I stand in the door and consider Grant and Marta's room. Nobody's in there right now, and I could easily go poke around, but not with Owen waiting for me.

Marta saw me last night. And now Owen found me at his dad's office. The last thing I need is for him to question what I'm doing in his parents' room.

It takes all of my strength to turn my back on the door. Grant or Marta could pop through at any time. Before grabbing my boots, I throw a glance over my shoulder.

Nobody's there.

It'll be great to get outside with Owen, to have it be just the two of us. I guess, in that way, it's a good thing this place is so much bigger than I believed it was.

I can't even imagine being stuck with Grant and Marta in a smaller house.

The thought gives me shivers. Now *that's* the stuff of nightmares.

I yank on my hiking boots—new ones Owen bought me just for this trip—then tie them and hurry back downstairs. Owen's waiting for me at the front door, and I let him slip a coat over my arms before zipping it up while he pulls on a heavy coat.

"You kids really heading out in this chill?" It's Grant, appearing in the hall like a ghost. He has a cup of coffee in a death grip, and no, I'm not entirely sure I'm right, but I'm fairly certain I smelled some whiskey in his cup earlier. That's one way to stay warm, I guess. His eyes flick from his son to me, then slide slowly down my body.

"It's better than staying cooped up inside." Owen throws his dad a winning smile. It's the same one that appeared on the cover of the hospital's latest quarterly report, and for good reason. If Owen hadn't decided to save lives, he could easily be a movie star.

Rich *and* good-looking? I want to pinch myself when I think about how lucky I got.

But even if he didn't look like a movie star, I would still have dumped my coffee on him. It was the only way to get what I wanted.

"That's always true. You want company?" Grant takes a sip of his coffee, watching his son over the rim.

"We're fine," Owen tells him, zipping up his own coat before turning to me. "We'll be back before we freeze, so tell Mom not to worry."

"Ten-four, kiddo." Grant salutes the two of us, then Owen and I are on the porch, the door closed firmly behind us.

"I didn't think your dad was a cop," I say, following him down the wide stairs to the driveway. "Wasn't he in sales?"

Owen shakes his head. "Yeah, definitely not a cop. Why?"

"Because he just used cop lingo." I frown. "I didn't think that was something people used unless they were cops."

This makes him laugh. "He always loved cop shows when I was growing up. None of the true crime stuff, really, but... what was that one? 'Bad boys, what is that you're about to do?' What show was that?"

It's my turn to laugh. "Well, you butchered it a little, but *Cops*. That was the theme song for *Cops*. You really don't know that?"

He shrugs. "Dad didn't watch those shows when he was home. Said he didn't want me seeing the bad behavior and thinking it was cool." He slips his hand into mine. "But he'd tell Mom about some of the episodes he'd watch while on the road, and she ate it up. She'd sing it after getting off the phone with him."

"No, she did not!" I can't help but grin.

"Why don't you believe me? Because she's just so hip that it's unfathomable?"

"That's exactly it." We're in the woods now on a path I hadn't noticed last night. It looks taken care of, with plants brushing up against the side of the trail but nothing growing in the middle of it. It's barely wide enough for the two of us to walk side by side, and only because we really like each other.

Our hips keep bumping, and I let go of his hand to wrap my arm around his waist and pull him closer while we walk.

"It's just strange to me that the queen of crosswords would find anything at all dangerous sexy." I look up at him as I speak.

"Please don't ever talk about my parents and use the word *sexy* in the same sentence." He squeezes my hip a little bit to let me know he's not really mad. "I don't think I can stomach it."

"Fair."

We brush through ferns that have grown over the path, then Owen clears his throat. "Gina, why didn't you just ask me for a tour of the house?"

I stumble but laugh it off when Owen wraps his arm around my waist. "You were busy, like I said. I didn't want to bother you, and it was a split-second decision on my way back from the bathroom."

He nods, then gestures for me to lead the way. I hate how impassive his face is.

Can he tell I'm lying to him?

We fall silent as we walk. The sound of running water is so quiet that, at first, I think I'm hearing things. As we draw closer, however, it gets louder until we're standing looking down into a stream. Isn't that what Owen called it? A stream?

There he goes again, underselling parts of this trip. He called the MiniMansion a cabin. This river a stream. Water boils over rocks and laps up against the bank. There's a flick of silver about twenty feet away, and I point. "What was that?"

"A fish probably. It's loaded with trout." He turns to me. "Hey! Why don't we fish for our dinner? I didn't even think about doing that earlier, but there really isn't anything quite like fresh fish. I'll teach you how to gut them."

My stomach twists. *Gutting* isn't on my to-do list.

"I'm glad you're okay with your hands in something's abdominal cavity," I say, "but that's not really my thing. I'm much better at getting a fish's information, finding out where they need to go, and pointing them in the right direction."

"It would be a lot of fun." He steps closer to me, blocking my view of the river. Right now, Owen is the only thing I can see. It was like that when I first met him. The first time I saw him, when I realized I'd found him, that all of our hard work had panned out, it felt like my vision shrank down to a tiny dot.

"If it's really important to you, I'll come with you," I say. Owen, like all surgeons, is used to getting his way. Surgeons are gods in the operating room and want to be treated as such when they're out of it. I knew that getting into this relationship. "But I won't hook a worm. And I'm not going to gut a fish."

He nods slowly. "Fine, but you can change your mind, okay? I'll let you."

"So noble," I tease.

He kisses me, cutting off whatever else I was going to say. When he steps away, he takes me by the hand to pull me down the trail.

"Wait, we haven't gone that way yet," I say, pointing behind us.

"I want to get my fishing stuff," he tells me. He's excited now, like a little kid on a mission to show someone their fort. Or maybe a frog in their pocket. It's a side of Owen I don't get to see at the hospital.

"I can't wait," I lie. "Hey, let me ask you something." He doesn't slow down. "You said yesterday that your parents have been wanting to meet me for months, but we've only been together, what, like seven weeks?"

A stutter in his step. Did he trip over a root?

I glance down to see what could have caught his toe, but there's nothing there.

"I was being facetious," he tells me, but he doesn't turn to look at me.

His voice is tight.

Looks like I'm not the only one in this relationship who can lie.

TEN

GINA

Styrofoam squeaks when I squeeze the side of the worm cup. After Owen and I got home from our walk and he told his dad he wanted to go fishing, Grant produced a cup of worms. No, not worms. *Nightcrawlers.* They're as thick as my finger, pink and pulsing, the rough band around them drawing my eye. I can only see three on top of the dirt, but Owen assured me there were a dozen or more so of them below.

As if I were worried. God forbid I hold a cup with only three worms.

"Hey, Owen?" I ask, looking up at him from my spot on the bank of the river. He and Grant are in the water, ignoring the way it covers the toes of their boots. Then again, they're in hip waders, so a little bit of water isn't going to get them wet.

He glances over at me, a grin on his face. "Everything okay?"

"Sure is. Hey, random question. Why is the cup cold?" I squeeze it again, and the worm on top turns, burrowing back into the dirt. If they're not moving around, I can't tell their heads from their butts.

Like a lot of people. I fight back a laugh.

"Oh, they were in the fridge." That's Grant, interrupting Owen to explain.

"I can't see Marta letting you put these next to her orange juice." *Gross.*

"Oh, no, I have a worm fridge. It's in my work area."

Grant's no longer looking at me. I watch with a mixture of surprise and revulsion as he stabs the worm he's holding with a fishhook, twisting it up and to the side before doing it again, attaching the squirming thing in just a few seconds.

My breath catches in my throat. A *work area.* I hadn't been sure what I'd be looking for when I came here with Owen, but I knew I needed to find... something. My little tours around the house last night and this morning didn't yield anything, although I did learn how much I want to get into their bedroom as well as Grant's office.

And I learned that Marta didn't want to share with Grant or Owen that I was up snooping in the middle of the night. No way she believed me as to why I was up, so why is she keeping it to herself?

I don't know. What I do know is that I need more time so I can poke around by myself, without Owen acting as a tour guide. And I'd like it to be during the day so I'm not relying on my flashlight to see. What I'm looking for isn't going to be on display. It's going to be locked up, hidden, protected. It'll be somewhere private. "I didn't know you have a work area." As I speak, I watch him.

He gives the worm a little tug, sending it into a spasm of fear and pain, then throws me a shrug. "It's not much, just a little space for me to go tinker away from Marta. Don't want to drive her nuts with my little toys."

"And your worm fridge," I offer, earning a laugh.

"Exactly." He finally looks over at Owen, who's standing

rapt, his fishing pole at the ready, his worm already stabbed through and squirming. "You ready?"

"Hell yeah."

Then, like they're ballerinas or something, the two of them turn and cast into the water, their movements synchronized. The worms land with soft *plinks*, then the bright red-and-yellow bobbers catch and float on the water.

As much as I hate to admit it, I can see why the two of them like fishing. It's quiet out here, the water the only real sound. There's company, but you don't have to talk. And each of them has a beer. Granted, the drinks are by me so they don't accidentally get knocked over into the water, but for an early afternoon drinking event, fishing might not be so bad.

Still, it's not for me.

"If it's cool with you guys, I think I'll leave you to it." I bend down and carefully put the cup on the ground by the beer. It would be easy to tip it over and let the little guys go free, but why not let Owen have his fun? Besides, the longer they stay out here, the more time I'll have in the house. If only Marta wasn't around, this would be working out perfectly. "Fishing really isn't my thing."

"Oh, but I wanted to spend some time with you." Owen hands his rod to his dad and hurries back to shore, splashing loudly. He moves quickly, cupping my cheek lightly with his hand. "I'm sorry, I brought you here to meet my family and spend some time together and all I've been doing today is playing Daniel Boone with my dad."

"It's fine. Seriously. I'm so tired from work that I don't mind a vacation. Besides, I don't want you to feel like you have to cater to me all the time. I'll just go back and see if your mom wants any help around the house."

I'd rather chew off my own arm, but he doesn't have to know that. Just like he doesn't have to know there's no way in hell I'm spending any bonding time with his mother.

I'm going to stay as far away from her as possible while also digging up dirt on her.

"She's gone to town," Grant calls. He's not even looking at the two of us and he still heard what I said. He keeps his eyes on the bobbers, so he doesn't turn to us when he speaks. I'm honestly surprised he could hear me over the sound of the water.

She's gone. I feel a flash of excitement.

"Hey, I don't want you rambling around in that big house by yourself. Stay with us." Owen squeezes my arm. He's standing so close to me I can feel the warmth radiating off him.

A thrill rushes through me, not because of the way Owen's looking at me but at the knowledge that his mother won't be in the house. I'll be alone. I can snoop without anyone seeing me.

"I won't be rambling around," I say, going up on my toes to surprise him with a kiss. "Do you have any idea how many books your parents have?"

He grins, capturing my mouth for another kiss, then lets me go. "As long as you're sure and you're not just leaving because you feel left out."

"Oh, I don't feel left out," I tell him.

I can't guarantee I'll have a lot of time, but I have to try to get into Grant's office. Their bedroom. Any locked cupboards in the kitchen. The garage. And I really want to find Grant's little hidey-hole. What did he call it? A *work area*. That could be so many things. It could be a space for him to woodwork, which is probably what it is, but there's just tinkering, there's writing, there's...

Well, there are a few things I can imagine a man like him wanting to do behind closed doors. Which leads me to another question: does Marta have a hidey-hole? Somewhere she likes to disappear when she needs a break; somewhere she might keep what I'm looking for? It doesn't have to be a room. It could be as small as a closet or a locked drawer. Someplace private. Secret.

Someplace locked, I'd bet on it. As controlling as she is? It makes sense.

"If you're sure." Owen's doing that thing with his voice where he draws out the words because he wants me to feel like he's on my side, like he's not-so-secretly excited about having some alone time with his dad. Or maybe he's just thrilled about the opportunity to go fishing, I'm not sure. Either way, it's the same twitch of the corners of his mouth he does when he's just nailed a difficult surgery.

And, yeah, I know he's hiding how he really feels from me, but it's impossible for me not to smile back.

"I'm sure," I tell him, giving him a quick kiss before waving to Grant, who still has his back to us. "You two have fun! Catch us something yummy for dinner." Then, as quickly as possible, I spin away, hurrying down the path back towards the house.

Owen calls out, but the words are unintelligible. I'm so focused on getting to the house that I don't turn back. Overhead, some birds call as they flit back and forth in the trees, but I don't slow down. I don't look up. The front door is unlocked and I step through, then toe off my shoes.

I slip out of my coat and close the door behind me. I consider locking it but don't want to make Grant and Owen question what I'm doing.

I take a deep breath. It still smells like quiche in here, the scent of it and fried bacon still lingering. I feel my face twist into a scowl and force myself to relax. Sure, Marta is a pill. I didn't know exactly what I was going to be getting into when I met Owen's parents, but I knew it might be tricky.

But this has every possibility of getting worse.

I'd tried to be pretty thorough looking for a hiding spot in the house last night. So where is Grant hiding his little work area? The attic? Basement? I hurry down the hall to his office and grab the door knob, turning it back and forth. Maybe, if I'm lucky, the door will swing open and I'll walk in, nobody around, nobody watching, and—

Locked. Of course. Just like last night. If he has anything hidden in there that will condemn him for what he did, what they did, there's no way he'd leave this door unlocked.

"But what about the garage?" I whisper, rushing down the hall and turning into the kitchen. I saw the door that leads out to the garage in here last night but didn't think anything of it. But why would they have a garage and park on the driveway? At least Marta does. I don't know if Grant has a car or if they share.

But maybe the garage isn't really a garage.

It could be Marta's space to disappear into when she needs a break. It is directly off the kitchen, after all. That means easy access for her when she's cooking. I can see it.

Or maybe it's Grant's *work area*.

Fear tickles the back of my neck and I turn, slowly taking in the entire kitchen. Surely there's no camera in here. I would have seen it. I've been so careful, looking for anything out of place. Surely, if anything, they have cameras outside to protect their property, but why would they need one in the kitchen? They wouldn't. And to get what I want, I don't need to go outside.

I need to get into the locked rooms of this house.

But I didn't see anything last night, and I don't see anything now. No flashing red light. No shiny black eye. I'm just being paranoid.

Holding my head high, I cross to the garage door and turn the handle.

It's locked.

"Of course it's locked. What normal person is going to leave their garage unlocked where just anyone can walk in?" I bend down and peer at the knob, looking for the little button to push or tab to turn to unlock it.

But there's just a keyhole.

"What in the world?" The door's locked—I was right about that much from the start. But I can't open it from inside the house without a key.

Whatever's in here, they really don't want anyone seeing it.

ELEVEN

GINA

I take a step back from the garage door, pulling my phone from my pocket. Surely there's a quick YouTube video that will talk me through how to pick this lock so I can get in.

My hands shake as I swipe on my screen. A graphic of an almost-empty battery flashes at me and I swear. How did I forget to plug it in last night? I do it every single night when I'm about to get in bed. Before I tuck in for the night, I plug in my phone, then put it on the bedside table.

But there isn't a bedside table upstairs. I close my eyes and try to think. Last night Owen and I went upstairs. His parents had already gone to bed, but the two of us were slower in winding down. By the time Owen and I made it to our room, I was too busy thinking about him to worry about my phone.

I'd yanked off my pants and left them there on the floor. And that's where I found my phone this morning. My heart sinks and I check my watch. I don't know how much longer I have until everyone will be back.

"Gina, you idiot," I say, smacking my head with my palm. I'm dying to learn how to pick this lock, but the last thing I need to do is for my battery to die when I have the lock only half-opened. And I need to get a bobby pin or something I can use to pick it. First I'll plug in my phone and use that time to poke around the house again. Maybe I'll find something interesting, and if not, I'll have more battery power to watch a video later.

That hope of finding a bobby pin inspires me, and I go up on my tiptoes, reaching up and running my fingers across the top of the doorframe to look for anything that could be used to open the lock.

Nothing.

"Not even a speck of dust," I grumble and wipe my fingers on my jeans anyway. Of course Marta would make sure every inch of the house was clean before we arrived. I have no doubt she was on her hands and knees wiping down the baseboards to ensure the house sparkled for her son.

I make a face. It's incredible to me, really it is, that Owen turned out as normal as he did. Marta makes herself out to be a saint and the perfect mother, but it's not true. I don't know the full extent of what she did, but I'm going to find out.

"'I didn't like interacting with the locals,'" I mutter as I rub a hand across my forehead. Whenever Marta talks about someone other than Owen, her words drip with derision. But that doesn't mean she's any better than her husband. Or my father.

I turn away from the locked door and hurry upstairs. At the top, I turn to the right and race to Owen's room, only pausing in the doorway for a moment.

I made the bed after we got up, but the comforter seems smoother, the corners tighter. Even the pillows, which I know I left in a messy stack leaning up against the headboard, are straight, orderly.

Did Marta come in here and straighten up after we'd left the house?

A chill works its way up my spine and I turn slowly, taking in the rest of the space.

I don't think anything else is out of place or different, but it's almost impossible to tell. We were only in here long enough to sleep and then get dressed this morning, so I don't know if I'd notice anything out of place. My suitcase is unzipped, clothes already exploding from it, but that's my doing.

Isn't it?

Slowly, like there's a snake that might strike, I walk to my suitcase and poke some of the clothes. I was in such a hurry to get dressed this morning that I barely paid attention to what I was doing as I pulled out my hoodie. It had been under the rest of my shirts and had taken half of them with it, so they now bulged from the suitcase.

It looks like it was ransacked. There's a creak from the hall, and I whip round, my heart hammering in my throat.

Nobody's there. Old houses settle, don't they? They creak and moan, groaning like the elderly getting into bed.

Nervous, I run a hand through my hair and turn back to the suitcases.

Owen's looks as neat as it did when he packed it. His clothes are all in perfect piles, his toiletries bag in the bathroom. There's a pair of slippers next to the suitcase, the two of them neatly laid out for him to put on tonight.

I know those weren't laid out for him earlier. I've never done that for him, and there's only one person I can think of who would go out of her way to pamper him like that.

I scoff, feeling more in control now that I've caught onto her. Marta was digging around where she shouldn't be, but I'm doing the same thing. And I have an advantage—I was prepared for her snooping. I tucked things out of the way where she's never going to find them.

Besides, I highly doubt she would have been able to keep her mouth shut if she'd found what I have hidden.

I push that thought from my head. I have plans to deal with Marta. What matters right now is finding my charger and getting my phone plugged in.

I use an old iPhone, one that doesn't use the C adapter, so I can't just mooch off Owen's power cable, which is conveniently plugged in right by his suitcase. I guess this is what I get for not allowing him to upgrade my phone to an iPhone 15 like his. He keeps offering, but I've told him a few times that I like my phone.

This could have all been avoided if I'd not been so stubborn, but I'm now forced to find my own charger.

And I don't see it.

I'd swear I had it on the top of my clothes last night so I wouldn't forget to charge my phone this morning, but maybe I'm wrong. Everything's a bit of a blur from when Owen and I made our way into the bedroom.

But then where is it?

I carefully pull each piece of clothing from the pile, fold it, and put it back in the suitcase. It's only when I've tucked the last pair of socks in place that I let myself pay attention to the panic building in the back of my mind.

My charger is gone.

I know it was here.

And that only means one thing.

Marta took it.

TWELVE

GINA

Marta and Grant know more about me than they're letting on.

I exhale hard, then squat down, putting my head between my knees. Vomit rises in the back of my throat, and I gasp for air, forcing myself to stand and run to the bathroom. It's only after I've thrown up and brushed my teeth that I sag down to the floor, the tile cool through my jeans.

They took my charger to cut me off from the outside world. That's the only thing that makes sense to me. Owen wouldn't. Grant... I don't think he's had the time alone to take it. But Marta hates me and has from the moment Owen and I pulled up in her driveway.

There's no way I think anyone other than her is behind this. The trouble with that line of thinking is that then it only makes sense if I admit to myself that she took it because she knows why I'm here.

"Oh God," I say. My stomach twists again, and I hurry to the toilet, grabbing the seat as I get sick again. *She knows. She knows. She knows. She knows.*

"Stop it," I say, smacking myself on the cheek. It stings, and

I do it again on the other side. Tears stream down my face, and I force myself to flush the toilet, then brush my teeth.

Getting hysterical isn't going to solve anything. Curling up on the bathroom tile won't help me get to the bottom of this. This time alone is a gift, and I have no idea how much longer I have. I can't waste it, not when this might be my only alone time in the house.

All I want to do is flee. Steal Owen's keys. Take his car and drive until I'm home, then tell Wade I couldn't do it, that it was too hard, that they're smarter than we gave them credit for, that Marta was onto me from the beginning.

But that won't fix what happened.

Besides, if I leave now, I'll never know the full extent of what Marta did.

I splash some water on my face and leave the bathroom, rolling my shoulders back as I hurry down the stairs. Without any idea of when Owen and Grant will finish fishing and Marta will get back from... wherever she is, I have to hurry.

Last night I decided there aren't any cameras in the house. At least, there weren't any I could easily see, and I'm not going to poke through every book on the shelf looking for a hidden camera I was missing. I ignore the fear tickling the back of my neck. *They could be watching me right now.* Instead of slowing down, I race for the front door, only pausing long enough to yank on some sneakers before heading outside.

Grant's office door is locked. The garage is locked. But maybe, just maybe there's a way to get into the garage from outside, and I don't mean through the big double door. It seems pretty common to have an outside door leading into the garage. If there is one, maybe it's unlocked.

Even if it's not unlocked, sometimes doors get damaged by the elements. Mentally, I cross my fingers, hoping the door will be bent, or warped, or not sit perfectly in the doorframe. All I need is a little space I can work my fingers in, or a stick, or something I can use to lever it open.

I'm not thinking straight, and I know it, but rage over my missing phone charger spurs me on. The driveway is clear of fallen leaves, which is bizarre to see in the fall, but of course Marta would have all errant leaves removed. I run along the front of the garage, barely glancing at it as I do. Without a garage door opener, I can't see a way to get in through there. Garage doors are incredibly heavy, and the springs are dangerous.

The grass has been mowed recently. It's the perfect height all the way around the yard, and I can't help but roll my eyes as I hurry across it and around the side of the house. Surely there will be an outside door here.

There has to be some way into that garage. If I can't get in there, can't get in the office, can't find the proof I'm looking for...

Well, Wade would tell me that I don't need proof. That we did all the hard work already. To accept what we've done and move on with the plan, and that's what I'll have to do. But I told him I needed more time to make sure of one thing.

Nobody innocent will be punished. That was my promise to myself.

There. A door. Just like I'd hoped there would be. If we'd gotten blueprints of the house, I wouldn't be out here wondering if there were another way in, but this is good enough. I exhale hard and grab the handle.

Please open, please open, please just swing open and I'll finally know what's in here—

It's locked. I swear, then run my hands along the edges, looking for any weak point I could use to open it. Sweat rolls down the back of my neck, but I ignore it as I search the door.

Nothing. There's nothing.

I step back, my shoulders falling forward. Tears spring to my eyes, and I angrily wipe them away. It was a long shot; that's what it was. Silly of me to pin my hopes on something like a busted door when this place looks like a museum. No way would Marta or Grant allow a broken door to remain unrepaired. They're the type of people to have a quarterly checklist to ensure the house is in great condition every season.

"Okay," I mutter to myself, "that means you'll have to find another way in. Or screw the garage, there's probably nothing important in there." But even as I say that, I think about how the inside door is locked.

Who does that?

It doesn't matter because I can't get into the garage right now. I'll have to come up with another plan, and fast. Time is running out here. Our visit is short, and while earlier I entertained the idea of fleeing this place, I can't do that. Not until it's finished.

I walk around the corner of the house and freeze. Owen and Grant exit the woods across from me at the same time. Owen's carrying a fishing pole and tackle box, while Grant is right behind him with a bucket and fishing pole.

They're laughing, Owen's saying something over his shoulder, but he's going to look over here and see me. He'll wonder what I'm doing outside. I plaster a smile on my face as he turns.

His eyes land on me. A grin spreads across his face but slowly slides off. "Gina? Are you okay?" He moves quickly, putting the tackle box and fishing pole down on the ground. "What are you doing?"

"Just enjoying the fresh air," I lie. "Glad you two are back—it's perfect timing."

He doesn't smile in response. Owen closes the gap between us and lifts my chin with one finger. His eyes are dark, his mouth tight.

Does he know I'm lying?

No, not Owen. He's so innocent, so sweet. He believes me, no matter what I tell him.

"Do you feel okay?" he asks.

"I'm great."

"Gina..." His voice trails off, and he clears his throat. "I know you're lying to me. I really wish you wouldn't do that."

I freeze. There's a little voice in the back of my head screaming at me to make a run for it.

"What?" My voice is strangled.

He drops his finger from my chin and plucks at my shirt. "Is this vomit?"

THIRTEEN

MARTA

What does she know?

Those four words are on repeat as I stand at the stove. I have my apron tied tightly around my waist, a fish spatula in one hand, a glass of white wine in the other. Grant and Owen made short work of the half dozen trout they pulled from the river, and after tossing them in cornmeal and spices and melting butter in my favorite cast iron skillet, I got them on the stove for a salubrious dinner.

I should be enjoying this. I'm in the kitchen; my son is home. And yet all I can think about is Gina. Gina snooping around the house last night. Her little rat eyes, beady and dark, darting around the house, drinking it all in. Looking for something, I'm sure of it.

I asked Grant if he worried she knew what we'd done, but he'd blown me off. But I'm not so sure she's as innocent as he thinks. She knows more than she's letting on, but how much?

I try to ignore the disquiet eating at me and instead focus on Owen. Nobody was really hungry for lunch. I'd bet it was because everyone loved the huge brunch I made this morning. As much as Owen inveighed about my taking over and making the quiche instead of allowing Gina to make a frittata, he sure ate plenty of it.

That makes me smile. My son might put on a brave face in front of Gina, but he's still my little boy. That's something women who don't have sons will never understand. Once you become the mother of a son, you're in a different echelon than everyone else. You have to learn how to handle the heart of a boy, how to turn him into a good man, and you have to do it without losing yourself in the process. There's a bond between a mother and her son that no one, not even his father, will understand. Will be able to replicate.

Especially not her. I have to find out how much she knows, and I have to use her to get what I really want. But how will I find out the truth of what she knows without giving anything up? It'll be hard, putting all the pieces in play before she ruins everything, but I've been planning for this ever since Owen told me he was bringing her home to visit.

Girls... I scoff and poke at the fish before taking another sip of my wine. "Girls are easy," I say.

"What did you say?" Owen pauses next to me, a fifth of rum in one hand, three shot glasses caught in the fingers of his other.

"Oh, I was just muttering to myself," I say, leaning over and giving him a kiss on the cheek. "Nothing to worry about, Owen, just an old lady talking to herself."

"You're not that old," he tells me with an eye roll. "You just act like you are when you get caught doing something you shouldn't."

My mouth falls open, and I snap it shut. "Owen Henry Whitlock. How dare you assail your mother like that?"

The cheeky grin he throws me makes my heart rate slow down. "Oh, Mom. I'm just teasing. I know how stressed out you are about having Gina here though. It's pretty obvious. At least to me."

That's fine. He can see that I'm stressed out as long as he

doesn't realize the real reason I'm on eggshells right now. It's more than him bringing home a girl. It's *which one* he brought home.

Gina. I knew it was going to happen—there really wasn't any other choice. She's been on my radar for years. Her visit has been in the works for much longer than Owen could ever guess. I've planned everything, including how to get her here in the first place, and I'm not going to let her ruin my plan. My poor son, having no idea what his role is in all of this. He's always been so hungry for his father's love that he's been willing to do whatever Grant asks.

Take a job at a hospital that didn't deserve him? *Whatever you say, Dad.*

Date a woman Grant picked out for him? *Of course—I'm happy to.*

Bring that woman home so Grant can do what he wants with her? *My calendar is open.*

My grip tightens on the spatula, and I force myself to take a deep breath. The original plan has been put in action, but my changes make it even better. I have to keep reminding myself that as soon as it's all done, it'll be like old times, the way I like it.

No Grant. No Gina.

Just Owen and me.

"Well, a mother only wants what's best for her son," I say, taking a sip of my wine. "That's all I've ever wanted for you, and if you feel like Gina is the thing that's best, then I don't know that I can argue with you."

"Thanks, Mom." His expression softens as he adjusts his grip on the bottle. From the living room I hear music.

Johnny Cash. Grant plans on drinking tonight then.

"Just be careful that you don't get hurt," I say, trying to sound as sincere as possible. "First love is hard."

"She's not my first love, Mom." He laughs and knocks into my hip with his own. "I've dated before. You know that."

"Yes, but you've never brought a girl home before. As long as you remember I'm always here for you. Nothing will ever stop me from loving you, Owen." I'm trying to tell him that no matter how much he likes this girl, he needs to be careful. Not because of what might happen if she decides she's no longer interested in him, or if he gets tired of her, but because of who she is.

Because of her past. Because of what will happen to her in the future. He'll never know my role in all of it. That's key: that he doesn't find out what I've done. Or what I'm willing to do to keep him all to myself.

"You've never wanted me to bring a woman home." There's a frown wrinkling his forehead, there and gone. Fleeting. Ephemeral. "You and Dad have never really made me feel like you wanted to get to know any of the women I've dated. Until Gina."

"She seems special. You know your dad only wants what's best for you. He wouldn't have encouraged you to date her if he didn't think she was a great choice for you." I put down my wineglass. It's empty anyway, and Owen's too focused on Gina to fill it up for me, which is more than a little vexing. The last time he was home to visit, he stayed on top of my drink, making sure I never went without. Now, though, just the thought of Gina pushes any concern of my well-being out of his mind.

Soon enough, she'll be gone. I have to remind myself of that.

"She is." His words are forceful. "She *is*, Mom, and I want you to see that. I see a future with her."

A pause, then he completely changes the subject. "Hey, this is going to sound random, but have you seen her phone charger lying around anywhere?"

"Her phone charger?" I frown; close my eyes. Picture it exactly where I saw it last before I cut it in half and shoved it in the bottom of the kitchen trashcan while she and Owen were enjoying their walk around the property. I couldn't have her calling for help, could I?

"Yeah, I helped her pack, so I know she brought it on the trip, but we can't find it, and her phone died this afternoon."

I cluck my tongue. "Oh dear. I don't know what to tell you. I guess the silver lining is that she's here on vacation and doesn't need to be concerned about social media or the news." I shrug, then turn the fish before continuing. "I'm sure you can stop in town when you two leave in a few days and get her one."

He shakes his head. "No, I can head in tomorrow and grab one for her. It's not that far of a drive."

"Owen, no." My words are sharper than I intended, and I smile gently to take the sting off them. From the other room, Johnny Cash croons about Folsom Prison. "Let her relax. Don't you think she's looked happier here as the day has gone on? It's probably because she hasn't been tethered to her phone. Besides, any store that will sell one is so far away. Walmart? At least an hour. I don't want to forsake any time with the two of you. She can use your phone if she needs to, right?"

He sighs. If his hands weren't full, he'd use one to push his hair back from his face, I know he would.

I know my son better than anyone.

"I guess you're right. But if she really wants a charger, I'm taking her to town, so don't worry about it if we head out, okay?" And then he's gone, whistling along with the song as he heads towards the living room.

Grant passes him on his way in through the kitchen door. He's grinning, but it slides off his face when he sees me.

"Marta? You okay?" He pulls me into a hug, and I rest my cheek on his shoulder. So strong, so caring. Grant has always done everything in his power to keep me safe, to watch over me.

I may not have always liked his... extracurricular activities, but deep in his heart, he's a good man. But I don't want to play his games. I had to when Owen was younger but not anymore.

I'm tired of letting him run the show.

"Gina's realized that her charger is missing," I tell him, speaking into the worn flannel shirt he's wearing. It smells vaguely of campfire and fish, the combination not totally unpleasant. "But they don't know I took it. Owen wants to take her into town to pick up a new one because her phone died."

"Well, that can't happen, especially now that you've got her cut off from calling anyone." Grant rubs my back, his knuckles pressing hard into my tight muscles. He's still so strong. After all these years. I let out a sigh and feel my body go limp against him.

"Don't worry, Marta, I can come up with plenty of things for us all to get into. I'm not letting them head to town."

"You're so good," I murmur. "Thank you for watching out for me. It's just better that we keep everyone here until everything's settled. There's no reason to let things get out of control. It's all going to be fine, and now we can move forward with the plan."

No response. Just his hands on my shoulders, pushing me back a bit, then his lips on mine. I close my eyes and force myself to lean into his kiss. Grant thinks I'm on his side. He has no idea that I want something totally different than he does. And he doesn't know I'm willing to do whatever it takes to get it.

There's a bang.

My eyes fly open, but Grant is so much taller than me that I can't see anything past him. My heart hammers in my chest and sweat prickles my underarms. I lean to the side, my free hand gripping Grant's bicep to help me keep my balance.

There. By the door. A flash of color, then someone hurries away down the hall.

Gina was eavesdropping.

FOURTEEN

GINA

My mind races as I walk back into the living room. Is my face flushed? It feels flushed. Self-conscious, I press the backs of my hands into my cheeks to try to cool them. They're blazing hot, and I take a deep breath. Then another.

I know what I just heard.

Until everything's settled.

Yeah, like that doesn't sound ominous. I've read enough creepy books and watched enough documentaries to know that when people are talking about *settling* things, it's not good. Before Owen and I got together, true crime documentaries were my bread and butter. But I wasn't just doing research while watching them.

I was learning how to survive.

So what does this mean for me? I close my eyes as I think. I came here with a clear plan, but if they're onto me... no, they can't be. There's no way they have any idea what I'm really doing here. For all they know, I fell head over heels for their son and desperately want to marry him. I know who they are, but there's no way they know who I am.

There's no way they could possibly guess the real reason I

ran into Owen, right? But what if they did? What if they know, and that's why my charger is missing? Why else would Marta be watching me in the middle of the night? My stomach twists into knots at the memory of her standing at the top of the stairs.

I need to be careful. Pay attention. I might have to change my plan, speed things up. Wade would be happy about that anyway.

When I open my eyes, I plaster a smile on my face. They might be onto me, but I can't let them know I suspect a thing.

Owen's sitting with his back to me, three shot glasses in front of him. He hasn't poured the rum yet, but I know he's itching to do just that. Five minutes ago, taking shots sounded like an okay idea, but now my stomach's churning.

"What did you need from the kitchen?" He turns a little to look at me and I throw him a grin, bend down, and plant a kiss on the top of his head.

"I was just making sure I hadn't sleepwalked last night and plugged my charger in by the coffeemaker. Not that I think I did that, but you know. Strange place. Not thinking quite right."

"I've never known you to sleepwalk." He gestures to the seat to his right, and I pull out the chair and sit down. Now I can see the deck of cards on the table.

"First time for everything," I say. At least it doesn't sound like Marta told him about my midnight wanderings. "Poker?" I gesture to the cards. "You've been saying you want to teach me." Owen has no idea how good I am at poker. He doesn't need to.

"Yeah, now should be a good time to do that. Dad taught me, and I figured he'd be pretty helpful making sure I don't miss anything. As long as you're sure you're okay. If you threw up earlier, maybe you shouldn't be drinking."

"I'm fine, seriously. It was just stress over your mom not liking me," I lie. I'd tried to pass the vomit on my shirt off as being an old stain, but the smell had given it away. Owen's more observant than I'd like him to be sometimes. "But poker might have to wait until later. From what I saw in the kitchen, dinner is almost ready. Don't want to upset your mom by having too much fun before we eat." I smile to lessen the blow from my words.

"One shot," he says, uncapping the rum and filling the three little glasses. I'm definitely more of a Captain Morgan's girl. Silver spiced, if I have the choice. This rum isn't one I've ever heard of before, probably because I'm about as likely to shop the top shelf at the ABC store as I am to run a marathon.

Neither of those things are gonna happen. I run for two reasons: fear and food, and I've only been scared enough to run once in my life, and what did I do? I hid.

No, that's not fair.

I survived.

"One shot." I take the proffered cut crystal shot glass and tap it to his. "To us," I say at the same time he speaks.

"To this trip."

I shoot the rum, fully expecting my chest to tighten, my body to heat like I've stepped into a furnace. I'm prepared to hold back a cough, to do everything in my power to keep from looking like a lightweight in front of his parents. *Is it better to look like a lush?* But the worry is there and gone before I can grasp it, and the rum is so smooth.

It goes down without a fight.

"Wow," I say, "that was—"

"Smooth," Grant interrupts, leaning between us to take the last shot glass. He drains it like it's water, then puts the glass down next to mine. "That's my favorite. Five hundred dollars a bottle."

Okay, *now* I feel like I'm going to choke.

"I'm sorry, what?" My fingers flutter at my throat. If the entire bottle is five hundred dollars, and a fifth of rum has about sixteen shots in it... my mind races to do the math. "Do you know how much that means each shot was?"

"It doesn't matter. I like it." Grant reaches down and takes me by the elbow. "Now, my dear, dinner is served, and it's a treat. You've never had anything quite like fresh fish. It beats anything in the store, especially that frozen crap."

I stand with him because what choice do I have? It's not that he's squeezing my elbow so tightly it hurts, but I definitely don't feel like I can pull away from him. He steps close enough to me that I can feel the heat from his body. When I look up at him, he's grinning down at me. His grip is stronger than I would have expected as he guides me from the mahogany game table into the dining room.

Again, this room looks like something out of a castle. A huge flower arrangement at the end of the table perfumes the air. Giant paintings hang on the wall, the closest one of a bird dog standing on top of a hill, its fur blowing in the wind, its nose up and sniffing. I fully expect a coat of arms in the corner, but there's just an ugly sculpture in a glass case.

The over-the-top décor? It's getting a little old, honestly. At least I know where Owen got his money, and it's from working long hours at the hospital and being the best of the best. His parents, however, are still something of a mystery. The place is a museum but without any of the modern touches Owen added at his place.

In lieu of heated floors, there are thick Persian rugs. Are there verbal controls over the air conditioning like Owen has? No, but there's a huge vase behind glass in the case across from where I'm standing, and I don't know much about art, but I'd wager it cost more than the car parked in the driveway.

"Fresh trout, bread, scalloped potatoes, and crème brûlée for dessert," Marta announces, waving her hand at the table.

"How in the world do you find time to cook like this and handle the house?" I ask, pulling out a chair next to Owen. He grabs the back of it from me and helps slide it in as I sit. "Are you sure you don't have a private chef stashed somewhere?" *Maybe locked in the basement?*

Owen chuckles and drops a kiss on the top of my head. The last thing I want is to sit here at a table with Marta after over-hearing her and Grant talk about me, but I have to keep up pretenses. For Owen. For the plan.

The smile she gives me is tight. "One of the greatest joys of my life has been keeping the house for Grant while he was gone at work. Putting a good meal on the table every day is a gift from me to my family."

She really needs to get out more.

"Well, you do a wonderful job." I glance at Owen, but he's staring down at the food like it's going to give him the secret to the universe.

Marta stares at me, her mouth pursed, a furrow growing between her eyebrows.

I hold her gaze. She and Grant are planning something, but I'm not going to let her intimidate me.

It's only when Grant helps Marta into her seat across from me that she looks away from me. He then sits in his chair, flour-ishing his napkin before putting it in his lap. I do the same, then wait to see how dinner is going to go. Is Marta going to serve all of us? Is it family style?

"Help yourselves," she announces, grabbing the platter of trout and taking the biggest filet. I'm sure she's going to put it on Grant's plate, but she leans across the table, narrowly avoiding dripping butter on the tablecloth, and puts it on Owen's. She then serves Grant, then herself, then pushes the serving platter towards me.

Charming.

"What did you get into while Owen and I were still fishing, Gina?" Grant hands me a slice of bread. "We were so sorry to see you head back to the house, but I understand not everyone is comfortable with all the aspects of fishing."

Marta looks up from her plate. "You didn't stay out fishing with the boys?"

"I cleaned up our room a little," I say. "It was so messy in there, so I remade the bed and repacked my suitcase."

Did her eye just twitch? It's hard to tell without looking directly at her, and I'm not going to give her that pleasure.

"Is that why our room looks so nice?" Owen nudges me with his elbow, then spoons some potatoes on my plate for me. "With a bed that nicely made, you could run a B&B."

"That's the last thing I want to do," I say with a laugh. "All those strangers coming in and out of your place? But yeah, I noticed the bed was messy and needed a little... tidying."

Now I do look up at Marta. Her lips are pressed tightly together, and she's staring at me. There's a pat of butter on her knife like she was about to butter her bread.

I smile at her. It's not returned.

"Thanks for taking care of it." Owen keeps smiling at me. He has no idea his mom is trying to shoot daggers out of her eyes.

"I'm glad it made you happy." I lean over to kiss Owen on the cheek. "You know I like to take care of you."

"You're the best." The look he gives me is so full of love that I feel a jolt of joy rush through me. It's not just because of the way he's looking at me, although I do enjoy knowing I have Owen wrapped around my finger. It's also because of the way Marta swallows so hard I can hear it.

She hates this, and that makes me love it more.

"Well, you've certainly made yourself at home here, haven't you, Gina? Wandering from room to room like a ghost. You'd think you were a reporter the way you linger at doors, poking your nose where it doesn't belong, hoping for some juicy tidbit to tide you over."

"Mom." Owen reaches out and touches her arm, but she doesn't look at him. "Whatever this is, you need to stop."

She saw me eavesdropping. She knows I heard what she and Grant were saying. I swallow hard, my mind racing. The food smelled amazing a few minutes ago, but now I feel like I'm going to be sick again. What are they going to do to me? Fear makes my stomach twist tighter. I knew listening at the door was dangerous, but sneaking around is the only way I'm going to find out the truth.

"It's true," Marta continues, ignoring Owen. "There's nothing like a houseguest who keeps creeping around, is there? It's akin to having a cockroach infestation. You just never know when they're going to turn up underfoot."

"Marta." Grant's voice has an edge to it. "That's enough."

"I don't think it's nearly enough." She's still staring at me. I force myself to meet her eyes.

"Marta, I'm sorry for whatever you think I've done wrong. But I promise you, I'm not sneaking around," I say, reaching out to take Owen's hand as I speak. He squeezes my fingers, and I make myself squeeze back. "I can't thank you enough for your hospitality and I hope whatever this is"—I wave my free hand in the air—"can be put behind us." Out of the corner of my eye, I see Owen give a little nod. "Now, Owen and I are going to head to Walmart in the morning to get a phone charger. Do you need us to pick anything up for you?"

"Oh, I don't need a thing." Her voice is a purr, but her eyes narrow as she looks at me, like a predator sizing up its prey. "But thank you for the offer. Still, I must insist the two of you stay here. We have so many wonderful things to do together as a family this weekend that it's silly for you and Owen to take up so much time tomorrow on a little errand like that. I think you should buy a charger on your way home; I wouldn't want you to miss any time with us. I mean, really? Who in the world could you want to call?"

I ignore her question. "If Owen wants to stay, we'll stay. In the meantime, do you mind if I look in the garage? See if you have an extra one stashed away? Everyone has a box of old cables and dead phones, right? Or is that just me?" I take a bit of fish, and *dammit,* it's really good. I don't want to enjoy anything this woman makes, but it's flaky and buttery and delicious.

"Well—" Grant begins, but Marta cuts him off.

"Oh, the garage is off-limits," she says. Her voice is light and breathy like she doesn't have a care in the world, but I'm still watching her, and I see the way she looks at Grant.

I see the expression that flits across his face. How her lips tighten. She gives her head a little shake.

Warning him to keep quiet?

Something. She's not any help with my charger, but she just narrowed down the areas in the house I want to search. No way would she act like this if there weren't some reason she didn't want me in the garage. I was suspicious about Grant's office, but now Marta has made the garage seem like a much bigger deal.

All I know is I need to get in there.

FIFTEEN

GINA

Then

Dinner was lasagna, and while the noodles were a bit rubbery from being nuked, I don't care. I ate five more cookies and washed them down with some milk, and my penny pile is bigger than it was when I got here. Wade wins this hand, and he's bragging about it as he pushes his pennies into his Crown Royal bag.

"I need to go," he says, glancing up at me and throwing me a wink as he pulls the gold tie tight. "You two have fun, but I have to get ready. Jeremy's mom will be here soon to get me."

The pang of sadness I felt when Aunt Bethany first told me he was going to leave for the night shoots through me again, but it's not nearly as powerful as it was at first. I'm excited about getting to spend one-on-one time with my aunt since that isn't something that happens very often.

Wade gets up, sighing as he pushes away from the table, then leaves the kitchen, his penny bag swinging in his fist. A moment later, I hear his footsteps on the stairs. Everything in the house creaks, which is why he and I have to be very careful when playing hide-and-seek. I know which steps to avoid if I'm trying to move through the house for another cookie. It's funny because I don't live here, but I feel like I know it better than my house.

"Okay, Gina." Aunt Bethany taps the deck of cards into place and wraps a rubber band around it before dropping it back on the table. "Poker isn't as fun with only two people, but I have a few ideas of what you and I can get into." She rests her chin on her hand and leans closer to me like we're about to share a big secret.

"Number one," she says, holding up a single finger. "Movie night. Now, I know you talk a big game about scary movies, but I don't like them, so I was thinking something a bit campier, like an action movie from the eighties."

I make a face.

"Two." Another finger joins the first. "Spa night."

I shake my head.

"Yeah, I didn't think so, but it wasn't something Wade ever wants to do, so I wanted to throw it out there and see how you felt about it. So, number three is... drum roll please."

I start banging on the table, a huge smile splitting my face.

"Crappy snacks and *Legally Blonde*."

"Yes!" The word bursts from me, and I raise my fists over my head in triumph. "Now you're speaking my love language, Aunt Bethany."

She laughs. "What in the world does an eight-year-old know about love languages?"

"Plenty. My mom made me read the book and tell her what mine were so she could *better meet my needs*." I make air quotes around the four words. Aunt Bethany rolls her eyes, and I laugh. "Hey, I'm not the one who came up with the idea! It was all hers."

"Oh, I'm sure it was. And let me guess, you receive quality time and you like to give words of affirmation."

My mouth drops open. Honestly, I'm shocked. How does Aunt Bethany know that when my own mom couldn't figure it out?

"You're right," I say, trying to keep my surprise from being obvious.

"I know I am. I always am." She gestures for me to help her clean up, and I stand, grabbing our glasses to take them to the sink. No dishwasher here, but that's okay. I've gotten really good at drying, which is the one job she has me do when I come over. Everything else is just taken care of, although I really like to help.

"You're the best, you know that, Aunt Bethany?" I watch as she plunges her hands into the soapy water, twisting the sponge around the plates, cups, and cutlery, before rinsing them off and handing them over to me. Once I felt how hot she makes the water and immediately jerked my hand back. I have no idea how she does it without burning off a layer of skin.

Wade said it's because she's used to really hot water at the diner where she works, that she had to get over not wanting to put her hands into hot water because she has to move quickly to wash dishes when they're running low and there's a lunch rush. He may be right, but I still can't imagine being comfortable in water that feels that close to boiling.

"I think you're the best too, Gina." Another swirl of soapy bubbles over a plate, then it's clean and in my hands. "I love it when you come over, and you know how much I love Wade, but I'm excited about a girls' night." She bumps her hip into mine, and I bump mine back.

"I was a little sad about Wade not being here at first," I admit because she's the type of person you can admit stuff like that to. Aunt Bethany hasn't ever judged me, and I don't think she's going to start now. "But I'm pretty excited about it. I like hanging out with just you."

"It'll be our secret," she says, then pulls the plug and rinses off her hands. The swirl of bubbles down the drain is mesmerizing, and we stand and watch it for a moment before the silence is broken by my cousin.

"I'm going to wait outside," Wade says, running into the kitchen. He has a backpack slung over his shoulder, but unlike mine, which was new last year, his is dirty and the zipper is broken. A paper clips hangs from the broken part so he can still use the backpack.

"Have fun," Aunt Bethany says, pulling him in for a hug. She kisses his forehead like she did to me, then squeezes him once more before letting him go. He rolls his eyes, but I know he likes the way his mom loves him.

"See ya, Gina." He hugs me, the moment swift, then he's gone, practically running out of the kitchen. There's a slight pause as he throws open the lock on the door, then it whines open and slams shut. A second slam a moment later is the screen door.

"Boys," Aunt Bethany says, and we both laugh. "Remind me to lock that later, okay?"

She throws her arm around my shoulders and leads me to the pantry. Well, it's not really a pantry, not like the one we have at home where I hid once during hide-and-seek, tucked back behind the big bags of flour Mom bought the time she said she might want to start baking bread.

They've been there for months now, but she only made one loaf, an inedible thing with a thick crust. Since then, she just swings by the store and picks up what we need. *It's easier*, she says. *Less stressful.*

I don't tell her Aunt Bethany makes her own bread on Saturdays, or that it's delicious with butter, or that it makes the entire house smell like heaven. She won't want to hear it, just like she doesn't want to talk about the credit card bills I found.

"Pick out what snacks you want. I'll get a tray and we'll load it up. Oh, do you want to put on your pajamas before we watch so we can be super comfy?"

"That sounds fun." I turn around with an armful of snacks. The chips are all off-brand, but I don't care. The name doesn't matter nearly as much as my mom thinks it does.

"Great. Let's go do that." She holds a tray out for me, and I dump the snacks on it. On the way out of the kitchen, she grabs two cans of Coke from the fridge and adds them to our stash. We're giggling as we hurry into the living room, drop off the food, then race to change, her in her bedroom, me in the bathroom.

Neither one of us thinks about the deadbolt.

SIXTEEN

GINA

Marta's more dangerous than I ever realized. Wade was wrong. He said Grant was the dangerous one given his history, and he is a concern, but Marta's the one I need to look out for.

That had been my fear, that she was the viper, hanging back in the shadows, waiting to strike when you least expect it. I'm not sure how to handle her. She runs this place with an iron fist. She's the one in control—I can tell from the way she shut down anything Grant was going to tell me about the garage.

What was that saying from the movie about a Greek wedding? The man might be the head, but the woman is the neck, and she can turn the head any way she wants?

It's something like that, and while I know it sounds silly, I'm pretty sure it's true. I see it at the hospital, when the men think they're the ones in control but it's obviously the women pulling the strings. It's like that in married couples all the time. It was even like that with my parents. My dad swore he was the one running the house, but it was clearly my mom.

Women control from behind the scenes. We work hard and ensure that everything runs smoothly. If I'm honest, isn't that what I've been doing with Owen? Wasn't that exactly what I did when I ran into him with coffee, spilling it all over him so he'd have to pay attention to me?

Because I'm confident there's no way he would have ever noticed me if I hadn't taken matters into my own hands. I hate that, hate the fact that it came down to me manipulating our first interaction, but after years of sitting on the sidelines of my own life, I was over it.

It was time for me to take control. Time for me to put aside the cloak of fear I'd been wearing for so long, *man up*, as they like to say, and be a woman.

"Are you two still on for poker?" I ask the question casually, leaning against the counter as I do. Grant's just finished putting leftovers in the fridge and Owen's about to load the last plate into the dishwasher. I stand ready with a box of dishwashing pods I found under the sink, and as soon as he steps away, I pop one in the door, close it, and press the start button.

It hums to life but is so quiet I can barely hear it.

"Poker? Are you sure?" Owen rubs my shoulder. "Dinner was... hard. I don't know what's gotten into my mom, Gina. But we can go upstairs and read. We don't have to spend more time as a family. Tomorrow we're all going to walk downtown, maybe drive to Walmart to get you a charger, but things will have blown over by then. I think maybe she's just tired."

"All of us are going to go?" Nope, no way. The one thing I need right now is time without anyone else in the house. I just have to figure out how to get it, and playing poker and pretending to be hungover is a wonderful idea.

"That's the plan. Why?"

"Just checking. It's a lot of together time, but I still really want to learn how to play poker. You said your dad could teach me, then we could play when we get back home. Come on, Owen." I lower my voice. "I don't want to punish you and your dad just because your mom hates me. It'll be a chance for me to get to know him."

"She doesn't—" he begins but stops when he sees the expression on my face. "Okay. You're right." He turns to speak to his dad. "What do you think?"

"I think it sounds fun." Grant wipes his hands on a kitchen towel, then tosses it back on the drying rack. It lands in a ball, and I can only imagine the way Marta's eye is going to twitch when she sees it later.

"Will your mom want to play with us when she gets out of the shower?" I turn to Owen, running my nails up the inside of his arm. "I don't want her to feel left out." That's a lie.

"Oh, she won't," Grant tells me. "Don't worry about her. She's never been one for cards, no matter how many times I offered to take her with me to Vegas on trips."

"You traveled a lot for work, didn't you?" I ask, following him out of the kitchen. "Owen told me you used to be on the road for... what? Weeks at a time sometimes? That had to be hard."

"It was, but I loved it." Grant pulls out a chair for me, then sits across from me. Owen's between us. Without being asked, he reaches for the rum and pours us each a shot. I pull mine closer to me, careful not to spill on the wood table, and wait.

No reason to start slamming shots and get messy. I only have to take enough for them to think I'm drinking as much as they are. If they think I'm hungover tomorrow, they'll leave me behind. That will give me more time to poke around without Marta hovering nearby.

"What about you?" I ask, turning to Owen. "Did you love having your dad gone all the time? I bet you and your mom had a lot of fun."

Owen shuffles the deck before answering, then deals out some cards, putting the rest of them face down in a pile in front of him. It's only when we've all picked up our cards and looked at them that he responds.

"I don't want to say I liked having him gone," he says, turning to look at his dad, who raises his shot glass in response.

My eyes flick back and forth between the two of them. I take the shot but barely taste it. I'm too busy watching Grant's face to stop Owen from filling the glasses back up.

Owen wipes his mouth with the back of his hand. "But Mom and I had a lot of fun together. Still wish Dad had been around for more of it, but what was I going to do? Get mad that he was out making a living for the two of us? Yell at him when he got home because I missed him? Sure, every kid wants to see their dad more, but you kept a roof over our head." This last part is directed at Grant, who smiles at his son.

"And I'd do it all again in a heartbeat," Grant says, lifting his shot glass again.

Another shot? This is going exactly how I hoped it would. This time, instead of downing the rum, I lift my glass, then grin at Owen after he and his dad take their shots. While they're still smiling, I quickly fill their glasses, holding the bottle over mine for a moment to mimic filling it up.

They never notice I'm not drinking with them.

"You never wanted to travel with him? Not even when you got older and he was still working?" I ask.

"Oh, I met up with him... what, once, Dad? I'm pretty sure it was just the once. We were actually in the same state, and I was on fall break from college. I'd just turned twenty-one and was desperate to go out for a drink with my old man." Owen's smile is tight.

"Let me guess," I say. "Vegas."

"Not Vegas," Grant says. "Not by a long shot."

They fall silent.

I clear my throat. "Well, at least you're retired now. And when we come visit, you and Owen can spend as much time together as you want." I hold up my shot glass. They both take theirs, and I refill their glasses before they notice mine is still full.

"And I can't thank you enough for letting me spend extra time with my son today," Grant tells me. "It was wonderful, and I really appreciate you stepping to the side so we could fish."

"Anytime," I say.

Owen holds up his shot glass. Grant and I raise ours in response. He drinks his rum; I only lift mine to my lips.

It goes like that for the next hour, Grant correcting me when I make a purposeful bad play, me filling up our shot glasses from time to time. I hadn't really tasted the rum at the beginning of the night, it was so smooth, but I'm not going to keep drinking, not going to let it get to my head. Tonight isn't about getting wasted; it's about letting them think I did.

And as for the game itself? It's been years since I've played, and while I got to be pretty good as a kid, they don't need to know that. I throw hands from time to time to ensure they don't pick up on just how good I really am.

When I finally speak after ten minutes of silence, I take my time to form my words, careful to sound like I've been drinking just as much as they have.

"So, Grant," I say, keeping my eyes on my cards, "tell me, what was your favorite city to travel to when you were working?"

"Vegas." His answer is immediate. "For obvious reasons."

I look up in time to catch the cheeky wink he throws at Owen, but his son doesn't return it. Owen looks... well, very interested in what his dad and I are talking about.

"Not Rosenville?" The two words roll off my tongue way too easily. I barely glance at the men before taking a pair of kings and putting them down on the table.

Owen raises his eyebrows.

"Rosenville was fine." Grant's words are measured. Slow. He beats my kings with a pair of aces.

"Not much to do there," I comment.

"There was always something to get into the few times I was there."

"Maybe you saw a different side of it than I did."

"Probably. I'm a lot older than you."

"You said you liked growing up in Rosenville," Owen says. His comment is an unwelcome interruption, and I have to fight my frustration. No reason to glare at him or make him feel bad for speaking up.

He's a part of this too.

"There were good things and bad things about it," I say. My next question is directed across the table from me. "What was your favorite thing about being in Rosenville?"

Grant pushes his empty glass away from him, but Owen doesn't move to fill it. "I'd be lying if I said the food," he says.

I force a laugh. "Not exactly a Mecca of great restaurants."

"No, but there was this great little diner. I can't remember its name."

"The Upside-Down Egg?" I offer. "Or Charlene's?"

He shrugs but doesn't respond.

Silence hangs in the air. Owen pulls two cards from his hand and throws them on the table, but I don't look at what they were. I'm too busy staring at Grant.

"There's fun nightlife," he finally says. "Although I think you were probably a little young to partake when you lived there." He drops his entire hand on the table. "And on that note, I'm bushed. Time for me to hit the hay, or Marta will come looking for me and break up our party anyway." He stands; raps his knuckles on the table. "Get this cleaned up, would you, Owen?"

And then he's gone without a backwards glance. I watch him leave, then turn to Owen, who's already shuffling the cards back together.

His face is impassive. It's the same expression he gets when he's worried about a patient at work or when something isn't going right around the house.

How much do you know?

I almost ask him. I want to reach out, across the chasm that's grown between us, but I don't move. And I certainly don't voice the words.

I'm not sure I want to know the answer.

He either knows everything and is even more dangerous than I ever imagined, or he's totally clueless.

But that doesn't mean he's innocent.

SEVENTEEN

GINA

Sunday

Owen honestly believes I'm hungover.

He hands me a mimosa. I'm sitting in front of the fire, my hood up over my head, a blanket pulled up to my chin. Without looking at him, I reach out and take the glass.

No, not a glass. This is a crystal flute, I'm sure of it.

"Hair of the dog," he says, crouching in front of me. He rests his hands on my knees and gives them a little squeeze. "I think it'll help. It's like being back in college."

"I didn't go to college," I remind him, then take a sip.

How would I act if I were really feeling close to vomiting? I close my eyes. Breathe through my nose.

So far, so good.

"Well, then this is you getting the full experience. Granted, it's harder on the body as you get older, but this is it. Welcome to college, Gina."

"Are you calling me old?"

"I'm just saying that twenty-eight isn't a spring chicken. Maybe we'll skip the keg stands I had planned for the afternoon." He chuckles, then takes my hand and kisses my knuckles. I have a death grip on the mimosa with the other hand, and I take a little sip.

I'm not a great actress. But I have to nail this.

"I'm just sorry if I've ruined the day," I say. That's what I would say if I hadn't orchestrated this. Pretending to be hungover was the only way I could think of to make sure Owen and his parents left me alone today. Nobody will expect me to hang out if I feel like crap, giving me the perfect opportunity to look around some more.

"You haven't. I think the three of us are still going to go to town, if that's okay with you. You can stay here, of course. No way would I put you in the car on these twisty backroads."

It's working. "Can you get me a phone charger?" I feel disconnected from my social media with my phone no more than a brick right now. Of course, Owen would happily let me use his to check my email, but it's not the same. I don't have my friends' contact information in his phone. I can't access my Instagram. I'm not completely cut off, of course, not with—

He interrupts me. "I don't know if there will be one downtown, and Walmart is an hour away. Mom already made it clear we're going to walk Main Street and check out the various shops that have opened up since I was last here, but I'll look. Without you coming, she's strong-arming me into being with her, not driving to Walmart."

"The shops will be open on a Sunday?"

He smiles at me and brushes my hair back. "It's nice, right? The shop owners realized a few years ago that they were shooting themselves in the collective foot by closing for half the weekend." He pauses. "Is there anything else you want before we go?"

I consider asking for a barf bowl to really play up how sick I feel. Would Owen bring me one of Marta's cut crystal serving bowls? The mental image of me vomiting in that makes me grin.

"See, you're feeling better already. Drink that up and I'll get you another before we leave. I bet you'll be up and about by the time we get home, but I don't want you to overdo it." He stands and plants a gentle kiss on my forehead. "Seriously, Gina, if you want to head right back to bed, feel free. There's no reason for you to be downstairs while we're gone. It's not like anyone's going to be judging you for sleeping it off."

"Oh, I have no doubt your mom is," I say without thinking.

He frowns. "Did she say something to make you feel that way?"

Oops. This is what happens when I let my mouth run without thinking first. I have to remember that Owen and his mom are close; closer than I'd like them to be.

"Owen." I take a deep breath. "I already told you—she hates me. Why can't you see that? Everything I do is wrong. I can't even walk around the house without a chaperone or she accuses me of snooping." I look up at him from under my eyelashes. "You know I wouldn't snoop, right? I don't get why she hates me."

"She doesn't hate you, and I don't want you making yourself sick thinking that again." He sits next to me and pulls me close. "My mom and I are so close; she'd probably have an issue with anyone I brought home. It's not personal."

Yes, it is.

"I would hate for you to have to choose between the two of us. I love you, Owen, but if she decides she doesn't like me, I don't know what will happen."

"Hey." He plants a kiss on my temple. "I love you. *You.* Okay? Don't you worry about my mom. She's... protective, but that doesn't mean she gets to be the one making decisions for my life. Trust me. She isn't going to change how I feel about you."

I lean against him, letting the silence draw out between us, then change the subject. Owen will keep thinking about this conversation, I know he will, but that doesn't mean we need to dwell on it right now. I've planted the seed of him choosing me over her. "Does your dad feel okay?"

"He's fine. He's also twice your size and closed deals in the bar every single day, Gina. It's not really fair to compare your tolerance to his. You're never going to come out on top."

"I can see that." I lean back against a cushion and close my eyes.

Owen clears his throat. "They've seen me hungover, okay?" I feel the cushions depress as he scoots closer to me. "They're not going to judge you for hitting the rum a little hard last night. It's not like you're supposed to get up and go to work this morning, right? If you had to help patients and families find their way around the hospital, then that would be different."

"I guess so."

He kisses me on the forehead. I can smell the bacon he had for breakfast, and my stomach rumbles.

"I know so, okay? Just rest. Take it easy. We might stay downtown for lunch, depending on how late we're out shopping, so I don't want you to worry."

"I would tell you to text me and let me know, but..." I let my voice fade off. He's already told me he's not going to get me a charger today. His mom is doing everything in her power to keep me from getting my hands on one. It makes me nervous. I'm clearly running out of time.

More and more I believe she's onto me, but how? It's simply not possible she could know why I'm really here, what I really want. But the way she watches me... I might have to speed up my timeline.

"How about I leave you my phone?"

My eyes pop open. "What?"

"Yeah, that's what I'll do. You can have my phone here, that way if you need me, you can call Mom or Dad and reach me that way. What do you think about that?" He stands, slips his phone from his pocket, and hands it to me.

"Really?" I ask, but I'm already taking it. "I don't know your passcode."

Surely he won't tell me that. Surely this was all just a show. Or maybe he'll tell me to hold on to the phone and he'll call me, that I don't really need to be able to reach out to him.

"Five-four-four-two." No hesitation. Just honesty.

I type it in, my thumb moving carefully over the screen.

There's a soft click as the phone unlocks and his home screen pops up.

"Are you sure?" I look up at him.

"Of course I'm sure. What, you think I'd ask you to move in with me and not trust you? This is nothing, Gina. I love you." He kisses me, using two fingers to lift my chin up.

I kiss him back. Of course I do.

But I'm not thinking about kissing him. All I can think about is his phone. Unlocked. Alone with me.

And I'll be in the house, alone, able to look for a way into the garage.

And not just the garage. There are so many places they might have stuff hidden, and since they won't be here, they can't stop me from looking. I can't wait to get into Marta's room. Look under her bed. See what skeletons she has in her closet.

"Call my mom if you need me, okay?" He steps back, his eyes locked on my face. I'm fully expecting him to change his mind, to tell me it was a joke, to take his phone back.

I mean, seriously. What kind of psychopath trusts another person with their unlocked phone? I can't think of anyone I'd give my passcode to, but maybe Owen doesn't have anything to hide.

"I'll call you. Have fun." Then, in a moment of brilliance: "Let me know when you're on your way home, okay? That way, if I'm still in my pajamas or something, I can change and your parents won't think I'm a total slacker."

He laughs. "They don't care, Gina, but I'll call you if that will keep you from worrying. Feel better, okay? I'm really sorry you have a hangover."

I would be too, if I really had one.

He takes my glass from me and leaves, returning a moment later with it topped up. More mimosa to help me through the morning. I kiss him and settle back into the sofa, making a show of leaving his cell phone out of reach on the coffee table.

Then the front door opens. Slams shut. I strain my ears for the sound of a key in the lock. The car starting and driving away.

They left me here alone.

That was a huge mistake.

EIGHTEEN

GINA

It's go time.

I gave it five minutes. Five minutes after they backed out of the driveway, and during that time I sat perfectly still. Even my breathing was shallow and quiet so I didn't miss anything.

And now that I'm completely confident they're gone and won't be returning for a while, I lean forward and grab Owen's phone.

In what world will a girlfriend not poke through her boyfriend's phone given the chance? It boggles the mind to think that's not a possibility Owen considered. If he ever got his hands on my phone, I'd fully expect him to go through my messages, my search history, my liked Instagram posts.

And that, ladies and gentlemen, is why I'll never let Owen anywhere near my phone without supervision.

"Okay, Owen," I say, my finger hovering over the screen. "How about messages first?"

A pang of guilt shoots through me as I tap the little icon on his home screen. As far as I know, Owen has never lied to me about anything. He's honest to a fault, never wanting to gossip about anyone, never wanting to do anything that could possibly hurt another person.

But that doesn't mean I can fully trust him, does it? Me opening his messages and reading them tells me one thing—that as much as Owen trusts me, I don't trust him that much.

At first, I'm disappointed. Owen apparently cleans out his text messages the same way he stays on top of his inbox. I've never met anyone sane who aims for zero emails in their inbox every day, but Owen does. Even if he's exhausted, he'll stay up a bit later, his finger flying over his screen, quickly deleting emails and moving the remaining ones to labeled folders.

If I didn't love him, it would drive me nuts.

Unfortunately, his text messages are just as picked through. I tap on the ones from *Lover*, not surprised to see the texts I've sent him.

There are also ones from *Mom*, and I eagerly click into them, my heart sinking when I see that there's only one from the day we arrived, after he let her know we were on our way. This means I can't get any information about what he and his mom were talking about prior to our arrival, but I was right.

He deletes his messages regularly. But why? Why would he clear out entire conversations unless there were something he didn't want me to know about? Did he delete his messages this morning before offering me his phone?

I glance up quickly, almost like I expect to see someone peering at me from behind another piece of furniture, but I'm alone. Still, this feels like a trap.

Back to his inbox and there are some texts from Chuck, one of the doctors he works with. He's told me time and time again how much he admires the man, how hard he works, what a good family man he is. I tap into the texts, and I'm not surprised to see it's just back-and-forth about grabbing lunch at the hospital last week.

There aren't any texts from his dad, which I find hard to

believe considering how close the two of them are. Besides Chuck, there aren't any from anyone else at the hospital.

I'm stumped, and I tap out of his text messages before clicking into his email. Not that I think I'll find anything in there. He's aggressive about weeding out junk mail. Still, I look through the various folders he has set up for emails, but there's nothing.

How about browser history?

Surely he's not so thorough with this as well—but it's all cleared. There's no search history to speak of.

I close the internet and flick my finger across the home screen. Owen isn't a fan of social media, so there isn't any Instagram, Facebook, or TikTok to worry about. No Reddit. Nothing that would take his time and attention away from whatever case he has coming up at the hospital.

Frustrated now, I lock his phone and put it back on the coffee table.

Okay. I'm not going to get anywhere with Owen's phone. As much as I would have liked to find something... damning maybe, there's nothing there. Owen's always been squeaky clean, at least according to my research. Wade did most of it, but I wasn't about to try to get Owen into bed without a little light internet stalking. No, I haven't ever seen his actual bank records, but he doesn't deal with shady people. He's never put himself in compromising situations. Owen isn't the type of guy to hurt someone else for his own personal gain, but I can't say the same about the rest of his family. I mean, really... where did they get the money for this house?

I glance around the room, the display of opulence appalling. Grant traveled for work as a drug rep, regularly taking doctors out to the bar to ensure they'd be willing to push his company's drugs when they were with patients.

But that job doesn't come with the same crazy paydays as being a doctor does, does it? Not if you're doing everything aboveboard, if you're not accepting kickbacks. So where exactly did Grant and Marta get their money? Maybe from family? It could be inherited money, I guess. That makes sense, especially since Marta didn't work.

Or perhaps Owen sends them money every month. I find that hard to believe, but with as close as he and Marta are, I might not be too far off.

I check my watch and hop off the sofa. They've barely been gone fifteen minutes, and I need to get a move on if I want to make the most of my time alone. The absolute last thing I need is for them to return when I'm halfway through unlocking the garage door, or trying to get into the attic.

This morning is a gift I worked hard for. I'm not going to waste it sitting on the sofa.

I know more about Grant and Marta than they could ever imagine. If Owen had any idea what I know about his parents, he'd never have agreed to bring me here.

There's just one question that remains, and I'll do anything to answer it before I make my final move.

Does Owen know what his parents did?

NINETEEN
GINA

It feels dangerous looking up how to pick a lock on Owen's phone.

But you know what? I'm going to look it up and then delete the search, just like Owen has been doing for who knows how long. I settle onto the sofa and click into the first video that pulls up on YouTube. It has a thousand comments with people thanking the guy for talking them through picking a lock.

Seriously, though, if Leroy can do it, how hard can it be? The man has a vape as his profile picture, for goodness' sake.

But ten minutes later, I'm scared this isn't going to work. After watching four videos, I'm not sure that I can do it, especially without the right tools. Anything's possible with the right tools, but I might be out of luck there. Ironic that the very tools I need to pick the garage lock are likely in... the garage.

Still, I have to do something.

Meeting Owen, coming here, getting into the house... it's all part of the plan. It's all so I can make things right from years ago. This small setback won't stop me from getting what I want.

Taking a deep breath, I press my fingers into my temples.

All I have to do is stick to the plan. I need to find out one key piece of information, then I can do what I came here to do.

I've already looked for a garage door opener and tried to get in from the outside using a door on the side of the house.

But there might be a better way. Maybe I can find a key and scrap the whole picking-the-lock plan. Chances are good there's a spare here somewhere. It could even be in their bedroom, and goodness knows I want to poke around in there. Time to kill two birds with one stone.

And that's why I hurry upstairs and stop right outside Grant and Marta's bedroom. I've been standing here for two minutes now, unsure of what to do. I need to be very, very careful. If I thought Marta did a nice job making our bed with tight corners, then I'd seen nothing. This is intense. An army drill sergeant would be thrilled with how tight the bedspread is pulled. You could bounce a quarter off it.

And as for the rest of the room? Nothing out of place. No stacks of books by the bed, no dirty socks on the floor. *As if I needed more proof there's a psychopath under this roof.*

So where to start? I rub my hands together to warm up a little, then lean against the doorframe. I walk to the bed. Without touching it, because goodness knows I don't want to accidentally mess up how the bed is made, I drop to my knees and look underneath.

Now, I don't know about most normal people, but under my bed? It's always been a bona fide warzone. Anything in my apartment that needed a place to go went under the bed. Shoes I'd kicked off and not put away were shoved under there along with pieces of junk mail I didn't want to deal with and boxes full of... well... junk.

That all changed when I moved in with Owen, and now I see where he got it. The man doesn't have anything under his bed, not even dust bunnies, although I'm going to attribute that more to the persistence of his housekeeper than to him. But

Marta doesn't have a housekeeper, and the only thing I see under the bed are floorboards so clean they seem to shine.

"Disgusting," I mutter, planting my hands on the floor and pushing myself back up to stand. I dust my hands off on my jeans, like there's anything to wipe off, then walk over to the wall of closets.

Four louvered doors make up one wall of the room. Directly across from them is a wall full of windows, and I turn my back on them as I survey the closets. Four doors and two adults? Surely Marta has two and Grant has two. It would be fair anyway, and I get the feeling the two of them like things to be very, very fair.

Taking a deep breath, I open the first door, then step back like I fully expect something to fall out at me, which is insane. The space isn't disorganized. In fact, it looks like an ad for IKEA or The Container Store. Men's dress shirts hang in front of me, in rainbow order, and underneath them is a rack of pants.

Shoes line the floor, but I barely glance at them. I step close enough to trigger the overhead light, and it snaps on, throwing a halo of light around me. My heart skips a beat at the sudden bright light and I have to calm myself down.

Nobody's here with me. It's just the way it's designed, to make it as bougie as possible. Nothing more, nothing less.

On to the next one.

I'm not surprised to see hanging ties and suit jackets when I open the second door. There's a shelf with a jewelry box, and I debate leaving it alone, but a second later I have it open.

Cufflinks. Watches. Even one gold necklace. It's all high-quality, all gorgeous, all perfectly matched to the man who wears it.

The lid snicks shut, and I pull out the drawer below it. More cufflinks. Two more watches. A money clip. I slide the drawer back, step back into the bedroom, and close that door.

I know I'm alone; still, this is terrifying. Marta doesn't like me, but her problem with me isn't just that she doesn't think I'm right for her son. It's that I threaten everything she has right now because I know the truth of what happened in the past.

On the surface of it, anyone would look at her and think she's a good person. They'd wonder why I'm concerned, why I'm tiptoeing around the house, why I'm looking for any dirt on her.

And on the rest of her family.

But that's only because they don't know the truth.

I exhale hard and grab the knob for the third door. Chances are really good that I'm not going to find anything in here that will give me the answers I want, and I know that. If Grant's closets are any indication, there won't be anything behind these doors that will be at all damning.

They're too smart for that.

But what other opportunity do I have to be alone in the house? That concern pushes me to move faster, and I throw open the door and step back, almost like I'm expecting something to be waiting inside for me.

Of course, nobody is. Not all shadows hide monsters, no matter what I might think.

I take a tentative step forward. Just like in the first closets, there are lights on the ceiling that come on when I step inside. Also just like Grant's, the entire thing is perfectly organized.

This closet houses her accessories. Purses. Shoes. Belts. There's a huge jewelry box right in front of me, but I barely glance at it. Instead, I reach out and run my fingers over the scarves hanging next to it. They're impossibly soft, maybe cashmere, all of them in bright, eye-catching shades.

Then the purses. I'm more of a Target girl myself, or I was until I started dating Owen. Now I carry a Coach bag he got for me specifically for our dates, but that feels like nothing compared to the thousands of dollars of purses in front of me. I know it's silly, but I can't help myself as I reach out and trace my fingers over the leather.

The stitching along the edges of the bags is perfect. The leather has been cared for—that much is obvious. All of them look brand new, but that makes sense because I highly doubt Marta's buying purses and then leaving them to rot. That just doesn't seem like her style. No, she'd labor over them, oil them, keep them in good condition. Or pay someone to do that work for her.

I find exactly what I expect when I open her jewelry box. There's a string of pearls carefully nestled in the velvet drawer next to a pair of diamond earrings. The next drawer down boasts rings—some sapphires, some emeralds, all set in gold.

Then the bracelets, coiled like snakes, nestled in velvet squares. My mind races as I try to imagine just how much money she has in jewelry.

There's a door on either side of the jewelry box, and I open the one on the right, setting the necklaces to dancing. Diamonds. Pearls. Shiny and gold and sparkling, and—

Something catches my eye.

A necklace, the charm on it a simple B. Not made of gold.

Not covered in diamonds.

Just a simple silver B.

My heart stops, and I grab the doorframe, leaning against it as I take a deep breath and try to fight the wave of dizziness that washes over me.

Nobody in Owen's immediate family has a name that starts with B.

But my aunt did.

TWENTY

GINA

Then

"We did it!" Elle Woods screeches the words from Aunt Bethany's tube TV, and she and I both laugh. I've got blankets up to my chin, and I snuggle down deeper into them as she grabs the remote and turns off the TV. There's a slight glow from the screen that slowly fades, then she leans over and turns on a small lamp.

"Well? How was girls' night?"

"I think we can do this every weekend." I think I can't possibly eat another thing, but I still pop a final chip in my mouth. "Do you think you can talk to my parents about going on dates more often? And we'll have to get rid of Wade, of course."

She laughs and sits, moaning a little as she stretches. "I think once Wade realizes how much fun the two of us had, he's going to want to join in in the future. But we probably won't be watching *Legally Blonde* with him."

"Probably not," I agree. I want to stay curled up on her sofa forever, but I force myself to sit up. The blanket puddles on my lap. When I yawn, I see Aunt Bethany do the same.

"Get on upstairs, Gina. I'll clean up out here, okay?" She stands, grabbing the tray before I can argue. "I'll be up in a bit; I just have a few things to take care of first."

"Do you need help?" I stand too, ignoring the way my right leg prickles as it regains feeling. "I don't mind helping you. You know that."

"I do know that, but it's bills, darling, and I'm not going to ask you to help me pay them. I just have to write out a few checks, balance my checkbook, that sort of thing. Do you want me to come tuck you in when I finish up down here? It'll probably be half an hour or so."

"That's fine," I say. When I get nervous, I tend to play with the hem of my shirt. My mom tells me all the time that I need to stop it, that people will think something's wrong with me, but I can't help it. I don't even realize I'm doing it half the time. Like right now.

I drop my hand to my side.

"Come here." She puts the tray down on the sofa and pulls me into a hug. I melt into her. She always smells good, and tonight it's a combination of fresh cookies and whatever detergent she uses. I asked Mom one time if we could use the same type Aunt Bethany does because I like it so much, and she just laughed.

"Love you," I tell her, giving her one more squeeze.

"Oh, sweet Gina." She lets me go and picks up the tray. "You are so, so special, my dear. Head on up. There's a surprise for you in your room that I think you're really going to love. See if you can find it."

With that, she turns away, and I race to the stairs, grabbing my backpack as I go.

A surprise in my room? Aunt Bethany is the queen of surprises. Sure, they tend to be rather small, but I don't care. She always downplays it, telling me it's the thought that counts, but her surprises are the best.

Before allowing myself to go to my bedroom, I stop at the bathroom to get ready for bed. Who knows what the surprise is, and I don't want to find out and then have to come back to brush my teeth.

After peeing and splashing some water on my face, I brush quickly, then hurry down the hall to my room.

Well, it's not *my* room. Aunt Bethany and I call it that because it makes it seem more special than it really is. There are only two bedrooms in the house and one's for Wade, but Aunt Bethany has a small space off her bedroom. She told me once it was designed for a nursery, so parents could have a crib in their room. It would make it easier for them to take care of a baby in the middle of the night, which makes sense.

At first, I figured it was a walk-in closet, but she has a tiny one on the other side of her bedroom. What it originally was doesn't matter because it's my room now.

There's a small cot inside with a pillow and a heap of blankets on top. Aunt Bethany hung a hook on the wall for me to put my backpack, and I have a tiny bookcase in here she got off the side of the road. There are some old copies of her favorite books from when she was a little girl, although most of the time when I'm here, I want to be with her.

But that's not the surprise. Nor are the twinkle lights that hang from the ceiling. Those have been here for a while, after I brought them over. My mom had bought all new Christmas decorations and she was giving all of the old ones to charity. I snuck the strand of lights into my backpack and brought it here to hang up in my room.

I think the lights are awesome, but the surprise Aunt Bethany was talking about is even better, no matter how impossible that seems.

It's a door.

For the longest time I've had a curtain hanging here. It was old and brown, probably a used sheet that came from a charity shop and she cut into shape, but it worked well enough to separate Aunt Bethany's bedroom from me. The only problem with it was that it didn't cut off the sound between the two rooms, so while I've always wanted a sibling to share a room with, I certainly don't want one that snores, and that's my aunt. She sounds like a freight train, but I've put up with it because I'd rather be here than at my own house. My parents would lose it if they knew that, which is why they can't ever find out.

But now I have a door.

I gasp and hang up my backpack, flick on the twinkle lights, then run my hands along its edge. It's heavy and thick, not like the thinner, flimsy ones that fill the rest of the house. It's also painted, white on the side that's in Aunt Bethany's room, a soft blue on the side in mine. And I love it.

I pull it shut after me. It clicks shut, and I turn the handle, pushing it back open. Silly to play with it like I've never seen a door before, I know that, but I can't help it. It's just so exciting. I close it again. This is my space, but it feels even more real now. If Wade is being a jerk, I can come in here and shut him out. And—I see it now—it has a barrel bolt.

Reaching up over my head, I slide it into place. A giddy, heady feeling washes over me, and I plunk down on my cot. It squeaks a little under my weight, but I came prepared this time. Last time I stayed, I asked Aunt Bethany if she had anything to make it stop squeaking, but she didn't. It wasn't hard to take the WD-40 from my garage at home. Mom and Dad won't ever notice that it's gone, and if they do, they'll think they misplaced it.

A moment later, the cot is fixed. I sit on it, feeling it sag under my weight, but it doesn't squeak.

"Perfect." For a moment, I consider getting up and unlocking the door, but I decide to wait until Aunt Bethany comes to check on me. How cool will it be to hear her knock, to get up and unlock the door, to invite her into my space?

I giggle.

Sure, this space is technically hers, but it feels like mine. It'll feel so cool to invite her in.

There's an old box in here full of Aunt Bethany's shoes, and I slide it back under the cot where it usually goes. Now I'm ready for her to come tuck me in. Mom says I'm old enough to not need her at bedtime and stopped a while ago, but Aunt Bethany offered. I'm not going to turn her down, no matter how old I'm getting.

I grab a book and settle back down on my cot. There's a soft pillow, and I punch it into place, then lean it up against the wall and tug some blankets up over me. I think I've read this book half a dozen times, but I don't care. It's not like Aunt Bethany has the money to go buy me a new one, and besides, it's comforting reading it over and over. I already know what's going to happen, so there aren't any surprises I have to worry about.

I want to stay awake for her to come tuck me in, but I'm already tired. It was a long day, and my stomach is really full. Like Aunt Bethany says, there's nothing quite like a full stomach to make you really sleepy. I roll over and prop my head up on my wrist, trying to focus on the book.

Yes, I could just go to sleep.

But I don't want to miss her coming to bed.

Sitting up, I force myself to stretch, then look at the time. She really should be up here any minute now, and I know she said she doesn't want my help, but there's no reason why I can't go keep her company. It's not like I'm going to get any sleep until she comes in anyway.

I put the book back on the bookcase and yank on a hoodie, then unlock the door and push it open. It's quiet in the house, but it always is at this time of night. Even if Wade were here, he'd likely already be in his room listening to music on his old CD player or reading a book.

I'm confident I can help Aunt Bethany so the two of us can

get to bed a little faster. Her stairs are rickety and steep, and I trail my hand down the railing as I carefully make my way down them, placing each foot exactly where I won't make a sound.

Halfway down though, I stop.

Someone's talking to Aunt Bethany, but I don't recognize their voice.

TWENTY-ONE

MARTA

Grant and Owen walk in front of me, the two of them matching step for step, and while we're going to have to go back home soon enough, I can't help but feel like everything is working out the way I want it to.

My son is home with me. It feels like all the pieces of my life are fitting back together, and that may be dramatic for some people, but it's the truth. Owen completes me. I know why Grant pushed for him to leave the hospital he was at and work at Mercy Mission. I know how important it was, and why he set him on that path, but it's nice to have my son home. That's all I've ever wanted.

That's the difference between Grant and me. He forced Mercy Mission on Owen because he's been watching Gina for years and knew she worked there. In his mind, if anyone could get Gina to our house, it would be our son. How he got Owen to quit his current job and switch hospitals, I don't think I'll ever understand. But just like Owen can never know why Grant and I are so interested in Gina, she can never know that Grant planned this all out.

And why not take care of things on our own? Why involve

our son? That's something I've asked him time after time, only to be told that I don't understand, that this is a family affair. That we all need to finish this together.

And you know what? He's right, but not in the way that he thinks. I just want to love Owen. That's all I've ever wanted from him. I've certainly never used him like his father does.

And now I have him back. Gina's sick at home, and I can pretend she didn't even come on this trip. All I have to do is use her to get rid of Grant and it'll be me and Owen again, just like it always should be.

Sure, Owen will be heartbroken when Gina is gone, but I can pick up all his pieces. I'm his mother. I carried him for nine months, and there isn't a single person in this world who knows what he needs more than I do.

The only thing that makes this morning less than perfect is the little bag Owen carries in his hand. He swings it like a small child on Halloween, gleeful over a bag crammed full of candy, and while I can pretend all I want to not know what's in there, I was there when he bought it.

A ring. A diamond ring. A flashy, over-the-top, ostentatious ring that I'm sure Gina will swoon over. Because what girl wouldn't jump at the opportunity to marry my son? What woman in their right mind would take one look at him and turn up their nose? Even a woman like Gina. *Especially* a woman like Gina.

He's everything she's never had. Living in that shit town, growing up with parents who didn't really want her. She worked hard to get to where she was, to snag my son for herself. Too bad she won't get to enjoy him much longer.

It's a dangerous game, letting Owen dream about a future with her when Grant and I have other plans. But that's my son for you—he's always seen the best in people, always believed in second chances. I warned Grant this might happen, that Owen might fall for Gina, and that it would cause problems later, but he hadn't been concerned.

And now look where we are. Buying an engagement ring for her.

"Gina," I scoff, without even realizing I'm speaking out loud.

"Do what, Mom?" Owen turns around, a grin slowly spreading across his face. "What did you say about Gina?"

"Oh, just that I wish she were here with us," I lie. "I'm sure she'd love strolling around downtown."

"I wish so too." He sounds so wistful that, for a moment, I feel bad for him. But then he continues, and I have to fight back a frown. "But it's probably better this way because I wouldn't have been able to pick out the ring for her. And I'm glad you two could be here to tell me what you think."

He wants to know what I think? I think he's making a huge mistake, but that's not what my son wants to hear so I keep my mouth shut. This baboonery will be over before too long anyway, so it's not like I need to worry about it. Let Owen think he's going to marry that frippet if that makes him happy.

Let him imagine their lives together, how she would wait on him hand and foot so she didn't have to keep a steady job. It will be painful for him when it all falls apart, but he won't ever know the role I played in it. This, all of this... pushing Grant towards Gina, making sure Owen will have me to turn to when he finds out what happened between the two of them, it's all for my son.

He can't know the truth. I've seen the way he looks at Gina, like she hung the moon. He's under her spell right now, and I need to free him from it so he can think clearly again. So he can know that I'm the one person in his life he needs.

"It's a lovely ring," I say because that's the only lie I can come up with on the spur of the moment.

"I'm so glad you think so." Owen gives a little sigh, then looks up at the sky. "It's so wonderful knowing that you and

Dad support this. That you like Gina. She really is special, don't you think?"

"One of a kind," Grant says, and Owen turns to look at his dad. I'm grateful for him taking our son's attention from me. "To survive the kind of things she has? Amazing."

There's a moment when I think that he didn't just say that, or maybe that Owen didn't hear him, but I can already see our son frowning.

"What did you say?"

Grant inhales, the sound sharp. A young couple walks past us, the shopping bag the woman's carrying knocking into my arm as she goes.

"You've told us before that she had a hard upbringing," Grant tells him, and I can hear the worry in his voice.

Don't sound desperate, Grant. That's when things fall apart.

"Did I?" His eyes flick to me, but I don't react. "I didn't want to share anything that Gina would have wanted me to keep private." A furrow appears between Owen's brows.

"Your mom isn't running around behind your back telling me your secrets, son. Don't worry about that. You know as well as I do that when you drink, things just come out."

Grant's words are painful—I can tell from the way Owen takes a step back. Nobody wants to have it implied that they should cut down on their drinking, especially not from their father.

"I didn't know." Owen's voice has changed, become flatter.

"Well, we all do it." Grant swings an arm around Owen's shoulders and gives him a little squeeze. "Really nothing to concern yourself about, son, okay? We all start talking when we've been drinking, and while you might feel bad about it, I don't want you to. It's not like I'm going to say anything to Gina."

"She'd be so upset with me."

I move forward. It's almost impossible to watch your son struggle—to know he's upset and you're part of the reason.

"She'll never know." Grant still has his arm around Owen. His fingers dig into his shoulder a little, but our son doesn't seem to notice. "Okay? I'm not going to tell her that you told me about her childhood."

Owen swallows. "What did I tell you exactly?"

This is huge. There's a precipice, and Grant and I are standing right on its apex. One wrong step and everything will come crashing down. What we've built together, what we're doing with Owen, his relationship with Gina... it will all fall apart if my husband isn't extremely careful.

More than that, the plans I made with Grant will fall apart. I won't let that happen, not when I've worked so hard to create the future I want.

Grant heaves a sigh and finally drops his arm from Owen's shoulders. "You told me she had a pretty traumatic childhood. Issues with her parents. You called, and had been drinking, and needed to get it off your chest. I told you I'm always here for you."

I can't seem to breathe normally. Owen seems to lean into Grant, and I feel my chest tighten. He should be turning to me for comfort, not his father. Not when Grant hasn't ever been there for him like I have.

Grant continues: "You also said there was a death when she was younger and she blamed herself for it, but I told you that kids don't have any control over something like that and that she needed to let it go. You agreed."

Owen nods but doesn't respond. He inhales, his breath shuddery, then exhales hard. "What else did I tell you?"

Grant raises an eyebrow as he looks at me. It's a silent plea for help, but honestly? He's the one who stepped in it. He can fix this.

"That's pretty much it, Owen. You've been all-in on this girl since I found her for you and you met her, and your mother and I are just so happy for you too. You wanted us to know a little bit about what she'd gone through when she was younger, so you told us that she'd lived through a pretty traumatic event but had gotten some help for it."

Grant is nodding but slowly. He still looks stressed out, like he can't quite believe the conversation he's having, but at least he no longer looks like he's going to freak out. For a moment there, I was afraid he was going to do something stupid.

"But I didn't tell you anything else? Like about the death itself?"

I look at Grant. He has to handle this perfectly or it's going to come back to bite us, I know it will. Owen is smart. Smarter than I think Grant is giving him credit for right now. You don't get to be head of cardiac surgery without knowing how to read people, at least a little bit.

"Son, I know nothing," Grant lies. "Anything I know, you've told me. There was a death. Gina feels bad about it, feels like it was her fault. She's been in therapy to handle those emotions, and you think she's handled them well enough to consider building a life with her. That's what I know, and that's all I care about."

"Please don't tell her I've told you any of that. I don't want her to think all I do is talk about her when that's not the case. Well, I want to talk about her but not tell her secrets. She's allowed to have them." Relief washes over Owen's face.

"Of course she is," Grant tells him. "And you and I are allowed to have ours too. I won't tell Gina anything that you've told me—you don't have to worry. It'll all be fine."

Those last words are aimed at me, not at our son. I lift my chin a little bit and stare at my husband.

It'll all be fine.

He better be right.

TWENTY-TWO

GINA

I know that necklace.

My mind races as I plant my hands against the kitchen counter and take deep breaths. I was looking for proof of what happened so many years ago, of what Wade is convinced he unearthed, but I'm still struggling to breathe. I knew there had to be proof here; what I didn't know is *what* that proof would be.

Twenty years. It's been twenty years since I've seen that necklace. Sweat breaks out on my brow, and I close my eyes. Wipe it away. Now's not the time to think about that. I can deal with the necklace later.

Another deep breath, then I run the sink and dip my hand under the stream for a drink. The water is cool, and I splash it on my face before turning off the tap and fumbling for a towel. I'm drying my face when a phone beeps. For a moment, I freeze, unsure of where the sound could be coming from, but then it hits me. I spring into action, dropping the towel on the kitchen counter, and race into the living room.

It's Owen's phone. Not mine, which is why the sound took me off guard for a moment.

My hands shake as I swipe on the screen and tap in his password. I'm not snooping, not technically, because he gave me permission to use his phone, but it still feels wrong to open it and see who texted him. If it's anything important, like about work, I might have to call Marta or Grant to let him know, but hopefully it won't be anything like that.

Then I see Marta's name on the screen and my heart does this weird flip-flop thing where at first I'm disappointed that she might be reaching out to me, then I remember that Owen could easily have used her phone to send me a text. I tap the notification.

Don't worry about your father. We just want what's best for you.

Clearly this text wasn't from Owen to me.

Which can only mean one of two things. Marta either doesn't know I have Owen's phone or she forgot. Either way, she wanted to tell him not to worry about something that happened with Grant.

But what is that all about?

I weigh the phone in my hand, tapping the screen to keep it from going dark. I feel like I should respond, should try to dig deeper into what's going on, but that's just dangerous, isn't it? What if she texted Owen because he was out of sight for a moment but now he's back? What if I respond with a text that makes her suspicious and she realizes that she's talking to me?

But how can I let this go?

I'm in the middle of looking for answers and it doesn't seem fair that I could have the opportunity to finally get some and I just... throw it away?

No. Not after I've come this far.

But still I hesitate, the different things I could say swirling around in my mind. They're all dangerous, no matter how I look at it. Marta and Owen could meet back up at any minute, she could realize I have his phone, she could know she's talking to me.

And then what?

"Oh, move on with it," I mutter, my thumbs flying across the screen. I only pause for a moment before I hit the send button, then I stare at the words, hoping that I didn't just make a huge mistake.

I know. And Gina is the thing that's best for me.

That sounds like something Owen would say, and I'm pretty sure I'm not just projecting. He loves me. I know he does. He knows some of the dark truth about my past, and yet, he still loves me. He invited me to live with him in his home, he's talked about our future, he wanted me to meet his parents. Love wasn't ever part of the plan when I met Owen, but I can't deny how we both feel.

I have no doubt he loves me. But would he if he knew the truth of why I'm here?

Not a chance. We'd be over.

I push that thought from my mind.

Her response is so quick I only have to tap the screen once to keep it from going dark.

I hope you're right. We don't want to see you make a mistake.

"Geez, spoken like a true monster-in-law." I don't know if there's anything I need to say in response to that. It's not like Owen would want to continue this line of conversation, I don't think. Who wants to hear from their parent that they think they're making a mistake with their partner?

Actually, Owen might fight this. Knowing him, he could

very well push his mother and tell her what he really thinks about her saying things like this about me.

But the last thing I need is for her to be walking with Owen or sitting across from him in a coffee shop while her phone goes off with texts from him. As soon as she realizes he left his cell with me, I'm done for.

I'll leave it alone.

Like it's a bomb, I put the phone back on the coffee table and hurry back into the kitchen, bringing my empty glass with me. I put it on the counter, then brace my hands next to it while I think. The necklace should be enough. I take a deep breath and consider what else I want to find. The fact that it was hanging in Marta's closet tells me she was involved. Somehow.

I have the proof I need. So why can't I stop? Why do I feel compelled to find more?

Maybe because my family isn't the only one that was hurt.

She's a bitch. But what if she was a victim in this? Nobody deserves to die because I don't like them personally. I refuse to have that much power.

I groan and rub my temples. This is bigger than me. Bigger than Wade. That means I need to push a little bit more for answers. Unfortunately, the locked doors in this house are a problem, and I'm running out of places to poke around without figuring how to get one of them open.

That means my only choice now is to follow one of the YouTube videos I watched. Honestly, though, the idea of trying to pick the lock terrifies me. Alternatively, I need to find a key. I didn't find it in Marta and Grant's bedroom, but to be fair, I didn't look as hard as I would have liked just because the room was so neat. There's no way I could put everything back the way it belonged.

Still, I'm going to give finding the key one more chance because I can't do much without tools.

Moving quickly, I walk around the kitchen, opening each

drawer as I go. The key rack hanging by the front door only holds Grant's and Marta's car keys, so if the garage key is on either of those key rings, I'm out of luck.

But everyone has a junk drawer. Surely the queen of clean, Marta Whitlock herself, will have one.

The first drawer is silverware. It jangles as I push it closed.

Napkins.

Placemats.

Spatulas, stirring spoons, a can opener.

I'm getting frustrated now, and I barely yank the drawers half open before slamming them closed again.

Paper and pens. Sticky notes. Tape.

Saran Wrap, tinfoil, plastic baggies.

Finally, in the last drawer: junk. It's glorious, the drawer crammed so full of stuff that I have to carefully shimmy it open so nothing falls out of the back and into the cupboard below.

Even someone as perfect as Marta has to have a place to throw her crap, I guess.

I'm careful as I pick through the stash. Rubber bands and paper clips are up front, the paper clips sliding all over the bottom of the drawer as I poke through them. Then there are some business cards, but I barely pay attention to these before pushing them out of the way. A box cutter, which is probably more normal than I realize, but feels strange to pick up and weigh in my hand.

Crumpled receipts. Old gum. A box of Tic Tacs that must have been in the drawer for years given how the little candies are all stuck together and to the side of the container.

Then, finally, like a freaking beacon of hope, a small box of loose keys. I lift it out and dump them unceremoniously on the counter. Bits of dirt and lint scatter, and I flick them to the floor.

There's a dozen keys, maybe a few more, but some of them I can discount right away. I lift out a small key that looks like it was designed for a diary lock and toss it back in the box. An old car key follows. There's one key that's broken, and I put it in the box without a second glance.

If that's the spare garage key and it's broken, then there's nothing I can do about that now. Better to focus on the things I can fix than mull over the ones I can't.

That leaves me with a handful of keys, and I sweep them into my palm, then hurry over to the garage door. I keep trying to temper my expectations and tell myself that the key might not be in this box, but my heart beats hard with excitement.

And with hope. I'll try the keys here, then head to Grant's office if none of them work. Things haven't worked out for me yet, but there's plenty of time for it to all turn around, for one of the keys to open the garage or the office.

I don't know what I'll do if I can't find what I'm looking for. I know what Wade would tell me to do, but he wants to go scorched earth. I'm trying to be a bit more careful.

I drop to my knees and put the keys in a small pile in front of me, then pluck the first one from the top and try to fit it into the knob. It slips right in, and I feel a moment of elation—*could it really be this easy?*—but when I try to turn it, the key remains in place.

It's slightly stuck, and I swear as I jimmy it out, then put it on the floor behind me.

Another key. This one doesn't even slip in. The tip of it catches in the lock, and I drop it behind me, swearing in frustration.

The third key. Third time's a charm? Hope rises in me as it slides easily into the lock. For just a moment I think it's turning, that it's catching the pins, pushing them into place, preparing to slide open, but then it sticks.

"Come on," I say, wiggling it back and forth. Frustration makes my heart pound in my ears. I close my eyes. Take a deep breath. Try wiggling it again, but now it's not moving at all. When I try to pull it out, it catches, the key trapped inside.

No.

I yank on the key, leaning back on my heels so I can put all of my weight into it. For a moment, the key feels like it's moving, then it's stuck again.

A slam behind me makes the hair on the back of my neck stand up.

"Gina? We're home!"

Fuck.

TWENTY-THREE

GINA

Sweat drips down my nose, but I don't reach up to wipe it away. Instead, I lean to the right, putting even more of my weight into pulling the key out of the lock.

But it won't slip out.

Frantic, I leave it. From the hallway I can hear Owen talking, his low voice almost comforting. This is good. If they're still out there, then they haven't made their way to the kitchen yet to see what I'm up to. I brush the keys into a pile, careful not to leave a single one, then dump them into the box.

Right as I throw the box into the drawer and slam my hip into it to close it, Marta appears in the kitchen. Her eyes are beady as she looks around, taking in the empty mimosa glass, the crumpled towel, how I lean against the counter. I can almost see her cataloging everything about the scene.

Can she tell how nervous I am right now?

"Is everything okay, Gina?" Her voice is high. Fake.

"It's great," I lie. "I was just looking for a safety pin. Figured if you had any, they'd be in a junk drawer, but I didn't see any in here." I pat the drawer behind me.

As Marta walks over to me, my eyes flick behind her.

The key is in the knob, right where I left it. If she were to walk over to the door, she'd see it, but as of right now, she hasn't noticed it. Only problem is I don't know how long my luck is going to hold.

"They're in there," she tells me, waving her hand at me to make me move. I'm all too happy to step to the side, and I watch as she pulls open the drawer, digs inside the mass of paper clips and rubber bands, and pulls out three safety pins. "What do you need them for?"

"I just needed one to work the tie of my pajama pants back through," I tell her. "You know how those things can get pulled out, and they're such a pain to get back. Thanks for getting this for me." I take a single safety pin from her and smile.

She nods, her lips a thin line. Before she can respond, Owen's here, wrapping his arms around me and pulling me close. "Hey, you. I missed you."

I turn in his arms and kiss him. "Missed you too." If I stand on my tiptoes and put my chin on his shoulder, I can look past him at the door into the garage.

It's silly, but it almost feels like I can keep the key there, without anyone else finding it, as long as I look at it from time to time. If I look away, something might happen to the key. Or—worse—Marta or Grant might see it.

"The mimosas worked their magic, huh? You'd never know that when I left you this morning, you looked like you'd welcome death."

"With open arms," I quip. "You were right about the hair of the dog though. I had three mimosas, I think. Definitely helped keep the vomity feeling away."

"Glad to hear it." He kisses me again, then steps back. "Hey, sorry for not calling you on our way home. I just lost track of what was going on, and didn't even think about asking to borrow Mom or Dad's phone."

No, don't say it.

"Why would you have had to borrow a phone? Gina's is dead, so you couldn't call her." Marta crosses her arms and looks at the two of us. She looks like a predator, and I'm hit with the sudden, horrid feeling that she can smell fear.

"I left her mine so she could reach us if she needed anything." Owen throws her a grin, then looks at me. Nods. "I didn't want her to be left here completely isolated just in case."

"You had Owen's phone?" Marta turns to face me. The expression on her face is clear. *She knows.* But Owen doesn't seem to pick up on how unhappy his mother is. That, or he just doesn't want to see it.

I can't seem to form any words, but Owen speaks up for me.

"Well, yeah. Gina had never been here before, and it's not like there are close neighbors. What if she started feeling worse? I needed to know she could get help if necessary." Owen frowns, and I can basically see the synapses in his brain working overtime. "Is there a problem?"

"No problem at all." Marta smiles at me, baring her teeth. It's weird that humans are the only animals that bare their teeth when they're happy, isn't it? When other animals show their teeth, you know you've really messed up. "Where is Owen's phone now, Gina?"

"On the coffee table." I swallow hard. "I left it in there while I was trying to find a safety pin for my pajamas."

"Right. Your pajamas." Marta takes a step closer to me at the same time Owen speaks.

"I'll go grab it." Owen squeezes my shoulder, then hurries from the room.

He's so clueless.

"You were the one texting me." Marta's mouth is so close to my ear I can feel her breath on my cheek. It smells like coffee.

"I don't know what you're talking about." I deleted those messages from his mom. If Owen were to check to see what I'd been doing with his phone, he wouldn't find any proof of them ever being sent. That is, of course, unless Marta decides to pony up her phone to prove her point, but for some reason, I don't think that's her MO.

She doesn't want to turn me over to her son. She wants something else.

"I don't trust you."

"I know." My palms are sweaty. I want to wipe them on my pants, but I fight the urge to move. Isn't that what you're supposed to do when faced with a predator out in the wild? Stay still?

Do I lie down and hope she'll leave me alone? Or is my best bet to fight and hope I can drive her away from me long enough to survive this trip?

"I'll be watching you." She puffs air at me, and I keep from flinching away.

"I'm sure you will be," I say, surprising myself. I'm trying to keep the peace for as long as possible, but this woman is insufferable. "Just like I'm watching you, Marta. Don't think I don't know who you are."

She blinks in surprise, but the expression is there and gone before I can really clock it. "I'd love to know who you think I am, Gina. Because it seems to me you don't know a lot about much."

I hate her. More than I've ever hated anyone. She's evil, but she keeps it hidden behind a perfect façade. "Believe me, Marta, I know what you—"

"Marta? Gina? Is everything okay?" It's Grant, the worry in his voice evident. He's behind Marta, and she steps back from me swiftly, her face changing.

What was a grimace is now a smile. The lines on her forehead have disappeared. She crinkles her eyes a little bit like she couldn't be happier.

"Oh, we're fine, Grant." Whipping around, she steps in front of me. To block him from seeing the expression on my face? I'm not sure. "Gina and I were just talking about her day. Sure wish she had been able to come with us, but at least she was able to keep in touch a little with Owen's phone."

"He's a good kid," Grant says.

"He sure is." She pauses, then turns back to me before reaching out and carefully tucking some hair behind my ear. The brush of her skin on mine is painful, and I freeze, my eyes locked on hers. "So pretty. Don't you think, Grant? Gina's the prettiest girl Owen's dated in a long time."

Grant takes a step closer to us. I don't have to look away from Marta to feel his gaze lock on me. I feel it sweep over me, from my eyes to my toes and back. He nods. "You are gorgeous, Gina. No wonder Owen loves you."

I force myself to swallow hard and step out around Marta. She stares at me, her lips curling into a smile.

It's hard to look away from her, but I finally do, my eyes landing on Grant. Best to pretend that didn't happen. That things are normal. That I didn't see the way she glared at me or how Grant's eyes flicked up and down my body. Again.

He has a white paper bag clutched in his hand, and I eye it. I'm still worried about my interaction with Marta, but I can't help but smell the delicious aroma coming from the bag. As much as I want to run screaming from this room, it's best to pretend like things are normal.

At least for now. Wade would tell me to end it all now, but I don't want anyone to be collateral damage, to deal with what I survived as a little kid.

Not even Marta.

"Did you bring donuts?" My mouth waters just thinking about what he might have in that bag. After everything—the stress of hiding that I wasn't drinking as much as I pretended last night, the champagne this morning, the run-in with Marta— I'm feeling a little sick to my stomach, but donuts? Those could help. Without meaning to, I glance past him at the garage door, then drag my eyes back to his face.

He's turning to see what I was looking at, and I reach out to grab his arm. As soon as my hand touches his bicep, he turns back to me. I let go when his eyes reach mine.

"Sure did. And we picked up some breakfast casserole, fruit, and biscuits." The smile he gives me is a mirror-image of the one Owen throws around when he wants people to do something for him. I notice again how his eyes drift down my body before he hefts the bag between us. "Why don't you head on out to the dining room, and Marta and I will bring plates?" He holds the bag out to me, and I take it, making sure not to touch his fingers or look at Marta as I walk past her.

I know they want me out of the kitchen so they can talk about me, but I don't care. I can't stop them from talking about me.

Just like I couldn't stop what happened to Aunt Bethany.

TWENTY-FOUR

GINA

Then

The first thing that crosses my mind is that Wade came home early from his sleepover and that he's talking with Aunt Bethany in the kitchen.

But as I make my way down to the first floor, I'm less and less convinced it's Wade.

This voice is angrier. There's gravel in it, like the man rolls each word around in his mouth before speaking. Then, when he does release the words into the air, they fall like stones, heavy and dark.

Painful.

I pause. There are still a few steps to go until I reach the first floor, but I'm afraid to go down them.

Lowering myself slowly, I sit on the edge of the step. My heart hammers away in my chest, and I feel a slick of sweat break out on my skin.

It could be the food. That's it. It has to be the food sweats; Wade told me those were a thing you could get. *Food sweats*. Sounds disgusting.

But I don't think that's what's going on. My stomach is twisting, sure, but it wasn't a few minutes ago when I was upstairs. This is different. I've not felt like this before, like I need to rip through my skin and step out of it, like running as far and fast as possible is the right thing to do.

It's not food sweats.

It's fear.

"Now, don't you act surprised. I saw the way you were looking at me at the diner." That's the voice I don't recognize. If my aunt responds, I don't hear her.

Hair on the back of my neck prickles, and all of my muscles tighten. I want to race into the kitchen and see who Aunt Bethany is talking to, but at the same time I want to turn and run. I want to burst through the front door and get outside where maybe the sky will be big enough to allow me to take a deep breath.

My eyes flick to the front door. It's partly ajar, some cool night air snaking through the crack. I can hear the gentle sound of rain and smell it too, but that doesn't calm me down any.

I have to know who's with my aunt.

There's a voice in my head screaming at me that I'm making a huge mistake as I carefully stand up and walk down the rest of the steps.

Maybe Aunt Bethany has a boyfriend.

I dismiss that out of hand. She would have told me if she had someone coming over—I know she would have. And a boyfriend doesn't explain why the front door was left open.

It doesn't explain anything.

Her voice now, high and tight. Fearful.

"Please don't."

That's it. Just two words and I freeze, my legs heavy, dipped in concrete. I need to see what's happening, but I can't move. My nostrils flare. There's fear in the air—I smell it, and the hair on my arms bristles. I couldn't hear her before and wanted to. Now I wish I hadn't.

The man's voice again, but murmuring in a way that means I can't make out the words. Chills race up my spine. My mouth goes dry.

I force myself down another step.

I'd love to stay right here and not go any closer to the kitchen, but what if Aunt Bethany needs me?

I have to make sure she's okay.

More steps, slow, placed carefully. I know this place like the back of my hand. How many times have Wade and I played around in here, each of us being as quiet as possible so the other person didn't find them? I'm nervous because the stakes are higher, but I still know my way around, and I have no doubt I can get closer to the kitchen without being seen or heard.

I keep moving. My feet are bare, and the wood floor is cool. I want to close the front door to keep the chill from entering. Instead, I take a deep breath, and I don't let myself walk over to it. I have to stay focused.

More steps.

I'm at the kitchen door now, and while part of me already knows this is bad, that something terrible is happening, that doesn't prepare me for what I see.

My gasp dies in my throat.

I reach up, grab it, squeeze tight.

I can't take my eyes off my aunt.

TWENTY-FIVE

MARTA

What I have planned for Gina isn't bad enough. She deserves much, much worse.

I slam a new bottle of orange juice down on the counter and angrily twist off the lid. Before I can throw it though, Grant's hand appears and covers mine.

"Hey." His voice is low. "You okay?"

"Am I okay?" I whip round to face him. "Are you serious right now? No, I'm not okay. Gina... she had Owen's phone, Grant."

He cocks an eyebrow at me. "And?"

"And I texted his phone, thinking I was talking to him. But I obviously wasn't. I was talking to *her*."

He gets it. I see the moment when the lightbulb flicks on in his brain. "What did you say?"

"Just that I want him to be careful. That we want him to be happy, but we want to make sure he isn't making a mistake. Nothing bad. Things any concerned mother would say."

"Did she tell you that you weren't texting Owen?"

I'm shaking my head before he finishes the question. "No.

She didn't. She pretended to be him." I pause, waiting to let that one sink in. "She's more dangerous than we knew."

This makes him scoff. His lip curls up a little, and he shakes his head. "No, she's not. She's a stupid, traumatized girl who thinks she hit the jackpot by making Owen fall in love with her. She's not a mastermind. She's nothing."

He's wrong.

It's not that I blame him for being wrong because I believed the same thing at first too. Gina seemed stupid. An easy mark to handle. Someone the two of us could deal with, especially with Owen's help in getting her here. The poor thing has no idea his father and I have been using him.

But now I'm wondering if we were wrong. She sneaks around. She watches and listens. These shenanigans with Owen's phone? Not for a second do I trust her. Maybe Grant is burying his head in the sand regarding her because he's being purposefully obtuse.

Or maybe my plan is working and he wants her for himself. The original plan... the one we agreed on? It ended in Gina's destruction.

But my plan changed. Did my husband's?

TWENTY-SIX

GINA

Hate radiates off Marta. Every time she looks at me, her face darkens. Her mouth presses into a thin line. I try to smile at her, but I can't force it.

This is all happening so much faster than I had planned. I was in control, or I believed I was, but now—

"So do we hear wedding bells in the future?" Marta takes a sip of coffee before pinning me in place with her stare. It's interesting that she directed that question at me and not her son.

"Wow, wedding bells," I say, grabbing my napkin and wiping my mouth. It's a good way to hide the expression on my face because I don't know what it looks like right now.

Do I want to marry Owen? Sure I do. It wasn't the original plan, and I had to get Wade on board, but I fought to do that. Wanting to marry Owen wasn't just because living with him has been living in the lap of luxury. I love the man. Yes, falling in love with him was an accident, but that doesn't mean how I feel about him isn't real. I'm not one of those pathetic girls who threw herself at an attractive man because she was already planning on walking down the aisle with him.

I threw myself at an attractive man because he was the key

to me getting what I wanted, and it wasn't a *Mrs.* before my name. It wasn't a ring on my finger. It was—

"Is that a no?" Marta asks, pulling me back to the conversation.

I swear I see a hint of hope there in her eyes. It makes me sit up straighter. I stiffen, slap a huge smile on my face, and reach for Owen's hand.

"Are you kidding me? There's nothing I'd love more than to marry your son." Even if it weren't true, I'd say it just to make Marta wince. Owen gives my fingers a squeeze, but I don't look away from his mother. Not until I get my point across. "Owen is everything I've ever wanted in a husband. No way would I want to live a single day of my life without him."

"Well, we're happy to hear that," Grant says, and I look at him, dragging my eyes away from Marta. For a moment there, it looked like she was going to break, that her face would fall, or she'd frown, but she's good. She'll show me who she really is in private but not in front of her precious son.

"Yeah?" I glance at Owen, who's grinning at his dad like the man hung the moon. "I'm glad to hear you approve."

"We'll look forward to meeting your parents," Grant tells me. "They must be pretty incredible people to have raised such a wonderful young lady."

I let go of Owen's hand and rip off a piece of donut, carefully nibbling on it before I speak. "That's so kind of you, Grant, but I don't know when that will happen."

"Not even for the wedding?"

I shake my head.

"Why not? You're an only child, right? I remember Owen telling me that."

I nod.

"So why in the world wouldn't they want to see you get married? Every parent wants to see their child happy and loved.

You can't tell me Owen isn't good enough for them." He forces a laugh but doesn't really smile.

"Gosh, no." I shake my head and pop the rest of the donut piece into my mouth. "Owen's way better than they are, trust me. It's just that we're not very close, and I don't know if they'll even want to come to the wedding. Sometimes we go for months without talking." I pause, thinking. "Once it was a year. It wasn't malicious or planned; it just... happened."

"Oh, Gina," Grant says, and the pain in his eyes is enough to make me talk faster.

"No, no pity," I say, holding up one hand. "Seriously, I don't want your pity. We're just not close."

"Owen told us you had a... tumultuous childhood," Marta offers.

I glance up at her but she's staring at Owen. "Yes, well." I rub my hands on my thighs to wipe off the sweat. "My childhood wasn't great. And my parents tried their best to help me out after what happened." I pause; look up at Owen. The expression on his face is one of pure love, and although I don't really want to talk about what happened when I was a little girl, these are his parents.

And they know more than they're letting on.

"My parents left me with my aunt one night when they went out on a date," I say, never looking away from Owen. It's nice to have his eyes on me, to know he already knows this story and isn't judging me or going to think less of me. "And while I was with my aunt, someone broke into the house. And killed her."

Silence.

It's pretty much the response I've grown to expect from people when I tell them my story. Nobody knows what to say to the girl who narrowly avoided dying along with her aunt. Nobody knows how to handle this bombshell, not even Grant and Marta.

"I'm fine," I say, giving a little shrug like that will undo the years of pain and trauma I suffered after Aunt Bethany died. "They didn't know I was there."

"That sounds horrible." A strange expression flits across Marta's face, but it's gone before I can clock it. Her lips press together into a hard line. At the same time, she glances up at Grant. Out of the corner of my eye, I see him give a little shrug.

"It was," I say, swallowing hard.

Nobody speaks. Owen's hand closes around my arm, and he holds me for a moment before letting go and putting his hand in his lap.

"I don't want to say my parents blame me for what happened," I say, desperate to fill the uncomfortable silence. "But there's friction there, and I don't know how we can move past that. At this point in my life, I don't know that it's worth the trouble, not when I have the rest of my life with Owen to look forward to. All that to say... I don't know if or when Owen will meet my parents."

It's Grant who speaks first. He clears his throat, and we all turn to look at him.

"That had to have been the most horrible experience, Gina. I'm really sorry you had to deal with that. Please tell me they caught the guy."

I shake my head. "No, they didn't. The cops tried, of course, and they said for a while they might have a few leads that would pan out, but so far, nothing."

"How many years ago was it?" Grant asks. He leans closer to me, his eyes locked on mine.

"Twenty," I answer without hesitation. They don't need to know how I've been counting the days, months, years. How hard it has been for me to move on when my favorite person in the world died. How my cousin, Wade, and I clung to each other to make it through the horror of losing someone we both cared so much for.

"Twenty years, wow. And to think you survived it. And now you're here, wanting to marry my son," Marta says. She pops a bite of donut in her mouth, but I don't look away from Owen. He's watching me carefully.

I've always been honest with Owen about what happened and how terrible it was, but never once have I told him the truth about what really happened to my aunt.

I know who killed her.

TWENTY-SEVEN

GINA

Then

The man standing in front of Aunt Bethany is so tall he towers over her. His shoulders are broad, like a football player, and even though his back is to me and I can't see his face, I have a very good feeling I can picture it exactly.

Dark eyes to match his dark hair. A slash of a mouth, angrily turned up at the corners. Nostrils flaring. His teeth bared.

I've seen enough horror movies to know what evil looks like.

Aunt Bethany's staring up at him, her eyes wide with fear. I can practically smell it rolling off her, and I take a step back, tucking my body behind the wall. If he turns around, if he sees me...

My mind is unable to finish that thought. It's so terrible, just the idea of what he might do, that I can't focus on it. It flits in and out of my mind, like a disoriented bat flying at dawn, and I can't seem to slow it down. Catch it. Mull it over.

There's movement off to the side, and I turn to look, but I don't see anything. The shadows are long, the kitchen light not throwing enough light into the space to illuminate the entire room.

Panic makes you see things.

"Please." It's Aunt Bethany, and my eyes snap back to her. She doesn't pray, but the word is a prayer on her lips. "I don't know what you want, but I don't have a lot of money. You can have it! You can take whatever you want." She swings her arm out to encompass the kitchen.

The table with cardboard under one leg to keep it from teetering back and forth. The mismatched dishes, most of them with chips, drying in the drying rack. The fridge covered in art from Wade and pictures of the three of us.

There's nothing here of value, and I see the moment she realizes it. Her cheeks go pale. She swallows hard. Her eyes flick around the room, desperate to land on something that will help her get rid of this man, but there isn't anything.

Then she sees me.

Fear flashes across her face the exact moment our eyes lock, and I dig my nails hard into the doorframe to keep from running to her. Her eyes widen, just a bit, an almost imperceptible amount, then she looks back at the man. When she speaks again, her voice doesn't shake as much.

"Just take what you want."

"You know what I want. I've wanted you since I saw you at the diner. Running around in your little apron and shorts, bending over the tables to pick up plates. You made me want it." His voice is low. Rumbling. A truck on a gravel road, spitting the words up at me, flinging them at me like they're going to make me crack.

Want... what?

"That smile of yours? What man wouldn't want to spend some time with it? Show me your smile."

Bethany's face twists. I'm rooting for her, mentally begging her to do what he wants. Maybe then he'll leave and we'll lock the door, we'll go to bed together, and nothing terrible will happen.

But she doesn't smile.

The man turns, raising his hand at the last second. He backhands her, and she's flung to the side. When she grabs the counter to keep from falling, she exhales, the sound coming from deep in her lungs.

I want to go to her, but my feet won't move.

There's a shifting of light in the corner of the room.

I'm seeing things. My brain isn't working the way it should. I know what happens when you're terrified—I've seen it in a documentary. Your eyes widen, increasing your field of vision. Your pupils expand, allowing as much light in as possible.

I know all of this. It's still terrifying.

"You think you deserve to live?" He grabs her by the shoulder. I see how his fingers sink into her skin; how he plucks her back up and puts her on her feet. Without realizing what I'm doing, I reach up and rub my own shoulder. "You're nothing. Trash. Just trash."

Another smack. This time, she goes sprawling, the sound of her palms hitting the linoleum floor making me wince. She's crying, huge tears running down her cheeks. Snot bubbles from her nose.

"Please!" The word sounds painful, and I know it's not just for him but also for me. She wants me to run, to hide, but I can't move.

The man stands over her, the cords in his neck sticking out. I glance up at his face and it sears into my memory. He seems rooted to the floor, his feet spread wide, his hands out from his body like he's daring her to get up and run at him.

Red rover, red rover, send Bethany on over, but she doesn't move. She's flat on the floor now, her cheek pressed to the linoleum. I want to scream at her to get up and fight back, to run, to let me take her by the hand so the two of us can get out of here, but anything I want to say is stuck in my throat.

"You don't deserve to live." He leans back, pulling his right leg behind him. When he kicks her, she jerks, her hands splayed on the floor like she's going to try to push up. All I can hear is her sobbing, his laugh, the sound of static in my ears.

No.

"You're nothing, you know that?" Another kick. The thud is loud, the sound making my stomach sink. Her body jerks to the side. She rolls over, curling up into a little ball, her arms wrapped around herself. I want to lie down with her, wrap my arms around her, keep her safe.

But I can't move.

"Please," she whispers, the word accompanied by blood. I watch in horror as she spits, red drops of blood flying from her lips. There's now a spray of it, like paint, around her mouth. "Please."

"You don't get to tell me what to do." He bends down; grabs her by the back of the hoodie with one hand. His meaty fingers twist in the fabric, and she gasps, reaching up to try to pull it away from the front of her throat.

He's going to choke her.

The buzzing in my head is louder. It's like cicadas, stupid insects screaming, the sound so overwhelming that I barely notice the man is laughing. It's no longer gravel from his throat —the sound now rolls out of him endlessly, a tsunami of it, washing over me, making me press my hands down over my ears.

But he still doesn't know I'm here. He only has eyes for my aunt. They're dark and beady and locked on her face as he twists his arm out to the side, turning her the way you might turn a kitten you're holding by the scruff of its neck. *Yes, that's the one I want, that one right there with the long whiskers and the blood leaking from its mouth and terror in its eyes.*

"Do you know what I do to whores like you?" His voice is softer now, velvet.

It's terrifying. Somehow, it's worse than when he was yelling. It feels more dangerous, like it's making me lean in to better hear what he's saying. I don't want to miss a word, and I realize I'm hanging on every word he's saying.

Aunt Bethany is too. She's stopped fighting. Two fingers are hooked in the neck of her hoodie, pulling out, giving her a little extra breathing room. Her other hand hangs limply at her side.

"I kill them." There's a moment of silence, then the soft *snick* of a knife opening.

He has a knife. Not a small pocketknife, not like the one I like to carry in my backpack, but bigger, a hunting knife, one that folds open and closed so you don't accidentally gut something. The blade is sharp, serrated, the little metal teeth menacing, and I feel all the spit in my mouth dry up.

Maybe this isn't going to happen, I manage to think, then he reaches up and holds the blade above her, moving it back and forth, letting it reflect the light.

I step back so I can't watch.

He's laughing, the sound following me.

I hear shifting. He's positioning himself right where he wants to be.

"Come here." Low. Deep. His voice is ridged with anger.

Maybe he's preparing himself, or maybe she's trying to pull away, or he's angling her just right so that—

"It'll be over in just a moment," he promises, and his tone almost sounds caring, the way a parent might speak to a child, how you coax someone scared into doing something they don't want to.

Silence, then there's a soft pattering noise that sounds like rain, only what's falling is too thick to be water.

He's still laughing. Loud. He's so loud.

There's a ringing in my ears, like someone screamed in

them, making my hearing feel wonky. His laugh is so loud, so all-consuming, it feels like it's coming from all around me, like there are multiple men in the house, the laughter coming from them enough to make me choke.

"I guess there's nothing else to do here." The voice is different now, less angry, not nearly as deep. Like killing my aunt has changed him from Dr. Jekyll back into Mr. Hyde.

This can't be happening, it isn't real, this isn't real. It's the only thing I can think, and then I remember the new door she put on my bedroom, and I hurry up the stairs, planting my bare feet where I know there won't be any sound. I lock my new door behind me and sink down to the floor, squeezing my head as tight as possible between my hands.

TWENTY-EIGHT

GINA

"I just don't understand how they didn't catch him."

It's Grant who breaks the silence, and my head snaps up to look at him. I'd been thinking about the key and how to get it out of the garage door without anyone seeing it. I take a sip of water before responding to him. Not because I'm thirsty or my throat is dry, but because... well, reasons.

I need time to think.

"It happens." I let the words hang in the air for a moment before continuing. My mind wanders to the key again, and I have to force it back to the conversation. "You'd be surprised at how many unsolved murders there are every single year. There's a stat that just over half of all murders in the US are solved each year. And I mean *just barely* over half." I measure a centimeter with my finger and thumb and hold it up to show him.

"Not great odds for the victims," Grant says, and I shake my head.

"Not at all. And when you're left behind trying to figure it all out because the police have moved on, it's even worse." My voice threatens to break, and I swallow hard.

"Gina still has hope they'll find the killer," Owen offers. "Her whole family does, I'm sure, but Gina especially."

"I know he's out there," I say, nodding at Owen. "And someone like him, someone who can break into a house and ruin everything, take a beloved family member from people? That man doesn't deserve to live. He took my favorite person from me and tore my family to pieces. No, I don't have the resources the police do, but that doesn't mean I'm going to sit back and ignore the fact he's still walking around free."

"You seem convinced it's a man." That's Marta, and I turn, surprised, to look at her. She's leaning back in her chair, a smile on her face. "You keep saying *him* and *he*, but you didn't see the killer, did you?"

I pause. This is where I have to be very careful. "It was really dark in the house," I admit. But how dark was it? The kitchen light was on, but the bulb wasn't very strong.

My brain works overtime. Remember the shadows in the corners of the room? I thought I'd seen movement there, even though I'm sure there wasn't anyone else in the kitchen.

The killer was a man. It had to be a man; it's the only thing that makes sense, and our entire plan hinges on me being right. Still, my palms grow sweaty, and I wipe them on my jeans as I try to think. If it wasn't a man... then everything Wade and I have been doing is for naught.

But I heard his voice. I know I'm right.

"So you don't know who killed your aunt. You're just... stumbling around blind, hoping you find some clue that will help you out." Marta grins, clearly pleased with herself.

"What steps are you taking to find him?" Grant asks, leaning forward to get my attention. I hear Marta *tsk* but don't turn to look at her. His coffee sits to the side, untouched for the past few minutes, and his eyes haven't left my face. "You sound so sure of yourself, so you must have some plan of action."

"Well—" begins Owen, but I cut him off.

"It's not so much a plan of action as it is blind hope." I give Owen a gentle kick under the table. Even he doesn't know all of the steps I've taken to find Aunt Bethany's killer, but what he does know might make me look crazy in front of Grant and Marta.

The long nights talking to Wade about where the killer might be.

Tracking him.

Hypnosis sessions to try to recall any tiny detail that might help me identify him.

The evidence board Wade has hung up in his apartment. It's got photos of multiple women we think the killer stalked and murdered. Information tying them together. A giant map with their locations marked. Wade traveled the country, devoting years of his life to finding this guy. He's interviewed people in the towns where he killed, spoken to retired police officers. Little by little, he's found the pieces needed to solve Aunt Bethany's murder.

Police reports on break-ins, stalkings, and murders. I can't even imagine how much he spent getting hotel records on guests so he could cross-reference them. Should they have given him information? Absolutely not, but when it's a mom-and-pop place and the kid working the front desk wants cash to score some weed, he was able to make it happen.

And as for why the cops didn't do that exact same thing? Good question, and it's one I asked myself over and over. Why couldn't the cops do this? Why didn't they?

The only answer I can come up with is that Wade dove into online message boards. He looked into the murder of any single woman across the country, which took him... well, years. I'd like to say he found the murderer through dogged determination, but there was luck involved.

Good or bad, there's always luck involved.

And the best part. All of this work, this hunting, this

research was done without letting anyone know how seriously we took it.

No way does Owen know about the murder map, not when I can easily imagine the expression he'd make if he saw it. He'd be horrified. Sweet Owen, who never has anything terrible happen to him, who can get his way with a smile or a swipe of his credit card, has never had anything consume him the way Aunt Bethany's murder has consumed Wade and me.

I force myself to take a bite, but the movement feels mechanical.

"Do the police have any idea why your aunt was targeted? Or was it just a random killing?" Grant asks. He must catch the strange look on my face because he pauses, then continues. "I'm sorry, Gina, it's just that I'm a bit of a true crime buff. Podcasts, documentaries, you name it, I love it. I know I probably shouldn't, but it's addictive, isn't it?"

I hold up one finger while I swallow, then run that same finger through the jelly on my plate, licking it off, before I respond. "I guess it's addictive for some people," I say, trying to choose my words carefully. "But when a crime like that affects your whole family? I don't want to say I'm a true crime fanatic. I just want answers. And the police don't have any ideas why Aunt Bethany was targeted," I finally say. "Although that was something they focused on. Why pick her? My cousin was out of the house that night, but it wasn't like she had social media to advertise that he was going to be gone. So how did this guy find her? Was he watching her for a while, making sure she was going to be alone? Only she wasn't, was she?"

"I just can't get over how horrible that must have been," Marta says.

"And you, just a little kid hiding from the killer," says Grant, shaking his head. "You must have been so scared."

"I was terrified," I say, speaking slowly. "Hiding was my only choice."

"Where did you hide?" Grant frowns.

"My room. Well, it was a little room I slept in right off her bedroom."

"That's why he couldn't find you." Grant gives a little nod like everything suddenly makes sense. "You said you came downstairs when you heard something, but did you see him?" He taps the table. "Or her, I guess, since you didn't get a good look at the killer."

I pause. This is where things can get real. It's where I need to be careful. "I was too scared to look."

A smile flickers on Marta's face.

"But Gina is so strong," interjects Owen, interrupting whatever Grant was about to say next. "What happened sucks, but you'd be impressed at how she's handled it. She doesn't let it drag her down, she's so kind and gracious, and is still one of the most trusting people I know." He grins at me, and I can't help but smile back. "I love her."

"I love you," I tell him. For a moment, both Marta and Grant seem to fall away. I even forget about the key, the proof I'm looking for. It's like it's just Owen and me, the two of us, and I could almost forget about the stress and pressure of meeting his parents, of talking about Aunt Bethany.

But then I give my head a little shake and all the pain comes racing back. I remember Aunt Bethany, how amazing she was. I remember what it was like losing the one place I really felt safe as a child.

My parents were barely holding it together before the murder. I didn't know about the affairs, about my father stepping out on my mother any chance he got, usually with women who were just passing through so they didn't expect a relationship. I had an inkling about the credit card debt, but there was no way I could ever know exactly how bad it was.

But when Aunt Bethany died, it was the straw that broke the camel's back. My parents fell apart, my dad blamed my mom, my mom blamed me. The entire town wanted a piece of *the girl who hid*, and all Wade and I wanted was Aunt Bethany back.

Nobody could bring her back. Not even Owen, with his skilled hands and his years of knowledge, could have saved her, not after the killer got his hands on her.

So I can't bring her back. But I can get her justice.

"Well, I wish you the best of luck in finding the killer," Grant tells me. "It's not fair for you or your family to live with that pain, to know she's gone, to have her taken from you like that."

"Thank you." I dip my head to him, my fingers finding the hem of my shirt. Thank goodness they can't see me worry the fabric. I hate it when people catch me doing this, when I see the pity on their faces. My mind flicks to the key in the door, but I force myself back to the present. "It's the one thing I keep focusing on. Finding him. Getting her justice."

"It must be exhausting."

I nod. "It is. He was so good, so careful. Like he'd done it before and knew he could get away with it. But he really screwed up when he left me alive."

"You think he might be a serial killer?"

I nod.

Silence falls around the table. I tend to do that, get too passionate about Aunt Bethany and what happened to her. It's never a surprise to me when people don't know what to say in response, when they get quiet and shift in their chairs, when they look at each other, eyebrows raised, but avoid making eye contact with me.

That's why none of this surprises me.

And I mean none of it.

Not the way Owen carefully kicks me right now, his lips pursed, a question on his face.

Yes, I'm fine.

And how Marta picks up her donut and turns it over in her hands like she's looking for the perfect place to take a nibble? Doesn't surprise me.

And how about the way Grant's slowly flushing, the red creeping up from the collar of his shirt, his neck slowly darkening, his dark eyes narrowing as he looks across the table at his wife.

That doesn't surprise me either.

TWENTY-NINE

GINA

I have to get the key out of the garage door before someone sees it.

It took some convincing to get Marta and Grant to let the two of us clean up the brunch dishes and pick up the kitchen after the world's most awkward meal, but they finally acquiesced, letting Owen and me carry the plates, cups, silverware, and leftovers into the kitchen. The dishwasher is on the other side of the kitchen from the garage door, thank God.

The key is still there. I have to force myself not to stare at it. How Owen, Grant, or Marta haven't noticed it yet, I have no idea, and I also have no idea how much longer my luck will hold out.

"Why don't you load the dishes since I know a lot of people are super particular about how they get put in there?" I glance at Owen, doing everything I can to tear my attention away from the door. If he sees me staring at it, then everything's going to fall apart.

"Oh, smart. Mom can be really funny about how the plates are put in the bottom rack." He kisses me on the temple. "You're so kind. I remember once, in high school, I loaded everything incorrectly and she made me take it all out and do it again. They were filthy, Gina. It was gross."

"Let's not have a repeat performance." I grab the orange juice and put it on the top shelf in the fridge. When I close the door and look over my shoulder at Owen, I'm pleased to see him loading the dishes.

The key.

The fear of it being found kept interrupting me during brunch, but each time I'd think up a clever way of escaping to the kitchen myself, it was thwarted.

There was more than enough orange juice and water on the table for everyone unless I drank so much I risked peeing myself. Marta had, of course, loaded the table to groaning with all the food they'd brought from Main Street. Unfortunately, the only option I had was to sit through the meal and wait until I could escape in here. Now my only focus is the key and how I'm going to get it out of the door. As long as Owen stays occupied, I should have a minute or two.

Even so, I cast one more glance over my shoulder before hurrying to the garage door. The key is still there, taunting me, and I grab it, then twist it hard to the side. "Come on," I mutter, wiping my other hand across my forehead. I'm sweating, an unfortunate combination of stress over talking about what happened to Aunt Bethany and the fear that someone will catch me with the key.

It doesn't move.

Another harried glance over my shoulder. Owen's whistling as he rinses the plates and loads them.

I twist the key to the other side. It's stuck now, fully lodged in there like only a locksmith is going to be able to get it out. I groan, squeeze my eyes shut, and exhale.

Then I yank. I plant my feet on the floor, then step forward with one to brace it against the door itself. When I pull, I feel my muscles stretch and complain, but I pull harder, squeezing my shoulder blades together like that's going to be enough to help me pull the stupid thing free.

I'm Arthur trying to pull the sword from the stone, only Sean Connery made it seem a hell of a lot easier.

There. Did it shift? Just a bit? I swear I've moved away from the door, but maybe that's my imagination.

"Last plate," Owen calls. "Then we have to decide what we want to do next. I know you missed going downtown this morning, and I'd be happy to go again if you want to."

"Mmhmm," I respond, trying to sound as non-committal as possible.

It's now or never.

I yank on the key as hard as possible. My fingers threaten to slip from it, but I manage to hold on to it. There's a soft metallic scrape, then a moment where all the pressure on the key is released. I try to step back to catch myself, but I'm yanking too hard and everything happens at once.

The key slips from the lock. My weight shifts. Owen shuts the dishwasher with a slam.

I hit the floor, tailbone first, then roll over onto my back, slamming my shoulder into the side of the lower cupboards. My breath flies from me with a loud exhale, and I cry out a moment later as two sharp pains—one from my butt, the other from my shoulder—shoot through me.

But I'm still holding the key.

"Gina!" Owen's next to me before I can take another breath. He bends down, grabs me by the armpits, then pulls me easily to my feet. "Are you okay? What happened?"

"I fell," I say, leaning into him as I slide the key into my back pocket. I'll have to get rid of it later, throw it away maybe, or flush it. The chance of getting it back into the drawer without someone seeing is slim to none and not worth the risk.

"How? Did you trip on something?" He pushes me away

from him and takes me by the shoulders, looking me up and down.

"Over my own feet." I'm trying for a rueful smile, one that will make him feel pity for me without making him question me more. "I'm so clumsy."

The sound of running makes me turn. Owen loops his arms around me, pulling me close. It's almost like he's afraid I'm going to fall again, like he has to do whatever it takes to keep me upright.

"What happened?" Grant asks, stepping into the kitchen. His eyes flick everywhere as he takes in the scene. I feel my face heat up as he looks at me. "Is everyone okay?"

"Gina tripped over her own feet," Owen says with a soft laugh. "But she's okay."

There's a thrumming pain in my shoulder, but I'm not about to complain. The best thing would be for everyone to forget this even happened. Fingers crossed.

"You poor thing." That's Marta. She approaches me slowly. Her eyes are locked on me. "You say you tripped over your own feet?"

My face burns. "Size ten," I say, scuffing one toe into the floor. "It comes with the territory." I'm in a real Princess and the Pea situation—I swear I can feel the key pressing into me through the fabric of my jeans. Without looking away from Marta, I reach back and lightly touch my back pocket.

It's still there. I'm going to be on high alert about it until I manage to get rid of it.

"What exactly were you doing?" Marta steps closer to me.

"I just tripped." I lift my chin a little as I look at her. "You've never tripped over your own foot?"

"No." Marta forces a smile to her face. It looks like it's going to make her skin crack, but she manages to hold it there for a moment. "I can't say I ever have." She doesn't look away from me, and I force myself to hold her gaze for as long as possible.

Owen murmurs something against the top of my head, then plants a kiss there. "Do you want ice on anything?"

"Ever the doctor," I tease, although, really? Ice sounds great. I'm not going to let either of them know how much pain I'm actually in because that will only invite Owen to look for bruising. If he insists on that, he might find the key. "But no, I'm fine. Seriously. More shocked than anything else, but it didn't hurt that bad. I got lucky."

"You really did. Why don't we head on into the living room? The table is all cleaned up, and there's no reason to stay at the scene of the crime."

"I'll meet you in there in a few. I'm going to pop upstairs and grab some painkillers. The pain isn't bad now, but maybe I can keep it at bay."

I grin at him, giving his fingers a little squeeze where they press into my side. Not for the first time, I feel a flash of guilt over what's happening.

None of this is Owen's fault. He's a pawn—that's all he is.

It isn't his fault his dad is a murderer.

THIRTY

MARTA

We're all silent as we watch Gina beat a quick retreat up the stairs.

I want her gone. Out of here, and out of Owen's life. She's a tool I can use to get what I want, but as long as Owen thinks she's the right person for him, she's standing in the way of my happiness.

I'll do anything to get rid of her.

Grant hasn't turned from watching Gina go up the stairs. It's like I can read his mind—I know exactly what he was thinking as he watched her ass in those tight jeans. Owen is oblivious, which blows my mind. How can a son of mine be so clueless when it comes to his father's proclivities? How could he bring Gina, of all people, here and think his father wouldn't want to get her on her own?

Or worse.

Grant's on the cusp of action, but we're running out of time. I need to push him to make it happen.

"Hey, Mom? Since we don't have any big plans for the afternoon, I wondered if you and I could dig out some of the old family photos," Owen says, and I feel my heart leap with excitement. "There's some baby picture contest among the doctors at the hospital, and I think I have a pretty good shot at winning."

"The photos are on the shelves over there," I say, gesturing across the room. "Do you see them? In the maroon leather-bound albums? Why don't you go grab some of the ones on the left—those are older—and we can start digging through them." Owen nods, eagerly hopping up to grab the albums. When he's across the room, I lean closer to Grant. "What are you doing?"

The words come out in a whisper, and Grant slowly turns to look at me. "What do you mean?"

I gesture at the stairs, keeping half an eye on Owen to ensure he doesn't return and overhear this conversation. "Gina. Touching her knee. Watching her walk away like you've never seen a woman before. She's your son's girlfriend, Grant. Almost his fiancée, if he gets what he wants."

It's a fine line to walk. I have to be careful. Do this perfectly. Push him just enough.

He shrugs, mollified, but not embarrassed enough. I want him to see what he's done to this family over the years has been destructive. The trips? And what about all the women? No way was I supposed to just turn my head, year after year, trip after trip, keep the home fires burning, and not ever feel like I was going to come out of my skin knowing what he was doing. Who he was with. It wasn't fair then, and it isn't fair now.

But now I can finally get what I want. I set the stage for him, encouraged him. Now I need him to make a move.

"I'm serious, Grant. You have to stop. Gina's off the table."

It's what my husband expects me to say. That Gina isn't someone he can have. That he has to keep his hands to himself. Gina should be so far off the table she's not even something for him to consider, but he's considered her, and that's always been the first step. Once he takes that first step, it's a slippery slope, this road to hell he's chosen to stay on, and he's already going down it. I can tell. Me telling him she's off-limits will only make him want her more.

But if my plan works, I can kill two birds with one stone. If Grant makes a move on Gina and she accepts... well, I'll have a reason to be a single woman and Owen will be free. All this *stand by your man* crap will go out the window if my husband sleeps with our son's girlfriend. He won't have a choice but to let me go.

Of course, he didn't let me go after his years of sleeping around when we were younger, did he? Even when I begged him for a divorce, to let me take Owen and allow him to do whatever he wanted, he wouldn't let me go. I do my best to push the memory away, but it's there, lingering. I'm just so sick of how he's treated me in the past, how he's walked all over me, taking me for granted.

It's time to get rid of them both.

"Gina is a grown woman," he says. "And you know just as well as I do that—"

"Okay, I think I have enough for us to start going through them," Owen announces. He steps between his father and me and drops half a dozen thick photo albums on the coffee table between us. They land with a thud, and the stack starts to glissade before Owen catches them. "Whew, that was close. These are the ones from when I was younger, so they should be the perfect place to find the cutest baby picture ever."

"This is not my idea of a good time," Grant says with a sigh. "I'm going to leave you two to it."

"What's your plan now?" I barely look up at Grant. Normally I pay him more attention, especially now, when I know what's on his mind, but if he doesn't get the attention he wants from me, he'll look for it elsewhere.

With Gina.

Besides, what mother doesn't want to relive the glory days of their child being young? I want to fall headfirst into these photos with Owen. I want to talk about what it was like when he was a little boy, how incredible it's always been to be his mother. I want to remember the cute outfits, the trips to the zoo, how oversized his backpack was when he first started school.

This is what happens when I have time with Owen. I jump in with both feet, happy to be important, happy for him to want to spend time with me. I was always an involved parent, and that helped me get through what my husband did when we were younger. It's been so many years since he looked at another woman.

Part of that is because he retired. He hasn't traveled in years, hasn't visited new cities and cozied up to women in bars. He hasn't watched them in the park, introduced himself to them while I was at home, chasing after our son, making sure dinner was nutritious and delicious, and washing his clothes when he returned home from work.

So many stains in his clothes, so hard to get that red out of the collar of his shirts. The smell of other women. Their perfume. And more.

Sure, I traveled with him a few times, unhappily leaving Owen with my mother so I could be with Grant. He wanted me to see what his job was like. He wanted me to partake in his extracurriculars. He told me it would bring us closer together.

And I tried.

I did.

But in the end, I left him to it. Spent time with Owen.

I've earned this time with my son. I've earned all the time with my son. Grant lived his best life when we were younger, and now it's time for me to get what I want.

Gina will be off the table for Owen. One way or another.

"A nap. Gina isn't the only one who might have had a bit too much to drink last night." Grant chuckles and stretches, twisting this way and that to work out his muscles.

I barely glance up, but Owen does.

"Are you hungover too?" There's a note of glee in his voice, pure pleasure that both his girlfriend and his father were hurting a little while he'd been so much smarter with not over-doing it last night.

"A little." Grant shrugs while he speaks, giving off an *aww, shucks* vibe. "I'm going to go rest my eyes for a bit, nothing crazy. Just long enough to feel like I'm a human again, and I'll be ready for whatever we plan to do this afternoon."

"Feel better." Owen flips the page in the album he's looking through. The expression on his face is greedy, like he can't quite get enough of what he's looking at. I glance at the photos in front of him. Us, at the park, him in a cute little blue hat, his mouth open in laughter on the swing. "Hey, Dad?"

Grant's almost to the stairs and he stops; turns around. "Yes?"

"Check in on Gina, would you? She's been in the room for longer than it should take to get painkillers. I just want to make sure she's okay up there."

Grant grins, his lips twisting up, his eyes dark with desire. Owen's back is to him and he's bent over the photo album, so he doesn't see the expression on his father's face.

But I do.

THIRTY-ONE

GINA

I hear footsteps in the hall, and I freeze, then turn slightly from where I'm sitting on the floor. My suitcase is open in front of me, my spare cell phone clutched in my right hand. There's a secret zippered pocket on the inside of the case. I'm sure it's designed for passports or money or even jewelry, but the burner phone I bought when Owen planned this trip fits perfectly inside. I sent Wade a text and am waiting for a response before I turn off my phone, but what if that was Owen coming to check on me?

He would. He's so kind. So good. Not at all like—

"Gina?" Grant's standing in my doorway, and he raps his knuckles on the frame, leaning in to grin at me. "Hey, I just wanted to check on you, make sure you were feeling okay. Everything alright up here?"

"Fine," I say, throwing my phone into my suitcase before flipping a hoodie over it. "I took some Tylenol and meant to bring a book with me to read on the trip, but I must have left it at home. No big deal—you guys have a library downstairs."

"Our books are your books." He walks into the room and sits on the edge of the bed, so close to me that I take a step back.

My suitcase pulls my attention, but I don't let myself look down at it. Best not to give him any reason to look at the suitcase, but what if Wade texts back right now? What if Grant hears the little ping that my hidden burner phone makes? Wade's the only person who has my number, and I never once considered putting it on silent. He knows not to reach out to me unless I reach out first.

"You and Marta are too kind." I walk past him, wanting to head back downstairs, but Grant pats the mattress next to him.

"Sit with me, Gina. You and I haven't had a lot of one-on-one time, and I'd love to get to know my son's girlfriend a little better. Although, if I'm honest, I don't know that you'll be just a girlfriend for much longer, will you?"

I don't feel like I have a choice. My throat feels dry, and I swallow hard, then force myself to walk over to him. Instead of sitting right next to him, however, which is clearly where he wants me, I sit a few feet away, on Owen's side of the bed, my knees straight ahead, every inch of my body angled as far away from Grant as I can be without coming across as rude.

He's a murderer. *Oh God, Aunt Bethany's murderer.* It's the first time I've been alone with him, and my heart hammers in my chest. My eyes flick to the door in hopes that Owen will be standing there, but he's still downstairs with his mother.

It's just Grant and me. Fear makes the hair on the back of my neck stand up. I have to close my eyes and take a deep breath, then I worry about him watching me without me knowing. *Or worse.* When I open my eyes, I can barely see him in my peripheral vision. He hasn't moved, but there's a smile on his face that makes my stomach twist.

Instead of getting up and running from the room, which is what I want to do, I rub my hands on my jeans once more. I'm sweating. I'm terrified.

Can he tell?

"Owen's mother and I haven't always had the best relationship," he says, and I slowly turn my head to look at him. He shrugs and nods, obviously taking my slight interest for an invitation to continue. "I know. I can't imagine it was easy for her to be married to me, not when I traveled all the time for work. She was always here, taking care of Owen, making sure I felt welcome the moment I came back home. I owe Marta everything, but sometimes it was hard to remember that. To remember her."

My mind races. I have to sound like I have no idea what he's talking about. "You're saying you had affairs?"

Again, I rub my palms on my jeans, and I think about what Owen would say if he were to enter the room right now. What in the world would go through his mind if he heard his father telling me about the affairs he had when he was younger? And does Owen even know about them?

Grant inclines his head but doesn't answer my question. I'm left to infer it, like not saying the words will keep them from being true, will keep me from having any power over him if I decide to go to Owen and tell him the truth.

"Why are you telling me this?"

"Owen is better than I am," Grant tells me.

Now he's staring straight at me, his dark eyes locked on mine. A shiver dances up my spine. Talking about the affairs he had is bad enough. But doing it while sitting on the bed I'm sharing with his son?

I don't see how this could get much worse.

"I don't think he'd cheat on you," Grant says, and now the words flow from him more easily, like the dam has broken and he can't stop them. "He's a good guy, Owen. But sometimes..." His voice trails off, but I can't speak to fill the silence.

Grant looks at me. *Really* looks at me. His eyes flick up and down my body, and I'm overcome by the sudden urge to cover up, to somehow make myself less than I am so that he won't be able to see all I am, won't be able to want what he sees. If only I had on that hoodie in my suitcase. It's too big for me; it hangs down over my butt, takes the shape I have and turns it into a floppy rectangle, and I'd feel more comfortable, more protected, more hidden. But I can't get up and get it, not when I'd have to walk right in front of Grant, not when I feel like I'm frozen in place.

"But sometimes what?"

Grant reaches out, his fingers resting lightly on my knee. I want to shift my leg away from him, but it's hypnotic, this feeling that he knows something I'm dying to know. That he might tell me something about Owen I didn't know.

Impossible. I know everything about him. About both of them.

Except I don't know what Grant's thinking right now. Does he know who I am? What I want? Does he want to hurt me? Or something else?

"Sometimes we all make mistakes. You're a beautiful girl, Gina." His fingers tighten, and my throat does as well, making it harder for me to breathe.

I inhale hard. "I love your son," I tell him, and he releases me.

"That's great, but don't feel like you can't explore other options." His eyes are dark when he looks at me. Hooded.

I clear my throat, and the moment between us, whatever it was, is broken. Gratitude washes over me, and I move to stand, but he beats me to it, striding past me to the door.

I can't move. He's up, he's occupying the space I want to be in, and any ability I had to get up, to flee the room, to hurry back down to Owen and, yes, even Marta is gone. I don't know what this was with Grant, don't know what he really wanted with me, but I'm glad it's over.

He's halfway out the door now. While it felt like he'd taken all the oxygen, made it impossible for me to breathe, every step he takes releases the tight band around my chest. I feel dizzy, like I've been underwater and can't breathe.

What was I even doing in here? I look around, then back at the door.

The phone.

A chill dances up my spine. Two more steps and he'll be completely out of the room. Ten more and he'll be at the stairs. Twenty steps and he'll be far enough away he won't be able to hear anything that happens in here.

He's almost gone. He glances back at me, his eyes curious when he looks at me, then he slowly turns away, his gaze locked on something down the hall.

He's almost gone.

He's almost—

The phone I've kept hidden beeps.

THIRTY-TWO

GINA

Grant turns back to face me, his movement slow. His hand is still gripping the doorframe, but now he's looking at me, step-ping into the room, his eyes flicking from me to my open suitcase.

I freeze.

The last time I was in a fight-or-flight moment, I fled. I saved myself. This time, however, there's nowhere to go. He's back in the room now, coming to stand in front of me, but he's still blocking the door. I could run, I guess, could get up and try to get past him, but I don't think I'd be able to escape.

Not when my legs feel like jelly. Not when my heart's beating so fast I feel like I might throw up. Not when he's looking at me, a dark expression on his face, like he's *daring* me to run. Like he wants me to. Like the chase is the most exciting part.

But I know, for him, it's not. I've seen what he does after the chase.

"Did you hear that?"

Of course I heard it. Of course I know what it was, but the idea of coming clean to him, of telling him I have a second phone that I've kept hidden all this time not only from him and Marta, but also from his precious golden boy son, is enough to make me feel like I'm going to throw up.

"It was my watch." I lift my wrist to show him the gadget. Funky and updated, Owen bought it for me two weeks ago. It not only tracks my steps but also my heart rate, how active I've been—or haven't been—my sleep, sun exposure, and even my fertility.

Yes, my fertility. There's something in there, some comment on women's bodies and how men are always trying to control them, but I can't think of what it is right now, not when Grant's staring at me like he doesn't believe a word out of my mouth.

"Your watch sounded like a text message."

He's spot on—he is. Give the guy a medal.

"Yeah, Owen got this for me," I say, twisting my arm up and around so he can get a slightly better look at the face of my watch. "It has more features than I know what to do with, and that was an alarm telling me I haven't gotten enough sun today. Have to make sure I get enough vitamin D, you know."

Grant stares at me. The wheels in his head are working hard, and I have no doubt he wants to call me out for lying to him, but he doesn't. "If you hadn't been so hungover this morning, you could have come with us to walk around downtown. That probably would have helped you out."

"Probably." I nod my agreement. "But that rum last night, woo boy." I throw him a grin.

I'm just a girl. A stupid girl. Just like all the other girls you've known, nothing to see here, nothing exceptional.

"Why don't you come on down with me and we can head outside? Get you that vitamin D. It's not like you found your book." He gestures to my suitcase.

I blink at him in surprise. "Thanks for the offer, but I'm going to read for now." I lower my voice; try to sound embarrassed. "I'm still feeling a bit hungover. But I'll be down in just a moment; I just have one more thing to do."

He crosses his arms and takes a step back so he can lean ever so casually against the doorframe. "I'm more than happy to wait for you."

Oh no. I need time alone without him watching me so I can get my phone out of my suitcase and hide it. The last thing I need is for him to come back up here and rummage through my things. Normally, that wouldn't be a concern. But Marta already did it. And Grant isn't like other men, is he? Once he found my phone, I don't think he'd be able to control himself.

He'd confront me, and I'm not ready for that.

"Well." I tuck a stray bit of hair behind my ear. Try to look concerned. "I'm sorry, Grant, I don't want to embarrass you, but I need to use the bathroom." I lower my voice and look down. "It's that time."

"Oh." He straightens up and gives his head a little shake before pinning me back in place with a stare. It's clear he's trying to tell if I'm lying. I'm looking up at him from under my lashes, and I see the way his neck darkens, the flush extending upwards. "Right. Of course. You take care of that, and I'll see you downstairs."

He turns and walks down the hall.

I spring into action and hurry to my suitcase. When I drop to my knees and pull out my phone, my hands are shaking. A quick glance over my shoulder to ensure Grant hasn't come back, then I carefully tap the screen to make it light up. This isn't the newest model by any stretch of the imagination. It's a bit more old-school, but still perfect for my use. I'm nervous and fumble through turning it on and clicking through to open the message I received.

Just let me know when.

That's it. That's the text. That alone wouldn't have been enough to upset Grant. If he'd only seen that text, he would have wondered why I lied about the sound not being a text message alert, why I had a secret burner kept from his son, but that single text wouldn't have been enough to make the whole thing blow up in my face.

But the one I sent Wade before that? That would have been a problem.

My hands are still shaking as I delete the text thread and power down the phone. Standing, I look around the room for a place to hide it. I don't want to keep it on me in case Owen pulls me in for a hug and notices it in my pocket. The way Grant was watching me, I have a very good feeling he's going to be on high alert now, doing everything he can to try to suss out whether or not I was telling the truth.

I have to hide it. Somewhere I can easily get to it when I need it, but not somewhere anyone else will accidentally or on purpose stumble upon it.

The first place I think of is in a dresser drawer, but I reject it immediately. That's one of the first places people look when they're trying to find something another person has hidden.

Not under the mattress, for the same reason.

I open the closet. The double doors swing out, and I blink in the sudden overhead light, look for the perfect place to stash the phone. There's a bunch of Owen's old clothes in here, stuff from when he was still living at home, stuff that probably doesn't even fit anymore. Or, even if it did, it's certainly not his style. I brush some hanging clothes out of the way, and my eyes fall on a row of old shoes.

There's a pair of hiking boots that look like they should have been throw out ages ago. They're dirty and dusty, and the laces are crusted with enough mud they could probably stand up on their own.

They're perfect.

I tuck my phone into the right boot, angling it and shoving so it ends up in the toe. Chances are good nobody will think to look there, but if they do, I hope the phone will stay caught in the toe. All I need is for it to be accessible while also hidden from the entire Whitlock family.

A moment later, I pull the key out of my back pocket and shove it into the toe of the boot.

There. It's hidden, and safe, and now I can move on with the next thing I have to do. I stand; close the closet doors. Before leaving the room, I hurry into the bathroom and flush, then run the water in the sink. Finally ready to face the family, I grab a slim volume from the same pocket in my suitcase where I kept my burner phone, stick it in the back waistband of my jeans, and head downstairs.

Grant, Marta, and Owen are all in the living room when I enter. They're bent over the coffee table, still looking at photos of Owen from when he was a little boy. For a moment, I pause, staring at them, trying to see them as if I didn't know everything about them.

They look like every normal family.

But Grant murdered my aunt.

More than just that, he's a serial killer.

He deserves everything he has coming to him.

"There you are!" Owen turns and grins when he catches my eye. He hurries to me before I can take another step and, like I knew he would, pulls me into an embrace. *Can he feel the book?* I lean into him, letting the smell of his cologne wash over me. It's smoky and rich and expensive. There's a reason men with money smell good, and it's because their cologne is the best. When he kisses me on the forehead and steps back, I exhale with relief.

It's still hidden.

"Hey, sorry about that," I say, giving him a half-smile. "I was looking for a book because I finished that other one I was reading, and then I had to pee."

"No apologies needed." He takes me by the hands. "Dad

said he couldn't sleep, so that means the four of us get to spend some time together. What do you think?"

"Sounds great," I lie. "What's the plan?"

"Mom and I want to finish looking at these photos," he says, "if you don't mind finding something to do for a bit. Of course, you can join us, but I don't know how interested you'd be in old family photos. Otherwise, we'll be done pretty soon."

"Not a problem." I throw him a grin and gesture to the bookcases behind him. "You better believe I can find a new book over here." I wander off and start looking at the titles. It's only after I glance over my shoulder to make sure nobody is looking at me that I pull the slim volume from the back of my pants, grab another book from the bookshelf to cover up what I've done, and sit in a squashy chair off to the side.

If this doesn't confirm what Owen does or doesn't know, I don't know what will.

THIRTY-THREE

GINA

Owen has a huge grin on his face when he sits down next to me in the squashy chair. There really isn't enough room for the two of us, so he helps me snuggle into his lap, looping one arm around my waist to pull me closer to him.

"Did you find anything good?" he asks.

"A few things," I say, turning the stack so he can see the spines. "But look at this one—it's so weird."

"A picture album?" Owen asks, flipping it open to the middle of the photos. "Was this over with all the family albums?"

I shake my head. "Nope, right over there on the shelf." I gesture with a jerk of my chin, then tap the picture the album opened to. "Any idea who this is? Family member? Friend?"

No, they're your dad's victims.

"I have no idea." Owen stares at the woman with me. She's young, probably a bit older than the two of us, dark hair pulled back into a ponytail. She's grinning at the camera, a soccer ball tucked under one arm, an ice cream cone in her other hand. Behind her is a river, and she's dressed in a swimming suit to beat the heat.

Her name is Megan Cornar.

"Maybe a long-lost cousin?" I offer, and Owen shrugs.

"Maybe. Let's see who else is in this thing." He flips the page. This photo is from a newspaper clipping, the headline and the caption both chopped off. Another woman stares out from the photo. She's rocking a short blonde pixie cut and holding up a set of car keys.

Jenny Zimmerman. I know all of their names.

"Okay, I have no idea who these women are. They must be family, but from where? I swear, I've never seen them before." He tries to take the album from me to close it, but I yank it back.

"I'm not done looking," I tell him.

He frowns. "But these people aren't anyone we know. If you want to look at pictures, come with me and I'll show you my baby ones." The grin he gives me is disarming. It's the one he uses all the time when he wants to get his way, but I'm not going to back down right now.

"Just let me look," I say, flipping one more page.

The face that stares up at me is so familiar my breath catches in my throat. It doesn't matter how many times I see a photo of Aunt Bethany, seeing her slows down time. She's so gorgeous, with laugh lines around her eyes, wearing the same apron I always remember her having on. In this photo, she's standing on her front porch, one hand blocking the sun, a grin on her face. It's the photo my mom chose to run in the paper after she died. It was also on display at her funeral, an 8x10 of it sitting on top of her casket.

There wasn't any way we could have had an open casket, not with her throat slit, not without putting a scarf around her neck to try to hide how she was murdered. That means the last time I saw her was on her kitchen floor, surrounded by blood, a veritable halo of it around her body.

Even though I knew this photo was in here, even though I'm the one who put it in here, seeing my aunt smile up at me from the page makes my heart skip a beat. I take a deep breath, trying to fight the wave of dizziness washing over me.

"Why is this in here?" My voice doesn't sound like my own. I reach out, touch Aunt Bethany's photo, then jerk my hand back like I've been burned. "Why? This photo? How?"

Owen yanks the album from me and turns it so he can get a better look. "Who is this?"

Who is this? Like I don't have the same straight nose she did. Like her hair and mine aren't exactly the same. Owen's stared into my eyes long enough to hopefully see the resemblance between them and the woman on the page.

"That's Aunt Bethany," I say. My voice is a whisper, and at first, I don't think Owen hears me, but then he stiffens, leaning away from me.

"What are you talking about?"

"Aunt Bethany," I say, snatching the album back from him. When I stand, my legs feel like jelly at first, but I manage to keep my balance. "This is Aunt Bethany. Right here. In this album. Why? How would she be in here?"

Owen glances to the side, then stands, pulling the photo album from me. "I don't know, Gina. Just... are you sure it's her? I know you're tired and you were hungover, and sometimes—"

"Are you seriously questioning me right now?" I hiss, aware that Grant and Marta are looking over at the two of us. Good. Let them look. This involves them, after all. When I stand up, he takes a step back. "You think I don't know what my aunt looks like?"

"Hey." He holds up his hands like he's trying to stop me from rushing him.

My eyes flick down to the album in his right hand. He's got a finger in it to mark the photo of Aunt Bethany. When I look back up at him, he exhales, sagging forward a little bit.

"If you're sure it's her—"

"I know it's her. What I don't know is why the hell your

parents would have a picture of her in a photo album. How did they get it? Is this some sick joke?"

His face burns red. "No, not at all. They wouldn't, okay? I don't know what's going on, but I can find out. I need you to calm down. There has to be a good reason why her photo would be in this album."

"You need me to *calm down*?" I growl. I knew this would be hard and I'd need to play up how I felt, but in reality... the horror and anger I feel right now isn't fake. Tears well up, and I don't move to brush them away.

"I mean... That was a poor choice of words. Let me handle this." He rubs my arms, the album momentarily abandoned in his lap. I glance down at it, but the cover is closed, hiding my aunt's face. "I'll get to the bottom of this, okay? Let me talk to my parents."

"I don't know what to do with myself. What's going on?" I take a deep breath and close my eyes, doing my best to keep from flinching when I feel his hands on my cheeks. He brushes the tears away, then kisses me on the forehead. "If your mom or your dad—"

"I'll get to the bottom of this." He's using his doctor voice now, the one that demands compliance. "Okay, Gina? Just sit tight. Right here. Let me figure out what's going on."

He sounds seriously worried, and I file that away as I stay where he left me.

What choice do I have? The burst of adrenaline I felt a moment ago fades, and I nod, stepping forward for Owen to wrap his arm around me. He does, of course he does. There's nothing this man wouldn't do for me, which is something I learned about him as soon as we started dating. Owen adores me, but more than that, he wants to protect me.

But I'm not seeing if he'll protect me. This little outburst isn't about checking if he's on my side. I have to know how much he knows, and there are two ways I can test it. This is just the first.

"Stay here," he tells me, and while I'm not normally one to follow orders, I sit down. My hands find the hem of my shirt, and I start playing with it, twisting the fabric around my fingers. He glances down at my hands but doesn't say anything.

"You're going to ask your parents?" My voice is small.

He reaches down; cups my cheek. His hand is warm, his skin soft, and I lean into him. "I promise you; I'm going to ask them right now. I'll get to the bottom of this." He pauses. "I have to be honest, Gina, I'm sure there's some sort of a reasonable explanation. I'll find out what it is."

I nod again, not trusting myself to respond. Owen fell for it hook, line, and sinker, just like I hoped he would. Now Grant... he's the one who will question me. Will question how the book really got here.

But that's fine. Pushing his buttons won't help me get what I want, but I enjoy it. It'll drive him nuts and bring me one step closer to finding out the truth of who knows what happened. Owen has no idea he's playing a part in that, that he's necessary for me to get the answers I need.

That is, if he doesn't already know the truth.

See, that's the problem. I have a lot of information.

But there are a few things I don't know. And I need to know exactly who to punish before I take my next step.

THIRTY-FOUR

MARTA

Owen's expression is dark as he walks over to Grant and me.

No, not *walks*. He *stalks*. His shoulders roll forward, and his eyes narrow as he focuses on the two of us. It's the same expression I used to see on his face before when he was completely focused on something at school. It's probably the same expression he makes when he has a big surgery and he's giving it his all.

I used to be proud of that expression. Of what it meant. Of how I knew it would result in the best possible score on a test, or the best possible outcome for a patient.

But now he's closing the gap between us, and I don't like it. I can see the way his jaw ticks, how his hand is clenched tightly, how he holds... Is that a photo album?

"Hi, darling," I say, but he turns from me and addresses Grant.

"What is this?" When he holds the photo album out to his father, Grant doesn't hesitate to take it.

He's either as clueless as I am or a very good actor. Or both.

"Looks like a photo album." Grant flips it open and immediately sucks in a breath. His eyes flick up to Owen's. "Where did you get this?"

"Where? Over there, on your bookshelf stuffed in between a bunch of random books." Owen juts his thumb over his shoulder towards Gina, the movement jerky with anger. "Gina found it when she was looking for something to read. Care to tell me why you have these photos and newspaper clippings and why there's one of her Aunt Bethany in there?"

"There's what?" I reach for the photo album, but Grant closes it and tucks it under his arm. "Grant. Why?"

He doesn't look at me. "This isn't mine."

"Bullshit." Owen spits the word like it burns. "You think I'm going to believe you? Come on, Dad, I'm not stupid. You might have been able to lie to me when I was younger, might have been able to convince me you were telling the truth, but not anymore. Drop the act for once in your life." The look he gives his father is searing.

"This. Isn't. Mine." Grant grits out each word. "Why would I have something like this?"

"I don't know, Dad, probably because you—"

"Stop it." I hate seeing them argue, hate especially when Owen gets so upset. "If your father says it isn't his, you need to believe him."

Owen turns on me, his shoulders hunched forward, his mouth dropping open. "Are you serious right now, Mom? Dad's obsession with true crime has gone too far. It's one thing to watch documentaries and listen to podcasts, but this?" He gestures at the book still tightly tucked under my husband's arm. "This is too much. Admit it."

"He wouldn't," I say, but even as I do, I know I'm wrong.

Look at what Grant has done: the sleeping around, the long work trips out of town, the photos I've found with him and other women. A photo album of his victims doesn't seem that far-fetched, does it?

But then why deny it to Owen? He could lie, tell him he put it together because he's true crime obsessed. But he didn't.

It hits me. Maybe it wasn't Grant who made it. Maybe it was Gina. I've been afraid from the beginning that she knows more than she's letting on, and what if I was right? What if she's here not by the hard work Grant and I have done to get her here, but because she's got her own agenda? I turn to stare at her, but she's not looking at us.

No. She's clueless.

"I think you need to take a deep breath." Grant and Owen are the same height, but he draws himself up, obviously trying to intimidate our son. "Why would I do this? What in the world do you think would possess me to put together something like this?"

Owen rolls his eyes. "I already said it. You're obsessed with true crime, like you're some bored housewife or something. It's unhealthy."

"Why don't you—" Grant begins, but whatever he wanted Owen to do falls by the wayside.

"Is everything alright?" Gina appears behind Owen, her eyes wide. She moved fast—I never saw her walking across the room. When she reaches out and lightly touches my son on the shoulder, he immediately relaxes. Instead of being held so taut, so tight, he folds in on himself a little bit, exhaling hard, some of the anger leaving his body with that breath. "That photo album is messed up, but I didn't mean for this to be—"

"We're fine," I say, probably speaking too quickly, but desperate to put an end to... whatever this is. I have to protect Owen, get Gina away from whatever this conversation is going to turn into. "Why don't you come with me and we can look at some of Owen's baby pictures? I'm sure you've never seen such a cute kid in your life. Trust me, Gina, he was darling."

Silence. It grows between the four of us, Gina staring at Owen like he's going to be able to fix this, me desperate to get her away from Grant. He's a loose cannon on a good day, and right now? It's not exactly a good day.

"Oo-kay," she says, but she doesn't immediately move. It takes her a moment to look away from my son and walk with me. We leave the men behind, their heated whispers reaching our ears as we sit down across from each other.

"Look at this," I say, speaking loudly. Even now, I can hear Owen's anger. As much as I want to keep the boat from rocking, he has every right to be angry. Grant knows better than to leave stuff like that lying around. You never know who's going to find it.

Case in point.

Gina barely glances at the photo. "Marta," she says, her voice low. "Do you think..." She pauses, shakes her head. "Why would Grant make that photo album?" She stares at me, her gaze boring into me, her eyes wide.

They glisten with tears.

I hate this woman except as a tool I can use. Her tears mean nothing to me; *she* means nothing to me. Even so, whatever I do right now, I have to be careful.

"Grant is very single-minded," I say. I put down the photo I'm holding so I don't bend it too much and crease it. "He loves true crime. I dare say he's obsessed." My mind races as I try to think how to handle this.

"But it was my Aunt Bethany..." She pauses, pressing her fingers to her throat. "Seeing her in that album? It took my breath away."

"She's a cold case, right? You said that." I don't give her an opportunity to respond. I'm speaking as quickly as possible, doing my best to overwhelm her with information so she won't have any reason to question me. "That's why Grant would have a photo of her. More than true crime, he loves cold cases. They..." *Excite him?* "Give him a lot to think about. I think he wishes he'd gone into law enforcement."

She remains silent, so I continue. "I'd suggest talking to Grant about this. He'll be able to put your mind at rest."

"Talk to him about Aunt Bethany?" The way she says the words sounds painful. "About what?"

"The case." I shrug. "If you spent more one-on-one time with him, really got to know him, you'll see that he wouldn't ever want to hurt you, Gina. Your aunt being in the album is unfortunate, but it wasn't vindictive. Give him a chance. He'd love to get to know you, and I know Owen would really appreciate you two spending time together."

She has to bite. Either for my plan or our original one, I need her to spend time alone with Grant.

"I don't know." She drags the words out, glancing over her shoulder as she does.

I could wring her scrawny little neck, I swear I could. Just wrap my hands around and squeeze, watch as her eyes bug out, feel her sink her nails into my arm to try to stop me, see the panic written across her face. Why won't she listen to me? Do the one thing I need her to do? Be useful for once in her stupid life?

"I know how much Owen loves you," I finally say, twisting my hands together in my lap. "But I have to be honest with you: he won't ever marry you if he doesn't think you're close with his father. You see how much they mean to each other, don't you?" She nods. "Then you understand you have to make nice with Grant, Gina."

Her mouth falls open.

"Grant and I were thrilled you came. But you have to make an effort with him." It's not a lie, not really. She's going to interpret it as me saying that we were both thrilled to meet her, and that's not exactly what I'm saying.

Grant was thrilled to have the opportunity to meet her. To tie up loose ends.

I was thrilled for the possibility that she might help me get out of the situation I find myself in. And then, after that, if he ties up loose ends? If he kills the one person he believes might have seen him that night? It's the original plan, after all, and it would be icing on the cake.

"I'm trying," she says, but I'm not finished.

"Are you really? Have you spent any time with him? Have you tried to get to know him, or did you come here secure in the fact that my son loves you? Freaking out about a photo album, about Grant's hobby, isn't going to endear you to him. He loves Owen so much and just wants to make sure you're a good fit for his son."

Gina chuckles. "I'm pretty sure I'm a perfect fit," she says, and her tone is so flirty, so *knowing* of my son, that I instantly get a bad taste in my mouth.

No matter. I'm not going to let her know that she got to me, not even a little bit. It's best if she has no idea what I'm thinking right now.

"What I'm trying to say," I tell her, reaching out and lightly touching her hand to keep her from flipping yet another page in the photo album, "is that Grant needs to have some alone time with you. It's the best way for him to feel really confident about you marrying his son. You want to marry him? Show his father how incredible you are."

"That's why I'm here," she says. "But I don't see a reason why the two of us have to have alone time. Isn't that the entire point of me coming to visit?"

She's not getting it. I can't afford to get really frustrated with her, can't afford for her to know that she's managing to rub me wrong, but I need to make my point very, very clear with her. If she wants to marry my son, she has to spend some time with my husband.

"Trust me," I say, making sure it doesn't sound like I'm threatening her. "If you want to marry Owen, which I know you do, and I fully support, you need to get his father on board." My hand is still on hers, and I give her one more squeeze before letting go. "It's that easy, Gina. Get Grant to fall for you, and there won't be anything standing in the way of you marrying Owen. He loves true crime. So what? Do you know how many men are obsessed with World War II? Would you get angry at him if he had a photo album with pictures from the war? I don't think you would. Not if you were being equitable. This is his thing."

Her mouth presses into a firm line. I'd kill to know what's going on in her head right now, but it doesn't really matter, does it? Because she finally gives me a nod.

Resolved. Determined. That's Gina, and I can see why Owen fell for her.

It was his father's doing that the two of them were in the same place at the same time.

It will also be his father's doing that they never speak again.

THIRTY-FIVE

GINA

The thought of spending time alone with Grant, without Owen —or, yes, even Marta—there to run interference, is enough to give me butterflies. But that doesn't mean I'm not going to go through with it.

It's all happening. It's one thing to come to this house with the evidence Wade and I found—that Grant not only killed Aunt Bethany but is a serial killer, and that Marta has covered for him for years. It's another thing to see proof. My aunt's necklace hanging in Marta's jewelry box shocked me. What did it mean? That she knew what was happening? Or that Grant gave it to her without an explanation?

Either one could be true, and that means it's time for me to handle Grant, to finally find out the truth of who was involved in his crimes. Being alone with him scares me: I know things about him that would terrify most people. But I'll do it for the plan. Even more than that, I'll do it for Owen.

Even though I never meant to fall for his money.

Even though I never meant to fall for him.

Running into him and getting into his life, into his bed... it was all part of a bigger plan, but that doesn't mean the feelings aren't real. It just means all of this is a lot more complicated than I ever imagined it would be.

But I have to look at it like this—this is my opportunity to spend time with the man who killed my aunt. I'll look him in the face. Then, later, when he doesn't see it coming, I'll punish him.

Marta sees the resolve on my face. "I'm glad to know you're willing to give it a shot," she tells me. "Trust me, the best way to get what you want in this family is to take control but let the men still think they're the ones in charge."

Yeah, I know.

"You're right," I say and give Marta my winning smile. It's my golly-gee-you're-so-smart-I-love-it smile, the one that got me through loads of classes when I was younger when all I really wanted to do was crawl back into my bed and forget that my life was real. Best if Marta thinks she has control over this situation.

As if on cue, Owen walks over and gently rests his hand on my shoulder. "You two getting on okay?" he asks, then groans, reaching down to snatch a photo from in front of me. "Not me in my underwear, Mom, really? Why do you think Gina wants to see this?"

I note the flush on his neck and cheeks, how tight he's holding his mouth, and speak quickly to take control of the situation. "Because you were so cute, and it gives me baby fever." I throw a wink at Marta before turning back to Owen. The movement is automatic, although fake. I have to swallow hard for the amount of lying I'm about to do. It shouldn't be difficult, not when I've been lying through my teeth to Owen from the moment I met him. But this feels different. Bigger.

Everything rests on him believing me.

"Did you straighten things out with your dad?" I ask.

Owen winces and runs his hand through his hair. "He... aw, hell. He's saying he didn't have anything to do with it. I don't know why he'd lie about that, but at this point, I don't know what to do. You deserve better, Gina. I'm so sorry."

I reach out and grab his arm. "Hey, what he did doesn't have anything to do with you, okay?" From the corner of my eye, I can see Marta watching me, but I don't look away from Owen. "Your dad... he obviously has issues. But I don't blame you for them."

Owen exhales hard and leans down to kiss me. His lips brush mine, then linger by my ear. "I'm so sorry, Gina. This is a nightmare. We can go if you want. We can just leave. Cut the trip short." He sounds desperate, and my heart aches for him.

He's hurting right now, but it's nothing compared to how much he's going to hurt very soon.

"I'm fine." I smile at him and squeeze his arm again. "Seriously, Owen. People make mistakes, and I forgive your dad."

He looks relieved, but the calm expression on his face slides right off when I continue talking. The words feel mechanical and fake, but I don't feel like I have a choice.

Right now, Grant is angry. Angry people make mistakes. If he slips up, he can tell me what I really need to know.

"I want to get to know him better. Your mom suggested what to do, and I think she's right. I'm going to spend some one-on-one time with him. See if he and I can't work out whatever this is." I gesture to him, then to myself. "I want to do that. For you. For our future."

Owen tilts his head to the side, the expression on his face almost comical.

Poor guy. Family relationships aren't nearly as easy as heart surgery. As brilliant as he is, he's having trouble keeping up.

"You don't have to do that, Gina. Dad screwed up. I'm not going to ask you to hang out with him when he just hurt you so badly. Stay with me, and I can keep him from hurting you again. I won't leave your side, okay?"

I take a deep breath while I think. Owen's acting exactly

how I would expect him to, but that doesn't tell me what he knows. "Nonsense. I know your mom would love to have some more alone time with you—isn't that right, Marta?" I ask her but then keep talking, unwilling to let her have a chance to get a word in edgewise. "Besides, once we go back home, who knows when we'll get back down here? We might not see your family again for... well, I hate to say years, but you know how quickly time passes." I shrug like that's going to remove the sting of what I'm saying. Marta has a small smile on her face, but it's clear to me she's burning up inside, and that thrills me. I smile at Owen, ignoring the pit in my stomach I get when I think about spending time with his dad. "You're so busy, and I don't want you two to feel like you didn't have enough time together."

"You're so astute, Gina," Marta says, interrupting the two of us. "I really appreciate you understanding that spending time with Owen is my top priority right now. Always has been, always will be, if I'm honest."

Ouch. Even Owen looks a little surprised.

I stand and give him a kiss. "Trust me," I tell him. "You and your mom can have some time to reminisce, and I'll be with your dad. I can't wait to get to know him better, and I have no doubt the two of us are really going to get along. You know me— I'm always willing to give second chances."

"Gina, I don't know." Owen pauses, raking his eyes over my body. There's pain in his gaze, and I wonder what he knows about his father. Finally, he exhales. "I really think we should be together as a family. That photo—" He pulls me closer, his lips by my ear. "I don't know what that was about. He acted like it was no big deal, like it wasn't something to worry about, but—"

"Owen. He was embarrassed. He's a huge true crime buff. He probably never thought twice about putting Aunt Bethany's photo in there. Why would he? He didn't know the two of us would meet and fall in love. What are the odds I'd find her picture? Your mom explained it all."

"Gina."

"I bet he forgot he even had it." I hate lying to Owen. The way he's looking at me, so full of love and concern, it's almost enough to make me stop what I'm doing.

But this isn't about him. It's about my family and getting revenge. So while spending time with Grant sounds terrible, I'm willing to do it. For Aunt Bethany.

"Gina." His voice is low. He glances at his mother, then takes me by the arm, pulling me a few feet away from her. "You're not listening. Dad told me the photo wasn't his. That none of it was. He's lying through his teeth about it. He has to be. I don't know why he would do that."

Damn. I take a deep breath and stare at Owen.

"Owen." I hesitate like I'm trying to mitigate how painful what I'm about to say is going to be. "Your dad... he's getting older. I didn't want to say this, but I've noticed a few things while we've been here that make me think he might not be as mentally sound as he once was. In fact, I have no doubt he put together that photo album and then forgot about it."

He looks surprised. His grip loosens on my arm, but he's still holding me tight enough that I'd have to jerk to get free from him.

"You think he put together that album and then, what, forgot?"

I nod. "I know you see the same thing happening with your patients, Owen. It's sad, but it happens. Trust me. I know how much both of your parents mean to you, and I want to spend time with both of them. Let me do this. You love your dad. He loves you. It was a mistake, that's all. I can forgive a mistake, especially since he doesn't remember doing it." I offer what I believe is a brave smile, then reach up with my free hand and dab under my eyes like I'm wiping away tears.

He exhales hard. Scrubs his hand down his cheeks. It's clear from the expression on his face that he's not happy about me spending time alone with his dad. "As long as you're sure," he says, then he gives his head a little shake and looks me in the eyes. "You need to know something, Gina. I'm never letting you go."

I give an involuntary shiver at his words. To be loved—to be *wanted*—by Owen is delicious, but before I can really bask in that, I have to finish this. I give him a kiss but don't linger, instead quickly turning to walk away from him. My eyes are on Grant, who's over at the other side of the room, carefully shelving the photo album Owen took from me. I could bring it up right now, but I opt for a different strategy.

Grant slowly turns to look at me when I approach.

"Owen and Marta want some time to hang out, so it might be the perfect time for the two of us to spend some time together, maybe get to know each other. What do you think about that?" I plant one hand on my hip and cock it out to the side.

I'm willing to pretend like nothing just happened. Is he?

The smile Grant throws me is disarming. "I think that sounds wonderful, Gina. If you're feeling better now, why don't you put on some shoes and I'll show you around the property? I know we got a start on doing that yesterday, but Owen and I got distracted fishing. That won't happen again. I'll take you towards the back field."

I look over my shoulder at Owen. He glances up at the two of us. I like that he's paying attention to where his dad is going to take me.

When I turn back to face Grant, I don't let my concern show on my face. "Wonderful." I'm prepared for a hike, and I hold up one finger. "Give me just a minute to pop upstairs and put on my hiking boots."

"Grab a coat," he calls after me. "It's chilly out there, and we don't want to have to turn back early because you're not dressed appropriately."

"No, we wouldn't want that," I mutter as I hurry upstairs. It only takes a minute for me to throw on a coat and pull on my hiking boots. When I meet Grant back downstairs, he's by the front door, his coat zipped all the way up, a hat yanked down over his ears. He gives me the once-over and nods.

"You approve?" I spin in a slow circle, letting him get a view from all angles. Goosebumps race up my arms as I do. The lecherous feeling of his eyes on me is uncomfortable, and I have to remind myself I'm playing a role. It's like *Romeo and Juliet* with more intrigue. More danger. "Hiking gear isn't really my style, but Owen made it pretty clear that I wouldn't be comfortable running around in flip-flops or in sneakers."

"He's a smart man," Grant says with a nod. When he opens the door and gestures for me to head out onto the porch, I hesitate.

It's cold out here. The clouds hang low in the sky, thick and dark, blocking out a lot of the sun. Whatever warmth there might have been earlier is now gone; it's a muted light outside, one that makes the air feel more like soup than anything else.

"Having second thoughts?" Grant's voice is light. Teasing. *He's willing to pretend nothing happened too.*

"Not at all," I announce, which definitely isn't the truth. I'm questioning a lot of things, if I'm being honest right now. But then I remember why I'm here, what my end goal is, and I feel my resolve strengthen. There's no way I'm turning back now, not when I'm so close to getting what I want.

Wind whips around the house, cutting down the driveway and making me bury my chin farther into the collar of my coat. When Grant brushes past me to take the lead, I don't fight him. I'm more than happy to let him show me the way. Not only does he know where we're going, but I'm also hoping he'll help block some of the wind from getting to me. Anything that helps decrease how uncomfortable I am right now is welcomed.

Even if that thing is Grant.

We cut sharply across the driveway in the opposite direction from where I walked with him and Owen before. This time, instead of following the river, he's leading me deeper into the woods.

Should I really follow this man into the woods knowing what I know?

No. I shouldn't. Wade would throw a fit. Going out into the woods with Grant is dangerous. Stupid. But this entire plan is dangerous and stupid. I want to look this man in the eye and see if he'll tell me the truth about what he did, about what Marta knows. I want to push him, make him scared, let him know I'm coming for him.

It's going to destroy Owen to lose his dad, and that hurts me because I love Owen so much. While I hate Marta, I don't want Owen to lose her too. Not unless she deserves it. Not unless she leaves me no choice.

But as for Grant? I've never been as terrified as I was when I saw him with Aunt Bethany. He deserves to be afraid, to worry that something bad is about to happen and he won't be able to stop it. The only reason I feel at all safe going out here with him is because I trust Owen. There's no way he'd let his father hurt me.

"There's a neat field back here," he tells me, calling over his shoulder. "This is where Owen and I used to play baseball when I was home on weekends. It didn't happen every weekend, but we always did our best to reconnect in between my trips."

"Did you ever regret it?"

He pauses. I watch as he plucks a briar from his jeans and tucks it against a bush so it won't snag me before continuing.

"Regret what?"

Everything you did. "Being away from your family all the time. It had to be hard knowing you weren't going to be there for all of Owen's firsts. I know when I have kids I want to make sure I'm there all the time. I don't ever want to miss anything."

"That's a noble goal," he tells me, but the tone of his voice tells me he's not entirely serious. "But when the alternative is not putting food on your table, you have to be willing to do what needs to be done."

"Sure, but look at this place." I pause, a little out of breath. Who knew Grant was in such good shape? He's leading the way like we're on an extreme hike and he's our overly excited, ruddy-cheeked leader. "I mean, you can't expect me to believe you were just making do. This place is gorgeous. It's the place of dreams."

"I'm really glad you think so." He finally stops walking and turns to look at me. There's about ten feet between us, but the intense expression on his face makes it feel like the two of us are standing a lot closer than we really are. "But part of me taking care of my family meant making sure they didn't live some-where crappy, like a derelict apartment. And now look at Owen. He's accustomed to the finer things in life. You think he's ever going to leave you wanting?"

"He doesn't," I say because it's the truth. "Never has. Never will."

"That's because he's just like me. Willing to do whatever it takes. Willing to go the extra mile. Willing to get his hands dirty." Grant lets the words hang there in the air between us. Neither one of us breaks the silence, not even when a burst of wind makes me shiver. A bird calls from somewhere deep in the woods, but I don't look away from Grant.

He's just like me.

No, Owen isn't just like him.

He isn't a killer.

THIRTY-SIX

MARTA

I stand at the window for a long time after watching Gina and Grant walk into the woods. I saw how he moved closer to her before taking the lead, how she pulled away, doing her best to put a little distance between them.

The way my stomach tenses and twists is familiar. I'm inured to this physical response to my husband's infidelity, but this time I'm happy for it. Without thinking about what I'm doing, I press my hand against the window.

It's frigid outside. The glass is cold, and I only leave my hand there for a moment before I tuck it into my pocket, but I stay at the window, watching until Gina and Grant are out of sight.

A thrill races through me, replacing the sick feeling I had a moment ago. This could be it—this could be when everything changes. It's a strange feeling being on a precipice, knowing everything in your life could get flipped upside down because of the actions of another person.

I'd theorized Grant might be able to sweet-talk his way into Gina's bed, but she's focused on Owen. Grant and Gina tumbling into bed together would mean I get what I want, but is it going to happen? Do I need to adjust my plan again? As much as an affair seemed like the best option at the time for me to have my son all to myself, maybe it's best if Grant continues with the original plan.

Kill Gina.

As long as Owen has no idea I was involved. I have to get him to point his finger at Grant to ensure my husband is locked up. Sure, he'll rave and claim I was involved, which is why I have to be so careful. In the original plan, it was Grant and me against Gina, but I have to be free of him, and this is the only way I get everything I want. I just have to keep adapting, being willing to change. Anything to get what I want.

Of course, Grant can't kill her right now, not when Owen's on high alert looking out for her. That's one thing I hadn't counted on—him falling for her. Grant picked her out for our son so he could find out what she knew about the night her aunt died.

I'd say she knows too much.

Kicking Grant and Gina out because they had an affair would be easiest. But if Gina turns up dead and all fingers point to Grant, I can still get what I want. I have to be careful, make sure I'm not implicated.

Thinking about that brings to mind the trophies Grant has brought me over the years. I'll need to get rid of them, but that will be easy to do in the ensuing chaos and will ensure Grant can't use them to pin any blame on me. Then it will be just my son and me, just like I've wanted it to be for years.

There's no more movement from where they entered the woods. From here, my view is completely blocked. No matter what happens, if they fight or if they fu—, I can't see it anymore.

Satisfied, I brush my hands together like I'm cleaning off dirt left there and turn, hurrying from the bedroom. Down the stairs, into the library, and I take a deep breath, trying to slow the pounding of my heart as I approach my son.

He's deep in a book—he must've picked it up while he was waiting for me to come back—his dark hair tousled, his eyes quick as they move back and forth across the page. I walk slowly up to him, a smile growing on my face as I watch him.

For all the hell Grant put me through, for all the pain and drama we caused each other, I can say it was worth it to have Owen.

"Hey, Mom." He looks up as I stop in front of him. "Everything okay? Your cheeks are bright pink." He frowns, then stands, dropping his book into his seat. "Do you need to sit down? Do you feel okay?"

"I feel great," I tell him, taking his hands and giving them a squeeze before lowering myself into the seat across from him. "I'm so glad we're getting to spend some time together. I don't get to see you nearly enough now that you're saving lives all the time."

He chuckles and dips his head before lowering himself back into his seat. "Well, I can't live at home the rest of my life. Like you said—I have lives to save."

I drink him in. God, he really is perfect. His dark hair is so thick, with a bit of curl, just like mine. His straight nose, his dark eyes... he's the best of me, with very little of Grant mixed in.

Thank goodness. When all this is over, I don't want to be reminded of my husband, of what he did for years and years, or how I turned on him.

"I know, but you know you always have a home here. You and Gina seem so in love right now, but I know how quickly things can change. And if they do, I'll be here for you."

He frowns. "What are you saying?"

I'm trying to prep him for what I know will happen. Poor Owen will never see it coming; I know he won't. He'll never understand that it was coming from the moment Grant found Gina. I still can't believe he didn't just go to her and end it. He likes to play with his food. My husband has always liked feeling in control, and believed bringing her here to kill her was the most poetic way to end her.

"I'm not saying anything," I lie. "You're my son, and I want to support you in any way I can. If something were to ever happen with Gina, you'd be welcome here. You're my son, which means you're the most important person in my life."

"You mean besides Dad." He stretches, grunting as he does, then fixes me in place with a stare. "You always said you were a Tammy Wynette fan."

"*Stand by your man* only goes so far. If he ever did anything to hurt you, I'd be there for you. I want you to know that."

"You're being weird." He picks up his book and riffles the pages. "Besides, Gina and I are in love. Just as in love as you and Dad are, in fact. Nothing bad's going to happen."

"I know—"

"So don't worry." The grin he throws me is casual. Behind him, the fire in the fireplace pops and cracks, but I don't look away from my son.

There are a lot of things in life that aren't a guarantee.

You never know when will be your last day on this earth.

You can't rest assured that the person you marry won't turn on you, won't hurt you.

But there's one thing I can guarantee, and that's this: I won't let anyone take my son from me.

THIRTY-SEVEN

GINA

Grant leads me deeper into the woods. Yes, I'm nervous, but I have to see this through. I've gone off book now, and Wade would have a fit if he knew I was out here in the woods with Grant. Alone. It was one thing he made me promise not to do, but he's not here, is he?

He's tucked away in a hotel in town, close enough to be involved when I need him but not so close he's in danger.

He doesn't get to have a say in how I handle this, and I want answers.

It's a trudge through the woods, following Grant out here, but I wanted to get to know Owen's parents, didn't I? After everything, I don't feel like I have a choice. I really pushed for this little visit, even bumping up the timeline so we could get here as soon as possible.

I always told myself I wasn't going to walk down the aisle with anyone until I knew their family. And while walking down the aisle with Owen wasn't the original plan... things can change. Feelings can develop. What's the saying? *Improvise. Adapt. Survive.*

Something like that.

Owen was simply a tool to help me get closer to Grant, until he wasn't; until he was more. I didn't mean to fall for him, but it did change the purpose of this trip. Now, the goal of our trip isn't just to make Grant pay for what he did to my family.

It's also to see how much his mother knew.

To make sure I punish who deserves it.

That, in a nutshell, is why I met Owen. Why I'm here. Why I was brave enough—or stupid enough—to come out here with Grant. At least one person is going to die here. I need to know if I have to kill two.

"This is the field." Grant stops walking and gestures at a huge expanse in front of us. It's close to winter, and the grasses have died back. It's a sea of brown and fading green, but there's still some life. A dozen deer at the other end of the field and a few crows watch us with beady black eyes.

"It's gorgeous." I'm serious too. Never have I pictured a field of dead grass as particularly pretty, but there's something about the dark sky, the way the wind is rustling through the leaves, how the deer are still staring at us like they've never seen people before.

"It is. I always loved coming home after traveling for work." Grant starts walking through the field, and I follow him, my head on a swivel.

There's just so much to take in. Growing up, we had a tiny backyard with more bare dirt than weeds. It was scrubby, and gross, and Wade and I spent more time reading books we'd checked out from the library than playing outside. But if I'd grown up in a place like this, wow; I don't think I would ever have gone inside.

"I'm glad you came, Gina." Grant pauses and turns to look at me. "It was such a pleasure to meet you after only seeing pictures of you."

"Owen loves selfies," I say, but Grant shakes his head.

"No, I meant on the hospital website. You know, I pushed

Owen to work at Mercy Mission, and then do you want to know what I did?" He keeps talking without giving me a chance to answer. "I told him to date you. Isn't that fun?"

I stop walking.

"Oh, yes. Owen has always been so focused on work, but I found you, Gina. I chose you for our son for a number of reasons."

My blood chills. Wade promised me that Grant had no idea who I was. He *promised* me, but what Grant is saying now goes against that promise.

"I ran into Owen and dumped a cup of coffee on him," I say, my voice flat, my words rote. "That's how we met."

"That's what you think?" A pause, then he continues, completely changing the subject and making my head spin as he turns and walks away. "Has Owen ever talked about moving back home?" He's slowed down enough that I'm walking next to him, and he glances at me while he waits for his response.

"Never."

"Really? I'm surprised. He always promised Marta he'd move back home. I told her she couldn't hold him to it, but you know sons and their mothers. There's a bond there you can't quite break through."

So I've heard.

His gloved hand brushes mine, and I step to the side, away from him. *Maybe this was a mistake.* I need to stay as far away from him as possible. I know Owen won't let anything happen to me, but how far are we from the house?

Would he hear me scream?

I unstick my tongue from the roof of my mouth. "He's never once mentioned it. And he's so good at what he does, he needs to be in a bigger city. He needs to be where he can really stretch his wings at a great hospital. Not that your hospital here isn't fine, I'm sure," I say.

But Grant just laughs. "Oh, you're not going to offend me,

Gina. Our hospital here isn't wonderful, but it works out for what we need."

His hand brushes mine again.

I step to the left.

He follows.

I feel the way my heart starts to race, how my palms become sweaty. Without slowing down, I shove them both into my coat pockets. There's lint in there. A rock. A penny. I grab the rock in my right hand and start to worry it.

"I really am grateful for the opportunity to get to know you. You seem... different from the other women Owen has dated."

"I didn't think Owen had brought any other women home," I say, doing my best to keep my voice level.

"He hasn't. But we've heard about them. And, of course, I look them up online."

"You stalk them?" I manage to chuckle when I say the words, trying to keep things light. But I can't ignore the way something wraps around my throat. I swallow hard to try to rid myself of the feeling. It won't disappear, and it's all due to the refrain running through my head.

He's a murderer, you idiot. He's a murderer, you idiot. He's a murderer, you idiot.

"Stalk them?" He shakes his head. Sounds offended. "Goodness, no, Gina, what do you think I am? A frat boy who got turned down for a date and doesn't know how to take no for an answer? I don't stalk them. But I do look them up. Make sure they seem like a good fit for our son."

I keep walking. My eyes are on the ground so I don't trip, but I'm keeping Grant in view in my periphery. "Maybe you're not an online stalker, but you mean you've never followed any beautiful woman home? Maybe from her job? Like at a diner?"

He doesn't immediately respond. "What are you really asking me, Gina?"

Fear tickles the back of my neck. I take a deep breath. "The police think my aunt was followed home from her job. That her killer found her there and couldn't help himself. I don't love the fact that men sometimes follow women like that." I'm going off script. This isn't the plan, but now that I'm alone with Grant, now that I can see how cocky he really is, I can't help myself. Wade would freak if he knew what I was doing right now.

I need to shut up, but he turns to face me, his dark eyes locked on mine, and I do everything in my power to keep from shrinking away from him.

"Are you saying I had something to do with your aunt's death?" There's a dark current under his words.

"You were in Rosenville. When was that again?"

"I don't remember."

"Sure you do." My brain is screaming at me to shut up and run, to get as far away from him as possible. I ignore that part of my brain and open my mouth to say something, but before I do, he reaches out and grabs my arm to pull me towards him. My first reaction is to yank away from him, but his grip tightens on my arm. "Look at the deer," he says, his voice low.

The hair on the back of my neck stands up. It's the way he's speaking, like he's trying to keep his voice quiet so it doesn't travel. It's how I swear I can feel each individual finger pressing into my arm. It's how close he's standing.

But it's also the deer. They're spooked, all of them standing completely still, their heads up, their necks taut. Even from this distance I can see how wide their eyes are, how their nostrils flare as they try to catch the scent of whatever's got them worried.

"What's happening?" That part of my brain telling me to run is now screaming at me. My muscles tense. My mouth goes dry.

"Oh, a bear. Coyote. Bobcat. Human."

"A human? You mean us? Could they smell us?"

"We're too far away." His voice is casual. Relaxed.

"So you're saying someone else could be out here?" Goosebumps break out on my arms. My coat is heavy enough to keep away the chill, but it's fear making me feel this way, not the cold. Why is it that the thought of another person out here creeps me out more than a large animal? Bears are huge, all sinew and muscles, sharp claws and teeth, but the idea of a human creeping through these woods, possibly watching us, makes me feel sick.

Unless it's Owen. Unless he followed us, making sure I'm okay.

"Sure, there are some people who don't pay attention to property lines. If they're following prey and think they can get away with it, they may very well come over here, to my place. Heck, they might not even notice they've left their property, not if their head is really in the hunt. I've felt that way before, so focused on what I was doing that everything else fell away. It's intoxicating, to lose yourself in the moment like that. In the hunt."

A shiver dances up my spine.

"We should turn back," I say, but Grant shakes his head. He hasn't looked at me since we stopped, since he grabbed my arm. I glance down to verify he's still holding tight to me.

"I want to see," he says, but I shake my head. Tug my arm away.

"Owen wouldn't like me out here with a hunter. It could be dangerous."

"Gina, for fuck's sake, you survived your aunt getting murdered by a serial killer. You're honestly afraid of someone out in the woods?"

I misjudged him. That races through my mind, and it terrifies me. I'd been so confident coming here, borderline cocky even, but what did I expect?

That a man like Grant would back down from something he saw as a challenge? That he'd let me walk into his house and walk all over him? No, I never should have hoped for that. The Grant I'm seeing now is different from the one I see when he's with his son. It's the same Grant I saw when he killed my aunt.

I screwed up, talking to him like this out here. I should have left well enough alone, should have stuck to the plan. What, did I think this wasn't going to backfire? Did I think he would let me accuse him of murdering my aunt and smile, then turn the other cheek?

I've never been great at controlling my actions. But never before has that inability put me in this much danger. I turn to him, doing my best to put on a brave face. *Never let them see you scared.* That's what Wade and I used to tell each other. I jerk out of his grasp. "That was uncalled for. You don't get to talk to me like that. I'm going back."

He doesn't look at me. "Oh, I don't know about that."

I wrap my arms around myself and whip round, my eyes searching the edge of the woods for the path we took to come out here, but the woods are thicker than I remembered them being. There has to be a path there, I'm sure of it, but... where?

"Shit," I say, choosing a direction and taking a step, but he shushes me, sliding a gloved hand around my cheek to my face and pressing it down over my mouth. Panic flares in me, a cold rush making my limbs feel numb.

"Shut that smart mouth of yours."

THIRTY-EIGHT

GINA

"Don't move."

I do what he tells me, ignoring the fact that every cell in my body is screaming for me to break away from him, to run, to fight—whatever it takes to flee. But it feels like I've grown roots. I don't think I could move even if he let me go right now.

"Look. Right there." He points and I turn, my eyes following the line of his finger.

It's a black bear, huge and shaggy, its nose low to the ground, snuffling and pushing its way through the thick woods to enter the field.

I still, my heart beating wildly, my eyes locked on the creature. Even from this far away I can tell how big it is. The bear is massive—its muscles and fat bunch and roll as it walks. Its head sways from side to side as it takes in its surroundings. I'm not sure if it's even noticed the deer standing there, or us, for that matter.

But the deer see it. There must have been some invisible signal we had no way of interpreting because they suddenly explode into action, bursting away from the bear, white tails up, long limbs stiff, eyes wide and fearful. Moving as one, they bound out of the field, hurrying away from the bear, crashing into the undergrowth of the forest, making their own path.

Grant slowly removes his hand from my mouth. I can still feel the heat from his gloved hand on my face. My skin feels like it's on fire from where he touched me.

"Is it going to hurt us?" I don't know anything about bears. Sure, I've seen them at the zoo before, sitting there fat and bored, knowing full well their next meal would drop right in front of them eventually, but this bear is nothing like anything I've ever seen in captivity before. It doesn't sit; it lumbers. It doesn't stare off into the distance with a bored expression; its beady eyes are quick and full of interest, and it's obviously very well aware of everything that's going on around it now that the deer have fled.

Its head is high, its nose working hard. I watch as it sniffs the air, slowly turning, before finally looking right at the two of us.

How good is a bear's vision? Can it really see us, or is it just looking in this direction because it smelled us?

I don't know, but now I wish more than anything we'd never come out here.

"That's not who you need to be afraid of hurting you," Grant says. "That little guy is way more afraid of us than we are of him."

I ignore the implied threat, my heart still hammering hard. "Little guy?"

"Sure, he's just a baby yet. Babies aren't what you need to fear."

"That means mom is around here somewhere." Fear nips at the nape of my neck, and I slowly look along the edge of the field, moving just my head, looking for another smudge of black.

Nothing.

"I want to go back to the house." The bear hasn't moved, and so I slowly turn around, looking again for any sign of a path through the woods. "I'm serious, Grant—this isn't what I had in mind when I came on this walk." My heart slams in my chest. "Point me in the right direction." How's my voice? Strong? Firm? All I had to do was stay in the house, keep to the plan.

Wade is gonna be pissed, but I can't worry about him yet. Not until I get out of this.

I'm terrified, and it certainly isn't because of the bear. I want Owen.

"You don't trust me?" He's turned around as well; now his arm is around my shoulders. I stiffen, but if he feels me pull away from him, he doesn't react. "Come on, Gina, you should know by now that I'll do anything for my son."

Alarm bells are going off in my head, but I force myself to nod. "Right. I know how close the two of you are."

"Hmm." He keeps his arm around my shoulder, and when I take a step forward, the weight of his arm holds me back. "Gina, you asked earlier about Rosenville. Don't you want to continue that discussion?"

"Not really." Fear makes my tongue feel thick in my mouth. "Really I just want to go back to the house." This was stupid. I thought I could get him out here, see some remorse in his eyes, get info about Marta's involvement, but all I did was willingly walk into secluded woods with a serial killer. Like an idiot. I glance over my shoulder to make sure the bear hasn't started in our direction. It hasn't, but it hits me there's something worse out here to be afraid of.

"Why? You've got me on my own now, Gina. Just like you've wanted. Sneaking around, peeking in my office. Now going on this walk with me." He must see the expression on my face because he forces a laugh. "Please don't act surprised. Or innocent. It's insulting."

This is a side of Grant he's kept hidden while I've been here with Owen. It's the side I expected to see, but it's still taking me off guard.

"Fine." I whirl away from him, pleased when his arm falls to his side. I'm sucking in tiny gasps of air, my heart hammering away. "You want to do this? Let's do this. When were you in Rosenville?"

He smiles, but the movement is slow. Lazy. The way he's looking at me is terrifying.

"I already told you I was in Rosenville a few times. It's a great town; does it matter exactly when I was there?"

"Tell me when was the last time you were there." I'm ignoring the little voice in the back of my head screaming at me to run for it. I'd be safer in the house, I know that much, but I already opened my mouth and now this conversation has to happen.

"It's been a while."

"Me too."

"You and I are more alike than you ever imagined, aren't we?" He reaches out like he's going to take my hand, but I step back from him. His hand hovers in the air for a moment, then he drops it back by his side.

"Gina!" Owen's voice travels through the woods. "Dad? You guys out here?"

I don't look away from Grant. His eyes are locked on mine, his mouth an angry slash, a red flush creeping up his neck.

"I looked outside and saw the deer go running by. There might be some bear out here. You two need to come in. Gina? Dad!" His voice is tight, but the sound of it makes relief rush through me.

Coming out here? It was stupid. What if Owen hadn't interrupted? What would Grant do to me? I give my head a little shake, pushing that fear from my mind. What matters is that I'm okay. I did something stupid, but I'm okay.

"Owen," I call back, still staring at his father. "We're right here. We're coming."

Grant shakes his head. When he speaks, he's quiet, his

words only for my ears. "Why did you come here? It wasn't because of my son."

"I came for the truth." My voice is low. Yes, I'm still terrified, but Grant won't do anything to me in front of his son. Why didn't I stay close to Owen? "And I found it."

He takes a deep breath, his dark eyes searching my face. I'm glad he can't read minds, that he has no idea what I'm thinking right now. Because if he could, I'd be screwed.

The only thing I can think about is how perfectly his expression mirrors the one I saw on his face before he killed Aunt Bethany.

THIRTY-NINE

GINA

Monday

Owen's beside himself, and it's all thanks to me.

"I'm going to talk to him, okay? Trust me, Gina, I don't know what this is, why he would do something like this, but I'm not going to look the other way. I'm so, so sorry this happened to you." Owen's murmuring the words, letting them wash over me, probably thinking they're comforting. He leans closer to me, pulling me tighter against his chest, then brushes his lips against my forehead.

That's good. With my cheek pressed against him like this, he can't see me smile.

"Thank you," I say. My voice breaks a little bit. "I thought they liked me, Owen. That they cared. Why would he do something like this? We walked in the woods together yesterday and smoothed things over. Then the evening was quiet but fine, and now I come downstairs to this? I just don't get it."

"He's obsessed with true crime," Owen tells me, and I nod like that explains it, but he isn't finished. "And he's always had this savior complex, like he's the only one who can make the right decision for your life. I guarantee you he wanted to piece things together for you, maybe solve the case, I don't know. There's no excuse for what he's done. I promise you—he won't ever hurt you like this again." He groans.

I almost feel bad. Poor Owen doesn't deserve to be dragged into this. But I'm here, and he's here, and nothing like this would be happening if it weren't for me bringing him into my life.

And now we're too deep into it to back out. Yes, I know the truth about Grant and Marta, and I honestly feel like I have enough proof to avenge my aunt. But Owen needs to see me as a victim first. He needs to be so head over heels for me that siding with his parents isn't something he would ever consider.

It's the only way this will work, no matter what Wade said.

"I've gone over the case piece by piece for years," I tell him. "And come up with nothing. There's *nothing*. Believe me, if there was a way to solve the case by reading her file, I would have done it."

"Maybe it's because you mentioned she may have been killed by a serial killer," Owen tells me. "And then he pulled out everything he had that might match the murders? I don't know, Gina, I really don't. I'd love to say I was in his head, but my dad has always been a bit of an enigma."

Instead of immediately answering, I wait to see if Owen will continue. He doesn't, so I clear my throat. "Okay, so maybe he had all this information on cold cases and saw how they might be linked. But I just don't get why he'd tape up all the pictures and newspaper clippings on the wall like that. Why he'd think that was something anyone in the family would want to see." Do I sound choked up enough? I wish I could cry on command.

"He's not a bad guy, Gina—I want you to believe that. But he's impetuous. He gets ideas in his head about what needs to happen, how he can help, and he acts on them. I hate to admit it, but he doesn't always think things through, and that can come across like carelessness." Owen sighs and scrubs his hand down his face. I can smell the coffee he started when he got me calmed down and put me here on the sofa to sit with me. My back is to the now-empty murder wall and ripped photos, like Owen turning me away from them will protect me.

"I guess not." I sniff, then give a sigh. "I feel all jittery, full of adrenaline. It's not as bad as the night she died, but it really brings it all back to me. It just hurts. Even if he didn't mean to hurt me, he did. That picture of her—" I let my voice break and trail off, then blink up at Owen, who reaches out and cups my cheek.

"Of course it hurts." His voice sounds thick. "If I could go back and stop this... tell him that this topic was off-limits, I would have."

"I know," I tell him, and I mean it. Owen doesn't have a mean bone in his body. What his father did doesn't involve him. I trust him to keep me safe from Grant.

I shiver and pull my legs up and hug my knees to my chest.

Owen stands up. "You stay here on the sofa and let me get you some coffee," he tells me. "Then I'm going to go talk to my dad. What he did? This isn't right. I don't know what he was thinking, but we're not supposed to leave until tomorrow, and I'm not about to let the rest of this day be a nightmare. Stay here, Gina."

I nod and give him a small smile, then watch as he hurries to the kitchen. A minute later, he's back, pressing a huge mug of coffee into my hand. "You stay down here, okay? He's still upstairs with Mom. I'm going to figure out what the hell is going on here. I just don't want you involved, okay?"

"No problem," I say, taking a sip of the coffee. Gosh, it's so good. Coming on this trip has been worth it for a few reasons, and the amazing coffee is one of them. "I'll wait right here."

He turns to leave, and I reach out, grab his hand. "Hey, I'm sorry this happened."

"Me too. You have no idea how sorry I am." He's having trouble looking me in the eyes. I know Owen, and this has got to be one of the most upsetting things he's ever gone through. The man is used to saving strangers' lives. He's not used to having to pick up the pieces of someone he loves because they got hurt.

And I'm sure he's not used to having to clean up his father's mess. That's never been his job, and of course he's going to struggle.

I shake my head. "No, you don't get what I'm saying. I'm sorry this happened, that this is how it all fell apart. I don't know why they'd do this to me, but I promise you, I don't blame you for any of it."

His face softens. His jaw has been tight since he heard me screaming in front of the murder wall, but it relaxes just a little bit. Taking my hand, he turns it over and runs his thumb along my palm.

"I don't deserve you; you know that?"

I'm already shaking my head before he finishes speaking.

"I'm serious, Gina. You're perfect for me. You're the one I want now and forever." A deep inhale as he stares at me. "I don't think anyone else would be as calm as you are, and while I hope to never have to ask you to be as patient and understanding about something like this again, I'm so glad you know it's not me. This isn't us. You and I can get through this, okay? And you're my top priority. Don't think for a moment you're not the most important thing to me. I would do anything for you, Gina. Anything."

Even look the other way while I handle your parents?

He has to. I want him, and I'm not leaving here without him.

I like seeing him this desperate to protect me, this willing to punish his parents, to show me how much I mean to him. It feels good, knowing I'm the most important thing in his life. And the fact that Grant and Marta will realize they lost him right before I handle them?

That's even sweeter.

"I'd do anything for you." I smile at him, hoping he can see just how much I love him. It's one thing for me to tell him I love him, to let him know how important he is to me, but this is the most important moment in our relationship. Owen's on a precipice right now, and I'm the one who put him there.

I have to know he's going to make the right choice.

That's part of the reason I wanted to come meet his parents. It can be so difficult, almost impossible, to tell if someone is innocent. If they're telling the truth. I needed them all in a room together. I needed to be able to look each of them in the eyes. Owen was supposed to be collateral damage, but I don't care what Wade thinks. Plans change. I'm not losing him.

"Let me handle this, Gina. I promise you—everything is going to work out."

He bends down and gives me a kiss, his tongue sweeping against mine. I kiss him back, hard, making sure he doesn't think I'm mad at him. I need Owen to believe we're on the same page, that I'm right there with him, that nothing will be able to separate the two of us.

"I love you," I say as he walks away.

He turns around. Repeats the words back to me.

Then he straightens his shoulders and heads for the stairs.

I settle back against a pillow. Something bites into the side of my thigh and I shift position.

The tape dispenser, almost empty after I taped up all of the photos and newspaper clippings.

I should have gotten rid of it last night but was too tired, so I brought it downstairs this morning to put it back in the junk drawer.

I have to get rid of it before Owen finds it on me.

FORTY

GINA

Breakfast is quiet. Owen sits next to me, his jaw tight, his back straight. He's giving off real don't-mess-with-me vibes, and I have to admit, I like it. I want him to choose me. Only me, always me. Part of me had worried it might be a battle between Marta and me, that he might struggle to choose me over her, but maybe I was wrong.

Man, I wish I could have heard what went on in their bedroom. Him throwing his parents under the bus for the artwork I hung up feels incredible, I'll tell you that.

Marta beats Grant downstairs. She sweeps past me on her way into the kitchen to start cooking. I watch her go, happy to sit here, let her wait on me. I want her to see Owen at *my* side, comforting *me*. He's chosen who he wants to be with. And, honestly, the last thing I want is to be caught with her in the kitchen.

Owen is blinded by love, but Marta isn't. I have no doubt she knows what I did.

It was one thing to come here knowing the truth of what happened to my Aunt Bethany. It was another entirely to try to sort through the lies, filter out the truth, figure out who was involved and who wasn't.

"What are your plans for after breakfast?" Marta asks. She puts her fork and knife down across her plate like we're in a fancy restaurant and she needs to signal to the waiter that she's finished her meal.

"I'm thinking we might head home early," Owen says, and I look up at him.

This... was not part of the plan, and I don't like him making changes to our schedule without consulting me. It makes sense though, after all I've done. I pushed him too far with my stunt last night and now I need to backtrack.

"Owen, no." My voice is quiet as I reach out and rest my hand on his arm. "No, I want you to have the rest of our scheduled time here with your family. I'm fine, okay? I'll read, I'll go for a walk, I'll figure something out."

"Gina." Owen matches my tone but then looks up at his mom. "Do you mind giving us a minute?"

She stares at him. "Right now?" When Owen nods, she sighs. "Fine. I'll check on your father. " She pushes back from the table, then hurries away. Grant opted not to join us for breakfast after his confrontation with Owen. No doubt the man is angry and about to lash out.

This is good. Angry people make mistakes.

"Gina, I'm not going to make you stay in this house one minute longer than necessary." Owen inhales, then shakes his head before exhaling. Hard. "It doesn't matter what Dad said, okay? Don't worry about it."

No way am I going to let him get away with that. "What did he tell you?"

Owen frowns. "Does it matter? I love you, and I'm not going to sit there while he talks bad about you." Owen spits out the words, then wads up his cloth napkin and tosses it on the table.

"He said I did it, didn't he?" I ask, but Owen's eyes are unfocused and he doesn't hear me.

"All he did was point the finger away from him. It doesn't matter, Gina. I love my parents, and I want them in my life, but not if he's going to act like this." He still isn't looking at me, and when he speaks again, his voice is quieter. "Like I can believe him, after everything."

I pause; let the words hang there in the air between us for a moment. "What do you mean, *after everything?*"

Owen has the grace to look admonished, then he shakes his head. "Nothing, Gina. It's just... my dad looks great on paper, doesn't he? So willing to do whatever it took to take care of his family, to put food on the table. But he's not an easy man to get along with, and I know he's not easy to be married to."

We fall silent. For a moment, we sit quiet, then I hear Grant and Marta's voices.

Owen stands and motions me to follow him into the kitchen. I do, watching as he refills our coffee mugs before leaning out into the hall, probably to check on where his parents are. I know he's hurting, but I can't undo what's been done.

And his pain will only get worse before it gets better.

He turns back to me, his cheeks flushed. "Did you do it?" The question takes me off guard, and I stare at him. "I'm sorry to even ask this, Gina, but you didn't hear my dad. He was so angry and convincing."

"Did I bring pictures of a bunch of murdered women, including my aunt, and hang them up in your living room in the middle of the night then pretend to find them this morning?" I have to fight to keep my voice low. "Are you seriously asking me that right now, Owen?"

He exhales hard and runs his hand through his hair. "I know, I know. It's insane of me to question that, but I want you to try to see it from my point of view."

"Your mother has hated me from the moment I walked in

this door." My back is against a wall, but I'm not going down without a fight. Putting up the murder wall last night felt like one last middle finger to Grant, but I'm beginning to regret it. I tend to overdo things when I'm trying to make a point. "Don't you place the blame of how things went down on this weekend on me." I pause, my mind racing. "Next thing, you're going to accuse me of putting together that photo album too."

"Forget it. Forget I said anything." He scrubs a hand down his face. "I just... This is insane. How could I predict that anything like this would happen?" He seems to deflate, and I pull him into a hug.

"I can't say this is the trip I expected it to be," I say, and he shrugs. "But I love you. And I would go anywhere with you. I'd do anything for you. We'll go home and forget all about this trip, okay? It's just a blip in our lives."

Owen takes a shaky breath. "It didn't cross my mind that my parents would hate you. Dad picked you out, you know? He said you'd be perfect for me."

"He wasn't wrong." I kiss him. "Everything's going to be fine, Owen."

"You're right." He pulls back a little bit to look at me. "But I still think we should leave earlier than we planned."

No. I can't let that happen. Frustration that I pushed it too far, that I might have shot myself in the foot when I was just trying to get what I wanted, surges through me. Any regular person would be thrilled at the opportunity to leave this house early, but I'm not ready. The plan is almost finished.

Do I want to stay? No. But I have to. Otherwise, this will all be for naught, and there's no way of knowing when Wade and I could orchestrate another plan. So, yes. I want to flee. But I can't.

I have to stay, and I have to keep Owen here. Just a little bit longer and it'll all be over.

"Let's stay through lunch, if not dinner," I suggest, and I'm not surprised when Owen starts shaking his head. "No, listen to me, Owen. These are your parents. Something happened here. Our wires got crossed somehow, but they're still your family. Even if you're mad at your dad, and you have every right to be, your mom loves you. Don't you think she deserves some time with you? Are you going to let your dad ruin that for the two of you?"

It's my final play, but I know it'll work.

"Are you sure?" His eyes search mine. I see love there, but it's clear he's already making up his mind. He wants to have that extra time with his mom. I should be hurt by that, should feel frustrated that he's willing to leave me in a position where I don't feel totally safe, but I'm not, and it's because it's what I want.

What I need is to get what I came here for.

"I'm so sure." I take his hand and give it a squeeze before leaning over to kiss him. "I want to do this for you. You deserve to have a bit more time with your mom because who knows when we'll see her again?"

"You're right. God, I love you." He cups my cheek, and I lean into his touch. "I'm obsessed with you, Gina, you know that?"

"I know." I can't help but smile at his words. Everything about Owen feels safe.

Except his parents.

"Great. Good. How about this? I can even make dinner if you want. You were so excited over the wine cellar, so why don't we go down there and pick something out? I don't know anything about wine, but you can show me around. We'll make the best of this, okay?"

As I should have expected, he frowns. "Gina, I don't know if drinking and then getting in the car to drive is such a good idea."

"I'll drive home. Being DD is no big deal—I want you to

have one more chance to be with your family." I'm laying it on thick, but Owen is just so happy to be the center of my attention that he either doesn't notice, or he doesn't care. "Seriously, Owen. You bend over backwards all the time not only for me but for your parents. Why don't you let me take care of you for a while? Go tell your mom I'm happy to make dinner. You and I can lay low today, maybe read, play cards. Your dad..." I shake my head. "He's something else. But I don't want to take you from your mom. Just don't be surprised if I make myself scarce when your dad is around."

"You got it." Owen pauses, staring at me, drinking me in. I shift under his gaze, but there's nothing malevolent there.

Relief washes over me. I only have to wait a few more hours.

It began two decades ago, but I'm ending it tonight.

FORTY-ONE

GINA

It's been harder than I expected getting Owen to stay when he's so desperate to leave. But I'm not walking out of here without ending this. Yes, I screwed up pushing it this far. Even as I hung up the photos of Grant's victims, I knew I was pushing it, but I'm impetuous. I've never been great at self-control.

Now I just have to hope I can see this through. Wade was right when he told me this was the one chance the two of us would get to take Marta and Grant by surprise, and I think I did, for the most part.

Just a few more hours.

Grant and Marta are quiet and leave Owen and me alone for most of the day. After lunch, we go for a walk around the property, then I'm ready to come back to the house and start packing. I'm usually a last-minute packer, but not today. Not when we have to get out of here as soon as possible once I'm finished.

"I'm ready to sleep in our own bed," Owen tells me, dropping onto the sofa next to me and throwing his arm around my shoulders. "There's nothing to make me appreciate my mattress like not sleeping on it for a few days."

"Same," I say, shifting position a little bit so I can look him in the eyes, "I can't wait for all of the luxury of your place." I pause, considering. "Hey, Owen, are we okay? I know this was hard and your parents are glad you came, but I don't know about me. About us. Where do we stand?"

"We're better than okay." He plants a kiss on my forehead. I should lean into it, should enjoy this PDA in his parents' house, but I'm wired. Every minute in this house, every second, it all brings me closer to finishing this. "Trust me. This was hard, and I know that. And I don't like the way you were treated, but that's between my parents and me, not you and me. I promise you, we won't come back until I know for sure they'll treat you better." He pauses. "They're going to miss us when we're gone."

Yeah, right. They'll miss me the way you miss an abscessed tooth after you get it pulled. I've seen the way his parents look at him compared to how they look at me. Both Marta and Grant look at Owen like they hung the moon, but me?

Marta hated me from day one. And I don't want to think about what could have happened to me if Owen hadn't come outside while Grant and I were on our walk. I screwed up, but that won't happen again. Putting myself in danger like that just to get under his skin and try to get some more info on Marta? It wasn't worth it.

"Well, it was really hard, but I'm glad we came," I tell him, snuggling into him. The tape dispenser digs into my hip, and I shift position a little bit. I really need to get rid of that before he notices, but Owen's so distracted right now, I could walk around naked and I don't think he'd bat an eye.

"You are? Why?" He rests his chin on the top of my head.

"Because your parents are important to you. Especially your mom. And now I know why you've always caved to the pressure your dad puts on you."

I feel him stiffen. When he doesn't say anything in response to that, I speak faster, wanting to make sure he understands what I'm trying to say.

"Not that you did anything wrong, Owen. But your dad is a force to be reckoned with. I can't imagine it was ever easy to stand up to him, to tell him no. Thanks for doing that for me. That's all I'm saying."

"He's never been an easy man," Owen admits. "But putting the blame on you? I don't know. I don't like the idea that one of them is lying to me, but it's clear that's what's happening here."

I nod. That's exactly what I hoped everyone would think when I snuck down here last night to hang up the photos and newspaper clippings. Owen never saw the slim manilla envelope of them in the bottom of my suitcase. Lucky for me, it was tucked inside the secret inside pocket with my burner phone, or Marta would have seen it when she rummaged through my things.

I'd been almost giddy hanging them up last night. Every time the house had settled or made a strange noise, the hair on the back of my neck had stood straight up. I'd crept through the house and tried the door to the garage and Grant's office, but both were locked tight. It was frustrating, but I still managed to get done what I planned to. Every time I snuck around in their house I was terrified. But last night, even more so.

It felt like I was doing something illegal, something I could get in a lot of trouble for doing, but I couldn't stop. I needed to see Owen's response, to know for sure that he was clueless about what happened to my aunt. I had to make sure he was going to take my side, and he did.

He passed the test.

"I talked to my mom," he says.

I'm surprised, and he must see the expression on my face because he continues. "While you were in the bathroom. I asked her if she could try for a few hours. To be nice to you, to act like she was happy we came."

"And she said?"

"That of course she would. She loves me, Gina—I know she does. And I want her to know how important you are to me."

"I'm glad," I lie.

Dating Owen wasn't ever about Owen, but that's not something I can explain to him now. Or ever, for that matter. Dating him was about getting to his family, learning more about them, then finally making it on this trip.

I never wanted Owen to get hurt, and I never meant to fall in love with him. But how could I not? He's gorgeous. Smart. Sexy. Driven. Sure, I would have dated him if he looked like a piece of gum on the bottom of my shoe, but it all worked out in the end that he's as attractive as he is, didn't it? I got off a lot better than I could have, and you want to know what that is?

Karma.

That's me finally getting what I deserve after so many years of having the rug ripped out from under me when things were going well. I've kept my head down, worked hard, done everything I could to not only make something of myself but try to get revenge for my aunt.

And it's all finally coming together. I just have to know for sure if Marta was also involved in my aunt's death. Wade was certain he had it figured out. After years of linking cold cases together and looking at evidence, he was confident in what he'd found.

"Gina." Marta stands in the door, fiddling with the bottom of her apron. Her face is drawn, and I wonder if she was involved in the discussion Owen had with his dad. "If you're not busy, I'd love to have you help in the kitchen. Owen loves my chicken and dumplings, and I planned on teaching you how to make them. That way, when you two go home, you can make him his comfort food after a long day at work."

"That sounds amazing," I say, and I swear, I can feel Owen relax a little. He sags against me some, like I was holding him up, and now he can finally relax. "I'd love to learn how to cook that. Thanks."

She smiles at me. It doesn't reach her eyes.

But that's fine because I'm almost out of her hair. There's only one thing I need to know, one thing I haven't figured out.

Does she know she's married to a serial killer?

FORTY-TWO

GINA

Every nerve in my body is on high alert while I'm in the kitchen with Marta.

She already had a roasted chicken in the fridge, and I picked the meat from the carcass while she talked me through mixing up the dumpling dough. In no time at all, the broth was simmering on the stove, and she talked me through how to cook the dumplings. It smells amazing in here, but that doesn't decrease the worry I feel.

I'd been curious why we needed to start cooking so early, but she explained that it takes a while to make and then to bake to ensure everything is nice and thick. There's part of me would have loved to snuggle up with Owen, to just wait out the few hours we had remaining in this house, but I need to talk to Marta.

I need to know what she knows.

I have to know who to punish.

I'm dropping bits of dough into the simmering broth, Marta right at my side.

"Marta," I say, keeping my voice even and my eyes focused on what I'm doing. "What's in the garage?"

She stills. "What do you mean?"

I jerk my head in the direction of the locked door. As far as I know, nobody ever found out I'd been trying to break in. My luck has held, and now I'm going to risk everything.

"Your garage," I repeat, making sure my voice is light. "You don't park in it, even with such a nice car. Why wouldn't you want to park in there? Keep your car out from under the trees in case a branch fell on it?"

There's a moment of quiet, just a beat, then she clears her throat. "That's Grant's space. I have the rest of the house to myself, but he wanted just a little room to spread his wings. So, the garage it is."

"Doesn't he also have a wine cellar?" Owen told me all about that before we came—how his parents love fancy wine, how they converted the basement into a climate-controlled area where their wine would be nice and safe until they were ready to drink it. "And his office. How much space does a man need?"

She narrows her eyes at me. "More than you'd expect, I know that much. You're sure to find out the same if you ever convince someone to marry you. But the wine cellar doesn't really count, does it, Gina? That's not a space he can go spend time in when he needs a break from everything. That's just a storage space. Think of it like a closet, the garage more like a workspace."

"For his woodworking," I suggest.

"Gina." Her voice takes on a bite, and I raise my eyebrows while scooping a floating dumpling from the broth. "What Grant does in the garage is none of your concern. It's none of mine either. He worked hard his entire life to give Owen and me the life we deserved, and if he wants the garage to himself, I'm not going to debate with him over it. Don't think you have any right to come to my house and try to upset the natural order of things."

The implication is clear: *I don't have a problem with what my husband is doing, and you shouldn't either.*

She wants me to drop it, but no way am I going to do that. Whenever I've watched a horror movie and the stupid protagonist is about to go upstairs and get murdered, or let an axe murderer sleep on her living room floor because there's a blizzard outside, or she tells the bad guy that she's about to call the cops if he won't stop being such a bad guy, I roll my eyes. It's ingrained in me, to judge other people for their survival skills—or lack thereof.

Yeah, as if I showed any survival skills yesterday walking with Grant into the woods. I shouldn't have done it, but I did. You think I'd have learned something from that.

And yet what am I doing? Marta has made it abundantly clear that I need to back off, need to leave her and her husband alone, and yet I'm completely unwilling to do just that. Where's my self-preservation instinct?

I left it upstairs in my little bedroom off Aunt Bethany's, I guess.

"You're right," I say, and while I know that sounds like a concession, it's not. Not entirely. "I was just curious because you seem totally okay with not having access to that space, and there must be some reason he doesn't want you in there."

The broth is really bubbling away now, and Marta reaches across me. Snaps off the flame. When she turns to me, her cheeks are red, her eyes wide.

"I would think you had more sagacity than this, Gina." Her voice has dropped so I'm the only one who can hear it. "I would think, after what you've been through, that you'd be more aware of how to protect yourself, of what you need to say, of not making people angry."

You and me both, Marta.

"Whatever you have in your mind about Grant, whatever

you believe about him, put it aside. My husband is a good man. He worked hard for our family."

"He hit on me." My voice is even quieter than hers.

She doesn't immediately respond, and I think for a second she hasn't heard me. Or is just ignoring me.

But she looks up at me, one eyebrow raised. "He does that."

I take a deep breath and clench my hands into fists so I don't poke her in the chest. She just confirmed everything I already suspected. "You knew he did. That he would. And you still wanted me to spend time alone with him."

She shrugs. "Grant has always had a wandering eye. He's never liked being tied down to just one person. That's the way all men are, Gina, and the sooner you realize that, the better off you'll be."

"Not Owen," I say, and she shrugs again.

"Maybe. Maybe not. I hope he's not a lot like his father, but you never know, do you?" She says the words with a smile, but that doesn't diminish the fact that each one feels like a knife.

No way am I going to give her the satisfaction of looking surprised. She can try all she wants; I'm not backing down. "Did you know about Grant's... proclivities before you two married?"

She bumps me out of the way with her hip and scoops the last of the dumplings from the broth. I watch as she layers them, cooked chicken, and poultry seasoning in a baking dish before pouring the broth over them. It smells amazing, but the beige color, the thick gloppy dumplings, the shredded meat... it makes my stomach turn.

I'll never make this for Owen. Never.

"Grant hid a lot of things from me before we were married," Marta says. She yanks open the oven and slides the baking dish inside before closing it and turning on me. "You have to understand that men do that. And when you find out their true selves, you don't have much of a choice."

"You mean to leave or stay?" I'm watching her eyes carefully for any sign of deception. She could be lying to me, but I don't know that she is. Marta was first honest with me when she told me she didn't trust me. This is the second bit of honesty I've experienced from her.

"Grant didn't hang up the photos and newspaper clippings," she says.

She's leaning close to me, and I take a step towards her, willingly closing the gap between the two of us. I want to know what she knows.

Or what she thinks she does.

"Nobody else would have," I counter.

She could be innocent. I have to know where she stands, what she knows. There's no way to make my final move without getting inside her head. I'm so ready to end this, but I have to be careful. I'm not throwing away two decades of work because this woman pisses me off.

"You would have. You did it. I know you did. Grant knows you did."

"But Owen doesn't believe you. He trusts me."

"My son is a fool." She hisses the words at me, taking me by surprise. I'm tense, my muscles all tight, ready for whatever else she's going to say to me, but before she gets a chance, Owen leans in the kitchen.

"Everything okay in here?"

Marta takes a step back like I burned her. She turns to him, and I see the way her face changes, how she smiles, how it spreads across her cheeks, reaching her eyes. Her body relaxes, and she grabs her apron, wiping her hands on it. The transformation is complete when she reaches up and tucks some stray hair behind her ear.

"Of course, darling."

He glances at me before looking back at his mother. "It was quiet in here. That's all."

"Oh, girl talk." Marta flaps her hand to shoo him from the kitchen. "I'm just making sure Gina knows all of your favorite meals before you leave. I want her taking care of you."

"She takes care of me," Owen says, right as Grant appears behind him.

"Was I not invited to the party?" Grant grins at his wife, then turns to me. "Gina, when you get a second, there's something I'd like to show you. In the garage."

FORTY-THREE

GINA

My stomach turns as Grant opens the door into the garage. He'd pulled the key from his pocket, yanking it out with a flourish actually, a magician producing a rabbit, then slipped it into the lock before throwing me a wink.

It turns my stomach, that wink. The flippant way he acts, like he's never done anything wrong in his entire life, like nobody could ever dare suspect he might not be perfect. The more I get to know him, the more I see him in his son.

I don't like it.

"This is my domain," Grant announces, reaching to the right to hit the lights. "I heard you and Marta talking about it, so I figured I might as well show you my space. She has her kitchen; I have the garage."

"And your office, and the wine cellar," I offer, and he chuckles.

"Right you are. I made the money. I get whatever space I want. Now. What did you want to see so badly in here? You keep poking around the house like you're dying to learn all of our secrets."

I ignore him.

I knew what I was expecting when I followed him into the garage, but it's not what I get. The room is immaculate, not a tool out of place, with a large band saw in the far corner, a planer next to it, and huge tool boxes lining the wall next to me. Past them are some filing cabinets, and I walk over to one, eschewing the half-finished chair in the middle of the floor.

"What's in here?" I try to sound casual as I yank on the top drawer. It rattles in place but doesn't open.

Locked.

"Patterns. User manuals for my tools." He gestures at the band saw. "Ordering information for when I need more wood. Boring stuff like that."

"All locked up?"

He doesn't answer.

"That your worm fridge?" I point to a small minifridge in the corner of the garage.

Grant nods.

There's a huge whiteboard hanging directly across from me, and I walk over to it. It's on a swivel, but when I reach out to touch it, Grant *tsks*.

"Now, Gina, how would you like it if I walked into your house and just showed myself around? Peeked in your closet maybe?"

That sounded pointed. *Does he know I was in his closet?*

"Fair enough." I turn to him with a smile. "What do you have written on here that you wouldn't want anyone else to see?"

He pauses. "Plans for my trip mostly. Tracking various cities I went to more than once to make sure I didn't miss any sights. When you visit a city a few times, it starts to feel like home."

"Like Rosenville."

"Just like it. I know that place like the back of my hand. I always did my best to hit up the locals' favorite spots instead of getting caught in tourist traps."

"You mentioned you liked the diners." I'm well aware of how dangerous this conversation is. There's part of my brain screaming at me to stop, to leave the garage, to get Owen and flee from the house, but I can't do any of that.

"Sure, diners, but not just those. Little coffeeshops. Dive bars. I love stuff like that. Every place I've been to has its own flavor, its own thing to really look forward to. I never want to miss something unique like that."

"Funny," I say, trailing my fingers across the worktable. No sawdust. Honestly, everything in here looks pristine, like it's for show. "I haven't seen a single souvenir in your house since I got here. You don't collect shot glasses or magnets or even postcards to help you remember the places you've been?"

He barks out a laugh. The sound is too loud in this small space. "No, nothing ugly like that. I do bring home souvenirs—you got me there. But I'd much rather bring home something like a nice piece of jewelry for Marta. Something we can really enjoy."

"Lucky Marta. You traveled so much; she must have a ton of jewelry to choose from."

"You better believe it. Necklaces. Watches. Sometimes it's something bigger, like a pair of diamond earrings. Sometimes it's just a small thing, like a keychain. But everything reminded her that I was thinking of her when traveling. And when I see the souvenirs, I think about how much fun I had out on the road. They're personal to me."

Anyone listening in on our conversation would think we're having a nice time catching up, but the air in here is electric. Grant will take a step towards me, and I'll shuffle back from him. His eyes are beady and flick up and down my body while I'm trying to soak in all the details of this space.

It's a weird dance, one where neither of us will come out on top, but I don't think we can stop. At least Owen is within shouting distance.

To verify that I'm right, I glance at the door. It's still open.

"Does she know where each souvenir came from?"

He chuckles. "You mean the name of the person I got it from?"

I nod.

"I told her. She might not remember, but I do. In fact, I guarantee I could tell you where I got each souvenir and who I got it from. The hospitality of some folks would just blow you away. You'd never believe how willing some people are to invite you into their homes, their lives. They just want you to be comfortable, to feel like they've made a connection with you somehow."

"So she really did know." The air in here is getting thin. I want to flee into the house. At the same time, I want to keep asking him questions.

This dance we're in? It's not healthy. I think I know all the steps, that I've heard the music before, but Grant is more than one step ahead of me. It doesn't matter how clever I think I am—he's in control.

"Marta?" He's not asking me. Instead, he's staring off into space. "Marta knows everything, Gina. Always has. You should have figured that out by now."

"I need air," I say, walking past him to the door. My palms are sweaty, but I refuse to wipe them on my jeans.

"Gina."

The hair on the back of my neck stands up.

"You saw me, didn't you?"

I don't answer. I *can't* answer.

"You don't really think you're going to leave here, do you?"

"Owen won't let you hurt me."

"Owen does what I tell him to. Always has. But you can't

seem to understand that, can you?" There's a low current in his words. I pause, glance back at him.

Grant isn't looking at me. He's staring off into the corner, right between the closest filing cabinet and the tool box next to it.

I don't know how I didn't see it.

That's what I tell myself, even though it's a lie.

I didn't see it because I was so dead-set on getting into the filing cabinet. And then I wanted to see on the other side of the whiteboard. I walked right past it without paying attention, but Grant gave the game away by staring at it and bringing my attention to it.

A map.

Not of the world, not an innocent map used to teach little kids the countries and capitals, where the oceans are, what seas you have to cross to go somewhere, but still a map.

One of the United States, covered in pins, clearly marking his travels over the years.

Like the one Wade and I have been working on for years. Exactly what I was hoping to find here. Exactly what I *knew* Grant would have locked up somewhere safe.

A murder map.

And there, in Rosenville, a pin.

The red head of it mocking me, like a drop of blood.

FORTY-FOUR

GINA

I feel like I can't breathe.

Walking past Grant, I stumble into the kitchen, then brace a hand on the counter to help keep my balance. I knew he'd have a murder map. I was looking for a murder map. Still, knowing it and coming face-to-face with it are two different things. A man like him, so organized, so involved in killing more than a dozen women over the years... he'd want to be able to see his work, to check in on it, to know what he did.

And then he told me I'm not going to leave here. My lungs are tight, like I can't take a deep breath. I close my eyes and breathe through my nose, trying to think through what just happened. My mind races as I try to come up with a way out of this.

Maybe go to Owen. Tell him everything. Beg him to help me.

I shake my head. As nice as that sounds, I can't rely on Owen to turn on his parents, despite how he defended me earlier. It's going to be tricky enough to ensure he stays with me after I get my revenge, and that will be when I have a very good reason for him to stay.

Without that reason, I can't guarantee he'll stay with me. And I refuse to lose him.

"What's wrong with you?" Marta takes one look at me, at my pale face, at the sweat I can feel beading on my forehead, and her lips curl into a smile. Any pretense has gone out the window.

"You knew," I tell her. I didn't want it to be true; honestly, I didn't. I hate her, but that doesn't mean I wanted to kill her.

A grin flicks across her face.

"Hmm." She crosses her arms and looks at me, tilting her head to the side a little. After a moment, she continues, like I'd never spoken. "See something that didn't sit right with you?"

I don't know how to respond to that. "I'm fine. I have something in my suitcase to help when I feel off like this." I know I don't need to explain myself to her. Not when we both know how the other feels. Owen isn't here for the two of us to pretend in front of.

Her eyes are quick as she looks me up and down. "What is it?"

"What's what?" I've already turned to walk away from her, and I have to turn back to look at her.

"What you have in your suitcase to help. I didn't see anything like that in there." She stares at me, one eyebrow cocked, and I feel my entire body go cold. When she leans closer to me to speak, she lowers her voice. "Keep Owen close, Gina. I don't know what you wanted to accomplish coming here, but you're out of your league."

I turn away from her and hurry out of the kitchen. I'm doing my best not to run, but there's a little voice in my head screaming at me to go faster, to get out of there.

I hate myself for it, but I glance over my shoulder.

She's standing in the doorway. Watching me.

I turn back. In the living room now, I try to slow down so Owen doesn't ask me why I'm running from the kitchen. Why

I'm pale. Why the way his mother was looking at me made me feel like I was going to throw up.

"Get it together, Gina," I tell myself.

Owen's reading, his long legs stretched out in front of him on a sleek leather ottoman. I pause as I walk by him, then drop a kiss on the top of his head.

"You okay?" he asks, looking up at me. "You'd think there's a fire or something, the way you're moving."

"Just popping up to our room to grab some headache medicine from my suitcase," I tell him.

He's on his feet in an instant. "You're cooking. I'll grab it."

"No, no, that's fine." Another glance towards the kitchen, but nobody has followed me. "You're reading, and it's such a small container that it can be tricky to find. Carry on with what you're doing, okay?"

He frowns. "If you're sure..."

"So sure!" My voice is too bright; I see the way he raises his eyebrows. "Don't think twice, I'll be right back down, okay?"

Now I move faster, practically running up the stairs. I don't pause at the top to listen for anyone following me, simply hurry down the hall to the room I'm sharing with Owen. Once inside, I close the door. Lock it.

Just in case.

I lean against the door for a moment, letting my heart rate come back down. Things are happening, and I have to stay calm to ensure they go off without a hitch.

After a minute, I feel like I can breathe easier, like I'm not so dizzy. I can think straight, which means I can do what needs to happen next.

Although, at this point, I'm not sure how I'm going to make it out of this in one piece. Not when I tipped my hand to both Grant and Marta. I have to stay close to Owen to stay safe.

I push away from the door. Instead of hurrying to my suitcase, however, I beeline for Owen's closet. The door swings open silently, and I kneel in front of his old boots. Dip my hand inside and pull out my burner.

My heart hammers in my ears, and I force myself to take a deep breath. Try to calm down.

It doesn't matter that I've texted Wade a dozen times from this phone; my hands still shake. I keep forcing myself to take deep breaths. It's one thing to come up with a plan, to figure out all the details and work it all out. It's another to be standing right on the precipice, close enough to see the end. I'm so close to getting what I want.

And finally I'm willing to do it.

It's time to put things in motion. No more waiting. Not when Grant looks at me like he wants to snap my neck. I want to ask him what he's waiting for, but I've baited him enough. Besides, I think I know the answer.

He wants to kill me, but he won't do it in front of Owen. Owen saved me when I was in the woods with his dad, and Marta just told me to keep him close.

She's playing with me. They're both playing with me.

Wade wanted me to kill both him and Marta the first night I was here, but I couldn't. I wasn't going to kill Marta for being a bitch. But now that I know the truth, she deserves to die for being complicit to Grant's crimes.

Thirty minutes.

Is that too long? Will I last that long?

After sending the text, I wait, rolling the phone over and over in my hands.

What if he doesn't respond? What if he's busy or if he was in a car accident and is now lying on the side of the road, the phone crushed and unusable, or—worse—fully functional, in the grass, just a few feet away from him?

I'm catastrophizing.

I stand. Pace. The room is large enough for me to gain some momentum walking back and forth across it, and I do, my feet quiet on the floor, the phone silent in my hands.

Just when I'm about to give up and make a call, the one thing we promised we wouldn't do, my phone buzzes in my hand. Relief floods through me, fast and almost overwhelming, and I turn the phone over.

Ok

That's it. Two letters, no punctuation, nothing that gives this moment the gravity that it should have.

I sink down to the bed and perch on the edge of it. My hands still shake as I select the text thread. Delete it. Power the phone off.

It's probably overkill at this point, but I still slip it back inside Owen's boot in the closet. When I close the closet doors, the overhead light flicks off, and I sigh, taking a deep breath, my hands still flat on the doors. This is a monumental moment, and I'm torn because I want to share it with Owen. I'd love nothing more than to rush back downstairs to him, fill him in, let him know how my plan is working out just the way I wanted it to. The way I *needed* it to.

But I can't do that. Owen was only supposed to be a pawn in this game, was only going to be used to help me get the thing I want, but I've stupidly fallen for him. He doesn't know the truth of who I am. Of what I'm capable of. If he did know, if he had even an inkling, he wouldn't have brought me here. I'm sure he wouldn't have moved me into his apartment with him.

Thinking about that right now isn't going to help me. I take a deep breath; hold it. Exhale.

It's almost time, and I'll be damned if anything stops me from getting the one thing I want.

Revenge.

FORTY-FIVE

GINA

I'd love nothing more than to leave right now, but I can't do that. Not while Owen's parents are still alive. Yes, I want to run away with him, and I will, but not yet. I need him here, with me, until Wade and I finish this. I already know what Wade is going to say about everything: that I should have listened to him and taken care of Owen's parents sooner.

If I'd followed my cousin's advice, this would all be over. I wouldn't be in this position, I wouldn't be staying as close to Owen as possible for safety.

If I'd listened to him, I'd be home. Instead, I have to stay here a little longer. And all because I thought his mother was worth saving?

It was a mistake.

"Dinner and a drink," I tell Owen, uncorking the bottle of wine. "And after that, we'll go."

"Sounds good." A slight pause, then he continues. "That's a good bottle." He takes the cork from me and flips it between his fingers before setting it down. "The perfect drink for a night to remember."

He has no idea.

"Every night with you is one to remember." I put the bottle down and hug him, snuggling up against his chest in the way I know he likes. "I love you. I can't wait to get home with you."

"Same here." He kisses me on the forehead, turning to look when we hear his mom laugh.

I pat his chest. "Go to them. I'll pour this and be right there."

"Are you sure? I can help."

"I've got it under control." I kiss him. "I'll be right there with the wine, don't worry."

Any time now, Wade. I'd love to text him, tell him to hurry up, but I can't. I glance at my watch. It's been twenty-nine minutes since I texted him.

Owen nods, before giving me another kiss. For a moment, I'm nervous he'll insist on helping me with the wine, but he turns and walks into the dining room. A moment later, I hear the sound of him sitting at the table. I move quickly, filling each glass of wine only half-full. It's time to put the pills in the glasses, but I'm afraid someone will see them. Instead, I walk to the door that leads into the dining room and hover there, watching, the glasses of wine in my hands.

"Owen, so glad you decided to come talk to us instead of—" Marta begins but she's cut off when the room is plunged into darkness.

"Son of a bitch." I can't make out the expression on Grant's face, but his frustration is evident. There's a shuffle, then the flashlight on his phone lights up. Marta does the same. "Come on, Owen—bring your flashlight and let's see what's going on. We probably blew a breaker. If that's the case, we'll get it figured out and have the power turned back on in no time."

Owen stands, his chair scraping on the wood floor. I'm silent as he pulls his phone from his pocket and thumbs on the flashlight. He finally turns towards me, the light hitting me straight in the eyes before he drops the beam to my waist. "You good?" he asks me, and I laugh. It sounds more normal than I could have imagined possible and hides how nervous I really am.

"Of course I am. You take care of the breaker with your dad." That earns me a kiss, then he and his dad hurry down the hall.

There's silence for a moment before Marta breaks it.

"I'm surprised you didn't want to help Grant with the breaker."

She's mocking me, and I ignore her. No way in hell am I spending any time alone with Grant. Not now, not when he knows I'm onto him.

When I stay silent, she speaks again. "I have candles in the kitchen." She stands, eyeballing me, her phone glowing in her hand. "You just going to stand there useless?"

"Nope." I swallow hard, my spit thick. "I was bringing the wine out so you guys have something to drink." Carefully, I put the wine down in the middle of the table.

She brushes past me and heads into the kitchen. It's only when she turns away from me that I reach into my pocket. There's a tiny envelope in there, a folded piece of paper with three pills. My hand shakes as I drop one each into Grant's, Owen's, and Marta's wineglasses.

When I did a practice run before our trip, the pills dissolved much faster than I thought they would. I pick up Owen's wine-glass and squint at it, bringing it close to my face for a good look. The light from Marta's phone filters through from the kitchen, and I can just make out the pill, still sitting in the bottom of the glass.

Crap.

I'm loath to leave them, but I force myself to quit messing with them for a moment. I'm well aware that Owen is gone and I'm on my own with Marta, but I don't think she's the real threat. Grant's the murderer.

I can see Marta through the open kitchen door—she's got her back to me, digging deep in a cupboard. She's muttering to herself, her voice muffled.

The front door opens and slams shut. I pause, waiting to hear if either Grant or Owen stayed inside while the other went to discover what happened, but they're both gone.

"What did you say?" I call through to her. Before she answers, I grab a butter knife and stir each glass of wine before wiping the blade on my pants. There. That should do it. Normally I'd fill the glasses up more, but I want to make sure they each can easily finish their wine, that they don't have too much to drink before they get the full effects.

"I said that of course this would happen on the last meal with my son. Why this weekend couldn't have worked out the way I wanted, I don't know." Marta's kneeling, holding something up to me as I walk up behind her. "Pretend to be helpful, would you?" I take it, surprised to find it heavier than I expected. "Candles are in there. There should be a box of matches as well. What mischance this is."

"It'll be fine," I murmur, carrying the box to the table and opening it. She was right—it's loaded with candles and a box of matches. Tea lights, tapers, thick squat ones. I pull half a dozen out and start lighting them as she walks up to the table next to me, reaching for her wine.

No, that can't happen.

I need them to all start drinking at the same time or chances are good someone will fall asleep before the others. "Do you think we even need candles?" I ask. She turns to look at me, and I blow one I just lit back out.

Her hand hovers by her glass for a moment, but she doesn't pick it up. "Are you stupid? Of course we need candles. What, are we going to eat by the light of our phones? Ridiculous." She snatches the candle from me and relights it.

"It does make it romantic."

This makes her pause. "Owen's making a fatuous choice being with you." She takes a step closer to me, the light from the candle in her hands creating a glow on her face. She should be pretty with the light flickering across her face, but her features are distorted.

"He loves me. And I love him. He can't stay at home with Mommy the rest of his life."

"You have no way of understanding what Owen and I mean to each other. You'll never be as important to him as I am." A pause, like she's debating saying more, but then she gives her head a shake as if to clear the thought. She glances at her wine as she turns to leave the dining room, giving the glass a once-over.

My palms grow clammy as I watch her.

Surely she can't tell it was tampered with. No. No way. She'd have to be psychic to know anything. Still, my heart is in my throat as she turns away. Before I can think of another way to keep her from drinking her wine before Grant and Owen are back, the front door swings open, a burst of cool autumn air flowing into the house.

"You'll never believe this," Grant says, his voice hard. There's anger there I haven't heard before, a note of it bubbling right below the surface. A chill races up my spine at the way his voice fills the house.

"Something wrong with the breaker?" Marta's unflappable. "Weren't you two able to fix it?"

"It wasn't the breaker." That's Owen, walking in around his dad but leaving the front door open. "Something else happened."

FORTY-SIX

MARTA

"Someone cut a tree so it came down on the power line." Grant's speaking to Gina and me, but his eyes never leave her face. He's watching her for any sign of weakness, any sign that she knows what happened out there.

But no. She's been trapped in the house. Cut off. No way was she involved in a tree coming down.

"How do you know it was cut and didn't fall on its own?" Gina sounds nervous.

"There was sawdust," Owen tells her. "It's pretty clear someone took a chainsaw to it.

"Who would do that?" I ask.

Owen turns to look at me, but Grant's gaze never leaves Gina's face. "Hard to say," he finally says. "But it feels pointed, doesn't it?"

I rub my hands up and down my arms. It's not chilly in the house, but I'm suddenly cold. Gina shifts position and steps closer to Owen, who reaches out and drapes his arm around her shoulders.

"I need a drink," my son announces. "Wine, anyone?"

"Wine sounds good." Grant finally looks away from Gina

and turns to me. His eyes search my face, and I know what he's thinking.

When are we doing this?

We've come so far.

But I won't kill her in front of my son.

That's why I sent the two of them out on a walk together, but I wasn't able to distract Owen long enough for his father to end Gina. Now they're planning to leave after dinner and we're running out of time.

But maybe some wine will relax Owen and he'll leave Gina's side long enough that Grant can take care of her. That'll have to work. I have to separate them. Warning her and telling her to keep Owen close was stupid, but everything about her enrages me.

I couldn't stop myself.

"Let's go," I say, making a shooing motion. The dining room seems to glow thanks to all the candles Gina and I lit. It's gorgeous, and I pause in the doorway, taking in the space. As long as I don't look at her, don't admit that she's here, it's perfect.

We sit, and I grab my glass. Of course Gina didn't fill it up enough, but that's fine. I'll start with this, then get Owen to go with me to the kitchen. Grant can... hell, I don't know how Grant is planning on taking care of Gina, but that's his problem.

Then, when Owen figures out what his father did, he'll be all mine.

There's a cloud hanging over the table, and I shiver before taking a sip. "To adventures," I say, holding out my glass.

For a moment, nobody moves. I look at Owen, sure he can see the expression on my face, how badly I need him to help me out here, and he finally sighs. Picks up his glass.

"To adventures and family."

Good boy. He's always been my good boy, always done what I asked of him. How I wished over the years that his father would shack up with one of the floozies he met when he was traveling instead of—but no matter. What Grant did is not my problem. I hoped to tempt him away with Gina, turn Owen away from her at the same time. When that didn't work, the only option was to let Grant do what he feels needs to be done.

He'll kill Gina, and Owen and I will live happily ever after.

There's a little voice in the back of my head reminding me that if Grant goes down, I'm going down too, but I ignore it. I'm not listening to it. I've got it under control.

"To adventures, and family, and candlelit dinners," Grant says, holding up his glass. He throws me a wink. I force a smile.

That's our thing, it's how we make toasts, and I look at Gina, who looks a little lost but holds up her glass of water.

Water. Like our wine isn't good enough for her.

"To adventures, and family, and candlelit dinners... and the future," Gina says.

Owen smiles at her, in love and truly happy. I down my wine in response, not wanting to see the expression on my son's face.

Grant does the same, and we put our glasses down on the table with a thud.

"More wine?" Gina's up before I can stop her. She hurries into the kitchen, humming to herself, using one of our candles to light the way.

I take the reprieve of her going away for a moment to touch Owen on the arm. He startles, then turns from watching Gina to look at me. "Owen, are you sure you want to—" But then she's back, chattering away about how *unbelievably dark* it is outside and can we believe *how cool it is* that we can't see our neighbors?

She's insufferable. I glare at Grant, but he's not looking at me.

Gina fills my glass. Then Grant's. Before topping off Owen's, she pops her hip out and grins at him. "Bottoms up.

Someone told me one time that adding more wine on top of stuff that's been in your glass for a little while makes it taste funny."

"That's not true," I begin, but Owen takes his glass and swallows the wine in two huge mouthfuls.

He puts the glass down, but I snatch it before Gina can pick it up. "What is this?" I ask, swirling the glass around. There are some dregs in the bottom of Owen's glass. Dregs that shouldn't be there.

My hand starts shaking, and I set his glass back down. When I pick up my glass, my hand shakes even more.

Why am I so nervous? This is *Gina*, not some mastermind. The wine shouldn't have dregs though, not when she just opened a bottle for dinner. Not unless...

"Gina." My head pounds. Nerves race through me, making it difficult for me to think through what I'm going to say. What I *should* say.

"Marta, are you okay? You look pale. Peaked." She reaches over and presses the back of her hand to my forehead. "Let me help you to the sofa. It might be a good idea for you to lie down."

I shake my head. That's a mistake. My stomach rolls, and I close my eyes, fighting against the wave of nausea threatening to overtake me. With my eyes closed, I feel like I can hold it all together.

That's what I'll do. I'll keep my eyes closed. Keep breathing slowly through my nose. In and out. In and out.

Grant says something. I wish I could hear what it was. There's a bite to his words, and I feel a corresponding flash of excitement. Good. Tell her she messed up. Whatever was wrong with the wine—

With the dregs.

They weren't dregs from the wine. They were something else. I force myself to look at her. She's grinning, still holding the bottle, her other hand resting on Owen's shoulder. He looks like I feel, like someone punched him in the side of the face, like his head is full of cotton, like every thought is more and more difficult.

"Owen," I say, but even to my ears I hear how it comes out. "Ohh-when."

"Owen's fine," Gina tells me. She rubs the back of his neck as he slowly lowers his head to the table. A thunk from the other side of the table tells me Grant's done the same thing. "He's totally fine. Now why don't you close your eyes, Marta? Take a little nap. I promise you—you'll feel better."

"Why?" My tongue is thick. It's a slug in my mouth, flopping around uselessly. I feel like I'm going to bite it off.

"Because you and your husband are killers." She lowers her face close to mine. If I had any control over my arms, I'd reach up. I'd grab her around the neck. I wouldn't let go until she stopped breathing, and even then I'd squeeze harder, just to make sure.

"I didn't," I say, but she shakes her head.

I have to close my eyes. She shouldn't do that. Not when I'm so close to being sick.

"He may have killed them, Marta, but you knew. You knew and you still got me alone with him. You knew he murdered my aunt and you still invited me to break bread with you. And Grant, picking me out to be Owen's girlfriend, making sure he worked at Mercy Mission. There was a reason for it, wasn't there? He wanted Owen to meet me."

I'm fading fast, my head drooping towards the table. She hurries around Grant, grabbing me by the hair, yanking me up so I have to look at her.

"I have questions, but maybe Grant can answer them. You're going to suffer the same fate she did," Gina tells me. "It's such a shame Grant killed you, isn't it?"

"What?" I'm fighting as hard as I can, but it's a losing battle.

I feel like I'm under water, caught in a current, my body pulling me down through layers of dark. I'm trying to kick and scream, trying to flail my arms to swim, but I can't move a single limb.

"Grant. He's a killer, Marta. One day he just... snapped. Killed you. Killed himself. That's what the papers will say. Good thing Owen and I had already left to go home, isn't it?" She glances at the table. "What a shame Owen will never want your chicken and dumplings again. Can you imagine him wanting to eat the last meal you made before your husband snapped?" She snaps her fingers, and I jerk a little, but I can't fight against the darkness bringing me down any longer.

My mouth moves. I want to beg her to stop. It's shameful, the fact that I would ever consider begging Gina. I can't do it. I can't make the words, can't think through what needs to be said.

"Don't you worry about a thing, Marta," she tells me. "I'm going to take care of Owen. It's such a shame his parents were terrible people, but I'll be there for him. I'll be the shoulder for him to cry on. And when he's ready to forget you, I'll make sure to help him with that too. He's mine, Marta. And I promise you, he'll never think fondly of you again."

And then I'm out.

FORTY-SEVEN

GINA

Marta's chin rests on her chest. Her mouth is open, her breathing slow and regular, but I can't get her to wake up.

"Marta," I say, grabbing her by the hair and pulling so her head angles up. "Hey, Marta." I blow in her face, but I don't get a response.

There's only one thing left for me to do, and I slap her as hard as I can. My palm stings, but gosh, it feels good. I've wanted to do that from the moment Owen and I arrived.

Marta deserves a lot worse than a slap, but she'll get it. I have some questions to ask her first.

"What?" She jerks, her head snapping back, her eyes flying open. "Gina?"

I don't respond. She takes a deep breath and reaches up to brush her hair out of her face but can't with her hands tied.

"What the hell? Gina! What did you do?"

"Hi, Marta." I'm squatting in front of her. Her back is against the kitchen cabinets, her feet out in front of her. I've tied her wrists and feet together, just like I've done to Owen and Grant. Marta can try all she wants, but she's not going anywhere.

"What did you do? Where's Owen?"

"With his dad." I lean closer to get a better look at her. Her pupils are returning to normal, but she still looks really pale, where I slapped her notwithstanding. "You don't have to worry about them right now, okay? You just have to worry about you."

"What's going on?" She squirms, twisting back and forth, but the combination of drugs in her system and restraints on her wrists and ankles keep her in place. "What do you want?"

"Just to talk." I sit back and reach out to the side, picking up a long knife I found in the knife block. It's not the one Grant used to kill Aunt Bethany, I'm confident of that, but it'll do the job.

Her eyes widen when she sees it. "Gina. Put that down." She stares at me and, when I don't oblige, tilts her head back to yell. "Owen! Grant! Where are you?"

"They're napping, Marta." I rest the knife on my knee and reach out to grab her hand. "Hey. I need you to talk to me and maybe we can figure something out. What do you think?"

"I think you're a crazy bitch!" She spits at me.

I wipe my cheek. "Same to you, Marta. Tell me, why did you push Grant to spend so much time with me?"

She eyeballs me. When she glances down to the knife, I chuckle.

"Your best bet for this going as smoothly and painlessly as possible is to answer my questions, Marta."

She lifts her chin and stares at me. All the anger I've felt since getting here, all of the rage over what they did to my family, the helplessness I felt as a young girl, everything bubbles up in me.

I grab the knife and stab it into her thigh.

There's a moment she's so shocked she doesn't respond, but then she starts screaming.

"Owen!" She's rocking back and forth now, twisting to try to get away from me. The knife is still in her thigh, and it jiggles with her movement. It's going to fall out, so I grab it.

Twist.

Pull it out.

She screams louder.

"Will you calm down?" I grab a towel from the counter and shove it in her mouth. Her eyes widen. She's sweating, the scent of fear making me wrinkle my nose. "Tell me the plan. I want to know all of it."

Marta keeps screaming against the towel. I straddle her, holding the towel in her mouth with one hand and pressing the knife into her neck with the other. I feel her blood soak into my jeans and make a mental note to change them before the grand finale.

"Marta, I'm going to give you one more chance. When I take this towel out of your mouth, I want you to tell me the entire plan. Do you understand?"

She's panting into the towel. I swear, if she passes out and ruins everything, I'm going to kill her.

Who am I kidding? I'm killing her no matter what.

"You and Grant pushed Owen to work at Mercy Mission to meet me, didn't you? After he stalked me online, you planned this out as the best way to make that happen, right?"

She nods, and I slowly remove the towel. The knife I keep pressed up to her throat.

"And then you wanted him to bring me home."

"Yes."

"Because Grant didn't know if I knew what he'd done, am I right?"

She pauses before responding. There's so much hatred in her stare that I can't help but grin. It would be different if she were in control, but she's not.

It's finally my time to shine.

"He wasn't sure. But he's been worried about you for years, and I told him we could take care of you."

"That's amazing." I throw my head back and laugh. "At the same time you two were thinking about how to destroy me, I was coming up with a plan to punish Grant. But I didn't know how much you knew. I didn't know if I should spare you. So you sent Owen to Mercy Mission, but he was already on my radar. Isn't that hysterical?"

She doesn't laugh, and the smile slides off my face.

"Your jewelry?"

"His trophies."

"You're sick." I stare at her, trying to stay calm. She's unbothered by this, like the two of us are having a cup of tea and catching up, not like I'm about to kill her. The fact that she's so calm makes me feel like I'm going to lose control.

I take a deep breath. Focus on what else I need to know.

"So Grant was going to kill me? But you sure didn't seem to mind him paying me a lot of attention, did you?"

At this, she juts out her chin. "He slept around, and him sleeping with you would sure turn Owen away from you, wouldn't it? I didn't care if you lived or died as long as Owen turned on you."

"You're disgusting, you know that?" I sit back, putting a little more space between us in case she decides to spit on me again. "This was all about Owen for you, wasn't it?"

"I love him. And he loves me. He'll never care about you, not like he does about me. You're nothing! You're trash! You're—"

I don't get to hear whatever else Marta thinks I am because I lean forward, pressing the knife into her neck. It slides in easily at first, the blade is so sharp, but then catches on something—her windpipe?—and I have to saw a little to get it moving again.

Blood bubbles out, hot and thick, the smell overwhelming. I

flick the blade to the side, sending spatters of red onto the cabinets, then get off her before dropping the knife to the floor.

God, I'm soaked. Her blood is on my jeans and my hoodie. I pluck the fabric away from my body. "Bitch. I loved this hoodie," I mutter, then nudge her leg with my foot.

She doesn't move.

Cocking my head to the side, I listen. The house is completely silent. Candlelight flickers in the dining room and here in the kitchen where I brought some candles in to talk to Marta.

I'm almost done here. I have to finish packing. Change my jeans. Get my phone. Take my aunt's necklace.

And finally deal with Grant.

FORTY-EIGHT

GINA

Blood pools on the kitchen floor just like my aunt's did when Grant killed her.

I ignore how it's spreading and focus on the task at hand. Steam rises from soapy water, and I plunge my hands into it, enjoying the way my skin seems to burn, how red it's becoming. I don't mind washing dishes by hand, especially when it's one of the last things I'll ever do at this house.

Our suitcases are ready to go and outside on the porch. It was fun getting ready to leave, much better than packing to come here. I enjoyed folding Owen's clothes and putting them in his suitcase before sitting on it to zip it closed. Mine was harder, but I managed to get it shut. I left a few things behind, like the photo album of Grant's greatest hits, but I wasn't planning to bring that home with me anyway.

It served its purpose.

My new necklace hangs around my neck. It's not like Marta's going to need it any longer, and it's a family heirloom. I deserve it after everything I've gone through.

I'm humming to myself as I yank the drain for the water. As if on cue, there's a shuffling sound from the dining room.

"Dad? Dad!" It's Owen. His voice is tight. Terrified. "Gina! Oh my God, Gina! Where are you? Dad, what did you do?"

A scraping sound. He's trying to move his chair, trying to loosen the ropes I used to tie him to it, but Wade and I practiced for hours. I know how to tie ropes that will keep someone in place for as long as I want them to be there. Those knots, in fact, will just get tighter and tighter the more Owen struggles against them.

I turn, stepping high to avoid the mess on the floor. I don't want to have to clean myself up again, and while these shoes might not look like much to the average person, Owen bought them for me on our first date. The last thing I want is to get his mother's blood on them.

"Gina, you're alive!" Owen rocks back and forth in his chair. His eyes are wide. There's a line of drool down his chin that he can't reach to wipe away. I'm embarrassed for him. He suddenly looks more like his patients than the great Dr. Whitlock, and I hurry to him to wipe it away with a napkin.

He jerks his head away from me. "Gina, what's going on? Where's my dad?" He eyeballs me, his gaze raking up and down my body. "Are you hurt? Did he do anything to you?"

"No, I'm not hurt." I hold out my hands and spin in a circle for him to get a good look at me. "See? I'm fine. Just fine."

"What's going on? Why am I tied up and you're not? And where are my parents?"

I don't immediately answer, and he tips his head back. "Dad! Mom!"

Now he calls for his mother. I can't hide the fact that I enjoy it took him this long to think of her.

"Owen? Hey, Owen." I sit on his lap and loop my arms around his neck. "Hey, look at me."

He finally does, his eyes wild. "Gina, what's going on? I need you to explain it to me."

"I will, I promise." I trace a finger down his chest, enjoying the way his muscles bunch and twist. Owen's beautiful. I have no idea how he came from Marta and Grant, but he's my reward for everything I've survived. He's made it all bearable. I won't say he's made it worth it because I still want Aunt Bethany back, but as far as consolation prizes go, he's incredible.

"You're not tied up." He's panting, twisting his head from left to right to try to look around me. "Where is he? Did he do this? Is he going to hurt you?"

"Owen."

"Gina, you need to run. If he left you untied, if he's going to come for you, you need to get out of here. Get out of here!" he screams at me, the cords in his neck popping out. His eyes are wide, and bits of his saliva fleck onto my cheek. When he takes a deep breath, his nostrils flare. "Something terrible is happening! Do you smell that?"

"Owen, listen to me." The man graduated top of his class in medical school but he can't figure this one out? I'm embarrassed for him. "Your dad didn't tie you up."

He freezes, then slowly turns his face to mine. "What did you say?"

"It wasn't your dad. Look." I grab his chin and force his head to the side. Grant is just in sight, in the living room, tied up, just like his son. After tying everyone up, I'd popped out to the car to get a pistol I'd hidden there. I need it for my plan.

Blood oozes from the cut on Grant's forehead where I hit him with the gun once he started to wake up too early. I couldn't have him waking up and making noise to alert Owen to what was going on, could I? He's so much bigger than I realized, and I miscalculated his dose. No harm no foul though, and I enjoyed hitting him a lot more than I imagined.

I needed him asleep so I could clean up the dining room table, make it look like only Grant and Marta had been sitting here. The last thing I needed was anything pointing to the idea that Owen and I were still here when it all hit the fan. "See? It wasn't Grant."

That's what finally makes Owen start screaming.

He's sucking in little breaths of air, panting as tears fall from his eyes. Snot bubbles from his nose, and I sit back a bit to put some space between the two of us. *Gross.* This is not how I pictured this going. Owen's being much more dramatic than I ever imagined.

I don't like it.

"Owen," I say, patting him lightly on the cheek. "Owen, hey, look at me."

He doesn't. He can barely breathe; he's crying so hard.

I slap him. The sound of my hand on his cheek snaps him out of his drama.

"Gina! What happened? What happened? Oh my God." He rocks forward, trying to pull his wrist out of the rope. When he sees there's no leeway, he looks at me. Desperate. Terrified.

I hate it. If there was a chance Owen would understand what I was doing without tying him up, without drugging him, without slapping him... I would have talked him through it. But how he's acting? It's disappointing.

"Owen," I say, "listen really carefully to me because what you say is going to make a huge difference in how this plays out."

He sniffles. Nods.

"Did you know your father was a serial killer?"

A sob bursts from him, and he shakes his head.

"Owen, don't lie to me."

"I didn't know she was your aunt!" He's desperate, leaning forward against his bonds, trying to get me to look him in the eyes. "I knew he was a bad guy, Gina, but how was I supposed know she was your aunt? It doesn't make any sense!"

"Sure it does." I rub his knee, then stand and rub his back. He's got to calm down so we can talk or I'm going to have to drug him again. This... blubbering isn't something I can deal with for much longer. "You know what? You don't have to hear this from me." I pause to make sure he's going to listen to me. He's breathing hard, and I continue. "Why don't we ask your dad?"

Owen moans. The sound rolls out of him, but I ignore it.

There's a shifting sound coming from my right. Grant's waking up, his son's panic loud enough to cut through whatever deep fog he's been in since I knocked him out.

Can't say I'm happy to see him alive, but at least he can answer Owen's questions. He lifts his head and groans. Once he looks at me, it takes his eyes a minute to focus.

Dang, I hit him harder than I meant to. I glance at the gun on the table, consider how heavy it is. I've never actually pistol whipped anyone before, but I'd seen it in so many movies I figured I could handle it. And you know what? It was more satisfying than I ever imagined it would be.

"Glad you could join us, Grant." I grin at him. Blood covers his right temple. It's gotten into his eye, and he blinks hard like that's going to clear his vision. "You believed you saw me, didn't you?" I walk over to him and squat to get a better look. He's tied to a chair just like Owen, a gag in his mouth. When he mumbles something, I sigh, then rip the dirty towel from his mouth.

Instead of answering me right away, he pants, sucking in huge lungfuls of air like he hasn't had oxygen in years.

Dramatic.

"You thought you saw me!" I stand and point at Grant, anger washing over me. It's hard to control my rage. "That's why you wanted Owen to get close to me, to find out what I knew about that night!"

"Gina, you can't do this." That's Owen, and he's begging. I have my back to him and I don't turn around. "Gina, please. Think about what you're doing. I love you, Gina. You're everything to me—please don't do this."

"Owen, now is not the time." My eyes don't leave Grant. He's staring at me, his chin lifted, his jaw tight. "Answer the question, Grant. You were afraid I saw you, weren't you? That's why you sent Owen to Mercy Mission—he had to work near me, right? You couldn't handle the chance that someone out there might know what you did, so you sent Owen to get close to me. What I want to know is why you didn't kill me yourself? You didn't have a problem killing so many other women, so what stopped you with me?"

"Gina, you have no idea what you're talking about. Please, if you just untie me, we can all work this out. The four of us will sit down, will talk—"

"The four of us aren't doing anything, Owen."

He finally falls silent.

Grant glances past me to look at his son, and when he looks at me again, his good eye narrows.

"I knew I saw something," he finally says. "But I was a little... preoccupied that night. Things... took a turn." He glances at Owen, then looks back at me. "The papers didn't mention anyone else in the house."

"Because I was just a little kid, and they were trying to protect me."

"Her son wasn't there. It was the perfect time."

A wave of anger washes over me. Never in my life did I think that seeing red was a real thing, but it's happening right now. The only thing I can think when I look at Grant is how much I can't wait to kill him.

"So, what? You worried someone was in the house but the papers didn't report anyone there, so then what did you do?"

"Gina—"

"Shut up, Owen!" I whip round to scream at him. This is the moment where all of my questions get answered, but he's going to ruin everything if he's not careful. I need him to shut up and listen.

Grant clears his throat, and I turn back to him.

"I looked into your family. I came back to town, more than once, to watch and see if you were going to go to the papers, if there was a rumor anyone else was in the house. But your town rallied around you. Still, I wasn't sure."

Grant shouldn't be enjoying this. He's tied up. There's no way he's going to walk away from this in one piece, but the expression on his face tells me he's not worried.

I hate him.

"You kept coming back after you killed her?" Goosebumps break out over my arms. "You *stalked me?* But what? You didn't have the balls to kill a little kid?"

"I wasn't sure if I was right or not. I wasn't going to kill you without knowing for sure if you saw me. I should have just done it, I guess. Killed you. But that's why we came up with the plan. It's why I chose you for Owen. I sent him to Mercy Mission, brought you here. It was all to find out what you know and end you if I had to. I haven't killed in a long time, and I wasn't going to start again without knowing for sure I had to. I stopped, okay? I'd stopped and was living my life." He exhales hard, his chest rising and falling as he sucks in air. "Do you know how many times I'd gotten away with it? But things change a lot in twenty years, and I didn't want to risk what I had, the life I'd built, just to kill you." He makes a movement like he's shrugging, but he can't lift his shoulders very much, not with how tightly I tied his ropes.

"Well, aren't you a saint." Sarcasm drips from my words. "But you probably should have killed me when you had the chance." I take a deep breath. Change gears for a minute. There's something in my pocket, something biting into my leg, and I pull it out and hold it out to Owen with a flourish.

FORTY-NINE

GINA

"Owen, open your eyes."

He does after a moment, blinking up at me like he thinks I'm actually going to hurt him. That's what he doesn't understand, and he's going to need to—this isn't about him. Sure, he was a pawn both his parents and I used to get what we want, but that doesn't mean I'm going to hurt him. I love him. Yes, at first, he was just a tool I had to use to get to his father. No way would Grant have ever let me get close to him if it wasn't under the guise of being with his son.

But then, honestly, I fell in love with Owen. It was easy. There's so much about him to love. I don't want to lose him during this. I don't want to lose him or his apartment. I love the life he's invited me into, and I've figured out a way to keep that life, keep Owen, and still punish his parents.

Because, no, Marta didn't kill my aunt. But she knew about it, and she stood by her husband the entire time. She never stopped him, and if she had, Aunt Bethany could still be alive.

Owen glances at what's in my hand, then up at my face. He frowns, his focus obviously struggling thanks to the drugs still working their way through his system.

"Gina, what is that?"

"You know what it is." I kneel in front of him, resting my hand on his knee to brace myself. The ring I found in his pocket is gorgeous. It's exactly the type of engagement ring I'd expect someone like Owen to give me. It's a single solitaire, but it more than makes up for only having one diamond thanks to the size of the rock.

Yes, I've already tried it on. I had to know what it would look like on my finger. And it fit perfectly, just like I knew it would.

He doesn't respond. "Is there something you want to ask me, Owen? Because I already know what my answer will be."

Owen blinks at the ring, then forces himself to look at me. "You want me to propose? Right now?"

I nod.

"You've got to be kidding." He shakes his head, his cheeks turning red. "Gina, whatever this is, it has to stop! You can't possibly think I'm going to propose right now, when you have the two of us tied up like this. And where's Mom? Did you do something to her? And what *is* that?" He sniffs the air, trying to place the smell.

I ignore that. It'll come into play soon enough.

"Owen." I'm disappointed in him, I have to be honest. Wade and I talked this out a dozen times, and I never once pictured him reacting like this. "Your father is a serial killer." I pause, letting that sink in. "Your mother knew about it. She also knew he was a cheater, and she tried to get me alone with him so maybe he would make a move. Isn't that right, Grant?" I glance over at him, and I'm pleased when he nods.

Look at us, finally getting along. All it took was drugging them and tying them up so they had to talk to me.

"Then call the police," Owen says. "I'm serious, Gina, let them handle it. They can deal with it. Just let me go. I love you!

We'll call the police and leave here. Okay? Call them—it'll be fine."

"Owen." Grant's voice is low, a warning. We both ignore him.

I'm already shaking my head. "No, no police. Owen, don't you get it? I'm handling this because the police were never able to. You think I'm going to tell them everything I found out and let them drop the ball again? Your dad killed more than a dozen women. And then he put you in my life to see what I knew. To bring me here." I glance back at Grant. His eyes are looking a little brighter now. He's waking up more. "Hey, Grant, what was your preference? To kill me? Or sleep with me?"

His jaw works before he nods. One quick movement, up and down. "Either. But I was definitely going to kill you. Still will, if I'm honest."

"See?" I turn back to Owen, then slip the ring on my finger. I'm tired of waiting for the proposal that's not going to come. No wonder women do whatever they can to push their man to get down on one knee. It shouldn't be this hard for him to commit to me. "And the answer is yes, Owen. Of course I'll marry you."

"I didn't propose." He pauses, his mouth working like he's trying to come up with what to say next. "Gina, please. Let us go. Or just let *me* go. I won't call the cops."

"No." I stare at him. Man, I'm more and more disappointed the longer he talks. I really thought this would be easier, but he's making it much more difficult than it has to be. "Here's what's going to happen, Owen. I'm going to wrap things up here, then we're leaving. We're going home. You're going back to work, you'll tell everyone what a wonderful time we had, how happy we are to be engaged. Then, when we get the tragic news of your parents, you're going to act surprised."

"Please, Gina." He's crying again, and since he can't move to wipe his face, snot and tears mingle on his chin. "Please, I love you. You don't have to do this, okay? We can be together. We can call the police, let them know what really—"

"No police!" I scream the words in his face, then immediately feel bad. Poor Owen has never had anyone tell him no in his life, has he? This is all new to him, all scary. "Owen. Hey, listen. I'm sorry. Look at me. I'm going to untie you."

Owen stops crying. He takes a deep breath and stares at me.

The change is uncanny.

"I'm going to untie you, and we're going to walk out of here. Together."

He nods. "Of course, Gina. I think that's a great idea."

"Good. I'm so glad." I stand; wipe my hands on my jeans. The gun is on the table, and I pick it up and turn to Grant. "Do you have anything you want to say to me?"

His gaze never wavers from my face, but I know he's clocked the gun. He has to have. It's huge.

"I wish I'd killed you in that house. You had no idea that we—"

I pull the trigger. The bullet slams into his temple at the same time Owen starts screaming.

Now I need to move. I put the gun back down on the table, then kneel by Grant and untie him. Adrenaline pushes me to move as fast as possible, but it also causes my hands to be a bit clumsy. I work as quickly as I can, untying him from the chair, then tipping his body over onto the floor. The chair scrapes against the wood floor as I drag it back to the table.

Owen's still screaming.

"Hey, Owen." I kneel in front of him and start untying his wrists and ankles. "I'm going to let you go, okay? We're getting out of here."

He's hysterical. As soon as I untie his hands, he smacks me away from him, bending down to untie his ankles.

That's fine. If he helps me, we can get out of here even

faster. But as soon as his legs are free, he's up, lunging past me for the gun.

"You killed him!" He swings round, the gun trained on me. "You killed him, Gina!"

"Whoa, Owen." I hold my hands up and slowly stand up. Honestly, this is what I expected, which is why I'm prepared for it. One hand stays up between us, but I reach round to my back pocket and pull my burner phone out with my other. A quick swipe of my thumb pulls up my camera app, and I snap a few pictures of Owen. "You're not thinking things through, honey."

"What are you doing?" The gun doesn't waver from my face.

"Texting these to someone." I send the photos off with the single push of a button. Wade did exactly what we planned. He cut down the tree, throwing the house into the dark. Now he'll hold on to the photos for me. Our little insurance plan. "Put the gun down, Owen."

He's crying again, but the gun doesn't waver. "Where's my mom?"

"In the kitchen. She died the same way my aunt did. It's poetic, right?"

He doesn't answer.

"Come on, Owen! You didn't think she was innocent, did you? Your parents are evil."

He swallows hard. "Gina, why? You said you loved me."

"Oh, I do love you," I tell him. I take a step closer to him and reach for the gun. "That's why I didn't turn this into a huge newspaper story. Do you know what the tabloids would have done? You'd be finished as a doctor. Nobody would want you to operate on them once they knew your father was a serial killer. But now you're just an orphan who survived a tragedy. Your dad got angry at your mom. He killed her. Then he killed himself."

"But he didn't do any of this!"

"Owen. He killed so many women and got away with it. This is the story, and we're sticking to it."

"Nobody will believe that. They'll check his hand for gunshot residue. They'll know he didn't kill himself, and they'll come looking for us. We were the last ones to see him alive. You didn't think that through, did you?"

Of course I did. I swear, sometimes people just think the worst of you. No way would I have taken a step into this house without having a plan A, plan B, and plan C.

It's so nice that my plan A is working the way I want it to.

"Owen, that thing you smell? That you can't quite place?" He doesn't respond. "It's gas. They won't be able to look for gunshot residue on your dad because there won't be any of your dad left."

He screams.

Pulls the trigger.

EPILOGUE

Owen sits across from me at the dining room table, a glass of wine in front of both of us. I see the slim gold band on his hand whenever he takes a drink and the sight fills me with joy. We've only been married a month, but I'm already sure I'll never get tired of seeing that flash of gold, of knowing he's my husband.

He'd been so surprised when there weren't any more bullets in the gun. I only needed one to take care of Grant so that's all I loaded. You know, if I'm honest, it's a little insulting he thought that I would leave a loaded gun within his reach. Of course he was going to pick it up. Of course he was going to try to shoot me. I saw the relationship he had with his mother, and I'd just killed both of his parents. If he hadn't tried to shoot me, I would have been surprised.

And if he hadn't tried, I wouldn't have a photo of him at the crime scene holding a gun and screaming.

Not great for optics, let me tell you. If you're going to trust a man to cut you open and fix whatever's wrong with you, you definitely don't want them to have been on a murder spree the weekend before. It wasn't hard to talk some sense into Owen, to explain to him what would happen if he went to the police.

And burning that place to the ground? I'd be lying if I didn't say it still gave me shivers. The sight of the flames licking up the building, how the entire thing seemed to explode in orange and yellow?

Amazing. It would be a religious experience if I believed in that.

Not that we stuck around to watch as much as I wanted, of course. I'm not stupid. I saw some of the fire, the way the flames licked and surged around the house. But the photos of the charred remains, the embers glowing in the ashes? I had to wait to see those on the news like everyone else. But even with neighbors so far away they can't hear you scream, someone eventually noticed that the house was a bonfire. The police and firefighters were called, but by the time they made it all the way out there to the middle of nowhere, it was too far gone.

And so were Owen and I. Wade was more than happy to be our alibi that we'd left earlier in the day, and Owen didn't breathe a word of what really happened.

And I don't think he will. Giving up his life as a surgeon would do him in. And no matter how he tried to spin it, there's no way he could take me down without going down with me.

"Cheers to a wonderful first month as husband and wife," I say, lifting my glass of wine.

Owen pauses, then does the same. He's still struggling a little with the loss of his parents and with, as he puts it, *being married to the woman who killed them*. But I remind him over and over how I love him. That I've forgiven him for his father killing my aunt. We're even.

And neither one of us is going anywhere.

"It's finally time for us to take a honeymoon," I say. "I know you didn't want to immediately after the accident, especially since we eloped right after, but nobody would judge us now. We can finally fly to the Maldives, see what all the fuss is about."

He puts his fork down and stares at me. There are dark circles under his eyes. His skin is dry.

I hate it. Not because it means my husband isn't as gorgeous as he should be, but because I don't like seeing him so torn up. It isn't his fault he got caught up in everything with his parents, just like it wasn't my fault. I know he has to mourn, has to try to find a way to move on. I dealt with the same shitty hand, but now look where I am. Madly in love and married to the man of my dreams. Doesn't hurt that he's ripped. Or rich.

Or that he can never leave me.

"I don't know if I can do this, Gina." There's so much exhaustion in his voice that I pause.

We've had some variation of this conversation at least twice a week since the accident. Honestly, it's getting a little old. It's the same back and forth of *I can't do this* and *you will, or your life is over,* and I'm really not one for threatening people I love.

"Owen." I reach out and take his hand. He lets me but doesn't return the squeeze I give him. "I love you. What happened at your parents' house has nothing to do with you, and everything to do with what your parents did to me."

"But my mom was innocent."

I bark out a laugh without meaning to. "Sorry. It's just... no, she wasn't. She knew, Owen. She knew what he was doing. I'm not going to look the other way, and you shouldn't either. You pride yourself on being a good human, on following the rules, on helping other people. But your parents were the opposite."

"My dad—"

"Your dad killed my aunt."

He's silent. Finally, he nods. "You know everything, don't you?"

I arch an eyebrow. That's the confirmation I've wanted to hear since everything went down, and while I should rejoice in that, I'm suspicious. I don't like how he's refusing to meet my eye, how he glances down at his plate, then over my shoulder.

"I do. I know about your dad killing those women. Cheating on your mom. I know your mom hated me. Your dad put you in my path; he brought us together. He was going to kill me if he got the chance."

He sighs. "But he didn't. It all worked out, Gina. Now we need to move on. Together. The past is the past." He gives me a smile, but it seems forced.

"You don't sound like you believe what you're saying." I pull my hand back. Take another sip of wine. When I narrow my eyes at my husband, he has the grace to blush.

"I don't want to live my life with something hanging over my head. I want to be happy. With you. You and I can do that, Gina. We can be happy; we can face whatever comes our way. Let's just move on from this."

Oh. I see where this is going. Dr. *I don't want something hanging over my head* is doing his best to get me to delete those photos.

"Owen."

"Hmm?" He takes a bite of steak while he waits for me to continue.

"I'm not deleting the photos."

His face falls, just like I knew it would. I watch as he tries to catch himself, tries to keep the smile on his face, but he can't do it. Instead, he gets up and walks into the kitchen. A moment later, he's back, and he carefully fills our wineglasses.

And yes, *photos*. More than one. There are a few shots of pissed off Owen with the gun coming at me. I got some of him by his dad, kneeling next to him, the useless gun at his side.

Oh, and when he saw the empty gas can and grabbed it like that was going to allow him to undo what I'd done? Yeah, I took pictures of that.

And they all went right to Wade. Insurance photos, that's all they are. Wade won't do anything with them unless he has to —I know that much. Out of everyone I've ever met in my life, he's the only person who hasn't tried to screw me over. It's because it's always been the two of us against the world. Reaching up, I play with the necklace I'm wearing.

B for Bethany.

All of the other trophies Grant stole from the women he killed went up in flames, but not this one.

I take a long drink of wine before putting down my glass and picking up my fork. "And before you get some crazy idea about going to the police and trying to convince them that what happened isn't your fault, that I'm the bad guy, remember: I'm five steps ahead of you. Nobody will believe you; I've made sure of that." I stab my fork through the air at him to make a point. When he doesn't respond, I put it down. Drain half of my wine. "Trust me, Owen, I've had decades to think this through. You're trying to think on your feet right now, but there's no way you'll come out on top. Just enjoy being married. Enjoy the life we can build together."

He nods, but I see something in his eyes, a fire that tells me he's not quite done poking around, looking for a way to bring this all tumbling down. "I guess there's nothing else to do here."

Chills race up my spine, freezing me in place. My eyes snap to my husband as I carefully put my fork down. Have another sip of wine.

He's staring at me. His chin is lifted, defiant. His eyes narrow as they lock on me. Owen has never looked at me like this before, like there's something evil in him.

My head spins. I've heard those words before. Heard that tone of voice before. I close my eyes. Try to slow my breathing. Try to picture what happened so many years ago.

The dark. The movement in the corner.

The footsteps echoing around the house.

No, not one set of footsteps *echoing*. Two sets. Two sets laid over each other. I hadn't seen it at the time, but I see it now.

"What did you say?" My voice is strangled, even to my ears.

"I said... I guess there's nothing else to do here." There's a low rumble in his voice; a warning.

"Owen." I reach up and grab my throat, feeling my heart beating there. It's hammering hard, slamming out an uneven rhythm.

I see it all now. How wrong I was.

There was a second voice. A second set of footsteps. A second *man*.

No. It can't be. But then I look at him—really look at him, at his build, his dark hair, his strong shoulders. He was younger then, sure, but even at twenty-one, he was huge, easily towering over the people he met.

"You," I say, pointing at him. My hand shakes. "You were there."

"I told you I visited Dad on one of his trips. Just once. It was all I could handle."

Did he tell me that? My head spins. I reach for my wine, but I hit the rim of it, knocking the glass over. Red spreads out, wicking quickly into the white tablecloth.

He *tsks*; tosses his napkin over the spill.

"You were in the house."

"I was in the house." He leans back in his chair and crosses his arms. I see his muscles twist and dance. I've felt so safe wrapped in his arms, but now...

I have to blink hard. My vision is blurry, but shock can do that, can't it? Make it so you think you're seeing double.

"You said you had it all figured out." There's a hint of a mocking tone there. It's at odds with the Owen I know.

I close my eyes. It doesn't stop the room from spinning, but I can better picture the kitchen that night. Aunt Bethany. The man holding her. I was sure that it was Grant. No, it *was* Grant.

But then he told someone to come here, didn't he? I'd always pictured him talking to Aunt Bethany, like maybe she was trying to get away, but he was talking to—

"You killed her." God, my head feels heavy. I want nothing more than to rest it on the table and close my eyes, but I can't look away from the man sitting across the table from me.

"I killed her. You killed my parents." He chuckles. "Looks like we're even, Gina. But there's one big difference between the two of us."

I don't want to know what it is, but I can't stop myself from asking. "What is it?" My words sound slurred, just like Marta's did when I—

I force myself to pick up my glass and swirl it. My arm feels like it weighs a hundred pounds, and I have to concentrate to keep from dropping it. There—at the bottom. Dregs. Only... Owen decants his wine. He would never drink wine with dregs.

"Ahh yes, I wanted to try out your little trick from dinner with my parents. It's a terrible feeling, isn't it? To know something's wrong but not be able to do anything about it? To feel darkness creeping in at the edges of your vision and not be able to fight it? I hated that feeling."

I drag my gaze up to his.

"You could have left well enough alone, Gina. We could have been happy. I love you, and I was more than willing to overlook what happened so many years ago. But then you had to kill my parents. You could have kept your mouth shut about seeing my dad, and we would have walked out of there without any problems! But you had to make it ugly! I had to clean up your mess, try to talk my dad down. But you kept pushing, didn't you? You just couldn't leave well enough alone. Come on, Gina! You did this!"

He slams his hand down on the table. My breath catches in my throat, and it takes me a minute to find my voice.

"You're a murderer."

"So are you."

I'm silent. My mind races, unable to settle on what I need to do. It's hard to think things through, to come up with a plan I think will work.

Maybe something with the photos? I could call Wade. Tell him to release them. There's enough there to end Owen. He deserves to pay for what he did to Aunt Bethany, to me, to Wade.

And then what?

My palms feel cold, and I rub them against my jeans. Even as I'm doing my best to think this through, the drugs that were in my wine are making it harder and harder.

Say Wade sends the photos to some news stations and Owen goes to jail for what I did. Then what happens to me? I don't know. I can't wrap my mind around it. It's impossible to think that far ahead without help.

Wade. I need Wade.

I fumble for my phone and dial my cousin. My hand shakes as I press the phone to my ear. There's ringing, but the sound is much louder than it should be, and I drop my phone to the table, confused.

"Oh, hang on." Owen pats his pocket. Pulls out a phone. "I'm getting a call, and during dinner. So rude of me not to turn this off." He taps the screen. "Hello?"

I hear his voice through my phone.

"What did you do?" It's almost impossible for me to manage those four words. "Owen, what—"

"Remember last week when I was at the cardiac care conference? I took a little detour to pay your cousin a visit." He powers down the phone and puts it on the table between us. "Those photos you've been holding over my head? They're no more. You had chance after chance to erase them, Gina. But you wanted to hang them over my head, so you left me no choice."

"And Wade?"

"Like mother, like son. Only nobody will ever find his body.

I made that mistake once. I'm not making it again." He stares at me. "What do you want to do now, Gina?"

I don't answer. I can't. My mind is foggy, my thinking slow.

"Make your decision. Before you pass out." He takes a sip of his wine. Everything is blurry, but I see the way he smirks at me.

"My decision?"

"Sure. I didn't mean to fall for you, Gina, just like I'm sure you didn't mean to fall for me. But I did. Crazy how life works out, isn't it?" He shrugs, like *aw shucks*. "We can stay together. Make this work."

"You killed my aunt." My tongue is thick when I speak, but I force the words out.

He stands, the movement so quick it takes me off guard. When he slams his hand down on the table, the loud sound helps to cut through the brain fog. "You're no better than I am! We're the same, Gina. Collateral damage. Broken. You can stay with me, keep your mouth shut, and we can be happy."

"Or?" When I blink, it takes way too long for me to open my eyes again.

"Or this ends when you're knocked out. You can't fight it forever. What a shame, when we just got married. But I know what meds will stop your heart, making it look like a heart attack. Nobody will question me." He pauses. "But it doesn't have to be like that. We're perfect together, Gina. My dad was right. Be with me."

That's my choice. With Owen, or dead.

I open my mouth to speak, but before I can, darkness pulls me under.

A LETTER FROM EMILY

Dear reader,

I want to say a huge thank you for choosing to read *Meet the Parents*. If you enjoyed it, and want to keep up to date with all my latest releases, just sign up at the following link. Your email address will never be shared and you can unsubscribe at any time.

www.bookouture.com/emily-shiner

Here's something a lot of people don't know: I come from a medical family. You need a surgeon, a hospice doctor, or an occupational therapist? We've got you covered! Even with all that medical knowledge being bandied about at the dinner table, nobody was surprised when I eschewed medical school and ended up writing books. (Me almost passing out while dissecting a deer heart in high school may have played a role in my eventual career choice.) Whatever the cause, I'd rather write about doctors and make up twisted stories about their lives than be an MD, myself.

Honestly, I think it's working out well. I'd rather write about blood than deal with it any day.

I hope you loved reading *Meet the Parents* as much as I loved writing it! If so, please consider leaving a review. I'd love to hear what you think, and it makes such a difference helping new readers to discover one of my books for the first time.

I love hearing from my readers – please email me at emily@authoremilyshiner.com, or you can get in touch on my social media or my website.

Thank you for everything!

Emily

www.authoremilyshiner.com

facebook.com/authoremilyshiner
x.com/authoreshiner
instagram.com/authoremilyshiner

ACKNOWLEDGMENTS

It's an incredible thing – knowing I can come to the Bookouture team with an idea and see it turn into something I'm so proud of. Thank you so much to everyone at Bookouture, especially Kelsie Marsden, who helps whip all of my books into shape!

To my husband and daughter for everything, including copious cups of tea. While I'm on that note, to Blue Lotus Chai for insanely good blends that are so simple to make, even a coffee drinking husband can deliver a great cup.

To my hiking friends who have learned that when I gasp on the trail it's less likely to mean "snake!", and more likely that I finally had a breakthrough on a particularly tricky part in a book.

And, as always, to my readers. Every tag or mention I get thrills me. Reading time is precious and to be invited into your lives over and over is a gift. Thank you!

PUBLISHING TEAM

Turning a manuscript into a book requires the efforts of many people. The publishing team at Bookouture would like to acknowledge everyone who contributed to this publication.

Audio
Alba Proko
Sinead O'Connor
Melissa Tran

Commercial
Lauren Morrissette
Hannah Richmond
Imogen Allport

Cover design
Eileen Carey

Data and analysis
Mark Alder
Mohamed Bussuri

Editorial
Kelsie Marsden
Nadia Michael